THE
MONEY
HARVEST

THE MONEY HARVEST

by Ross Thomas

WILLIAM MORROW AND COMPANY, INC.
NEW YORK 1975

Printed in the United States of America.

1 2 3 4 5   79 78 77 76 75

Library of Congress Cataloging in Publication Data

Thomas, Ross (date)
    The money harvest.

    I. Title.
PZ4.T4595Mo   [PS3570.H58]   813'.5'4   74-31025
ISBN 0-688-02912-4

Book design by Helen Roberts

THE
MONEY
HARVEST

1

THE HAMMERTOED FRIEND AND ADVISER OF SIX PRESIDENTS wasn't dead, of course. Not yet. If he had been dead, he couldn't have wiggled his big toe under the bedclothes, the right one, which, like the left, was twisted all out of shape because of those shoes he had been made to wear when he was seven.

After his right toe finally obeyed his brain's slow signal, he wiggled the left one. He didn't open his eyes until then, until he was sure that he hadn't suffered a stroke or something worse during the night that might have left him paralyzed. There would be no point in opening his eyes if he were paralyzed—no point at all at ninety-three.

He lay there remembering once again those shoes that poverty had made him wear when he was seven. They had been of yellow calfskin, women's shoes really, with heels and highbuttoned tops and long, pointed toes that at seven had formed a cruel, unmerciful vise even after he sawed off the heels and dyed them black with stove polish and slit their sides with a razor.

By the time he was eight his toes were permanently deformed and he walked with a sliding scuttle, some-

1

thing like a pigeon-toed crab, which had earned him the nickname Crawdad from his schoolmates. He still walked that way, but ever so slowly now, and people still called him Crawdad, although seldom to his face unless they were extremely old friends, except that at ninety-three most of his extremely old friends were withered vegetables who were wheeled out of their rooms once a day for what might well be their last look at the sun.

Certain now that he wasn't dead, or worse, he examined the familiar blur of his room. There was the light from the floor lamp in the corner that was never turned off. He could make out the light. The rest of the room was filled with dark shapes. Since they didn't move he assumed that they weren't angels in waiting although he had lived too long to place much faith in angels—or in devils or saints for that matter. Sinners, yes. There was always a raft of them around.

The dark shapes were the room's furniture—the bureau, the writing desk, the chair that went with the desk, and the big upholstered chair in the corner under the floor lamp that nobody ever turned off. He continued to lie in bed trying to decide how he felt now that he wasn't dead. There was no pain; not yet anyhow. That would come later in the afternoon. Long ago he had discovered that there really wasn't much to be done about pain, since it refused to be ignored, other than be polite to it—maybe offer it a toddy or two and hope that it would go back where it came from, probably next door, because he now thought of pain as some nasty, despised neighbor that time had turned into his last acquaintance.

He moved his arm, which, winter and summer, was encased in the cotton flannel of his nightgown sleeve.

He had never worn pajamas, and never would, considering them to be both wicked and licentious, although he wasn't sure why, except that he had felt that way in his long-ago youth and now clung to the conviction out of habit or stubbornness. He remembered that someone had told him that men's flannel nightgowns were hard to find now. Well, he had enough to last forever because he knew that his forever had now been shrunk to a week or a month or a couple of years at most.

The wrist he moved was nothing much more than old bone covered with loose, greyish skin, hairless, but adorned with brown liver spots the size of quarters. The fingers of his hands were almost useless. Arthritis had bent his hands into bony tongs but his thumbs still worked all right and that's all you really need, he thought, a working thumb.

His hand moved until it discovered his thick glasses on the bedside table. He put them on. He could see now. He picked up the heavy gold pocket watch that had lain next to the glasses. Its black hands told him that it was 5:35, something he already knew. He wound the watch and put it back on the table by the bed.

Lying there, staring at the ceiling through his glasses, he decided that he should tell his wife before he told anyone else. He caught himself then and gave his head a small, hard shake of mild exasperation because his wife was dead, and had been for thirty years, although not a day went by that he didn't catch himself thinking of something that he needed to tell her.

He had told her everything, of course, not only about himself, but also about the others—deep, dark wicked secrets that he had sworn never to tell anyone and hadn't, except her. And she, a quiet, soft woman, not overly intelligent, but certainly not dumb, and still mildly pretty even then at sixty-one, had gone to her grave not quite convinced of the awful things she had been told.

Because he was one of the few men in Washington, if not the only one, who could be trusted absolutely to keep a confidence, no matter how wretched and despicable, or even dangerous, he had been burdened with more than his share of them by those who had come to the capital this past half-century seeking power or fame or wealth—or more often all three. Sometimes as he heard them out they would glare at him, their eyes defiant, their chins up and thrusting forward in an almost embarrassing attempt to turn confession into conspiracy.

But usually they would sit quietly, glass in hand, a bottle within easy reach, their eyes fixed on some distant point or sliding restlessly about, and their voices would be low and flat, almost a whispered monotone, as they recounted the rotten deeds of their days.

And sweet Jesus, he thought, how rotten some of them were. Conspiracy was their most frequently confessed transgression, of course. He knew that in this town they started conspiring first thing in the morning so that they could have it out of the way by lunch. They conspired for profit, for personal gain, for legislative advantage, for national and international power, and sometimes just for the hell of it.

But conspiracy was the least of the crimes he had been made privy to. He held up one hand and counted on his fingers. There were five instances of treason, he thought. At least five. And there were those three murders, all made to look like accidents, all in the name of what, national security? The public interest?

And your crime, of course, was your silence that granted consent, if not approval.

But it wasn't your approval that they had come seeking, he thought. It was absolution really and they seemed to feel that if they told you what they had done, had really done, then the very act of telling or confessing would somehow absolve them, and let them climb up there on the stool of redemption.

He could never fully understand this reasoning, perhaps because those who had come to him with their tales of high crimes and misdemeanors had not been brilliant men. He knew that not too many brilliant men ever made their way to Washington. Most of the truly brilliant ones, he had decided, were off writing poetry somewhere or making money in New York. For the most part, Washington got those who were merely smart or too often, just half smart. These were the ones who were just dumb enough to do something that they shouldn't, clever enough not to get caught at it, but neurotic enough to have to confess it to somebody. Still, he thought, they had been smart enough to confess it to you and not to their wives.

But this time is different, he thought. This time you're nobody's confessor. This time you just happened to be an eavesdropper and so you can spill it all. Anyhow, you committed yourself last night and they're sending a car for you at nine. By half past nine you'll be a talebearer, a ninety-three-year-old snitch. And maybe that's how they'll finally write you up in all the history books, if they write you up at all: William Makepeace "Crawdad" Gilmore, economic sage, sometime Cabinet member (twice), and would-be political maverick, at ninety-three turned stool pigeon thus saving his country from—well, from what?

He refused to think about it, not because it was so awful; he had heard far worse. He refused to think about it because it made him angry with himself. At seventy, you could have handled it, he thought. You would've had to have been slick, but at seventy you were still the slickest article around. But not at ninety-three. You're not well enough at ninety-three. Now that's a goddamn lie, too, he thought as he swung his legs over the side of the bed. You're well enough all right. You're just not smart enough anymore.

So last night he had called the smartest man in Washington and the smartest man in Washington was sending a car for him at nine. Meanwhile, he thought, you've got to get dressed. And that's going to take a while.

It took half an hour. It would have taken even longer except that the familiar clothes were neatly arranged on a chair by the bed. Once the nightgown was off the long underwear could be shrugged into and most of the buttons fastened. He rested after that to catch his breath. Next came his shirt. It was blue broadcloth and fairly clean and it buttoned up the front, but most of the buttons were already buttoned so all he had to do was slip it on over his head. The pants came next. They had only one button and a zipper, which he always ignored until later. The sweater vest was next. He put the gold watch into one of its pockets. Then he put his coat on, not his overcoat, but the suit coat whose trousers had worn out a quarter of a century before. It was still a good coat though.

Socks were always a problem. They were white, of course, made out of thick cotton and sometimes they got twisted. But once they were on he jammed his feet into his slippers and shuffled with his sliding crablike gait to the bathroom where he dropped his pants and sat down to find out whether his ninety-three-year-old bladder wanted to be emptied. Sometimes it did and sometimes it didn't. Although it vaguely embarrassed him, he found it less tiring to sit down like a woman than to stand up and wait for five or ten minutes until his bladder made up its mind.

By 6:19 he was downstairs at his front door sliding back the bolts and unlocking the locks. They were all relatively new, not over eight years old. He had never been quite able to accept the fact that his doors needed to be locked and bolted and that his first floor windows needed to be barred. That's because you grew up where you did, he sometimes told himself. In Missouri of a hot summer night we'd leave the front and back doors wide open and all the windows up and nobody ever stole anything. Except your dog. They stole your dog that time.

He opened the door and saw that the kid had missed with the *Post* again. It lay at the bottom of the six wrought-iron steps that led to the sidewalk. The sidewalk bordered O Street in Georgetown. He had bought his house cheap back in thirty-three and had lived in it ever since. Only a month ago somebody had offered him exactly twenty-four times what he had paid for it.

He went down the steps slowly and even more slowly bent down for the paper. He didn't hear them until one of them said, "Doan yell or nothin', ol' man. Doan do nothin' like that."

He straightened up, the *Post* in his hands. There were two of them. Niggers, he thought. You say black now like everybody else, but you still think nigger.

The taller one held a knife. It was a kitchen knife with an eight-inch blade. The other held a pistol. It's a little pistol, Crawdad Gilmore thought. Maybe it's a toy.

"See wha' he got," the taller one said. The watch was quickly found and pocketed. So was the money.

"Shit, man, he oney got thutty-two cents."

"You bettuh git us moah money, ol' man," the taller one said, moving his knife around in a tight little circle.

Crawdad Gilmore started to gesture with the *Post* toward his house, indicating that more money lay inside on top of the bedroom bureau, fourteen dollars to be exact. The smaller black took the gesture as the threatening kind and jerked the trigger of his small gun, a .22 caliber automatic made in Vitoria, Spain, exclusively for export. There was a bang, about the kind of a bang that a cap pistol would make.

The .22 long slug struck Crawdad Gilmore in his right side, coming to rest in his liver. He staggered and said, "Goddamn," murmured it really, and then took a step toward the black with the pistol. He took the step to keep from falling, but the black apparently regarded it as another move full of menace because he pulled the trigger again. There was another mild bang and this time the slug entered Crawdad Gilmore's body just below the breastbone, penetrating his heart. He died shortly after he fell to the sidewalk, his head cushioned by the 134 pages of Thursday's *Washington Post*, a fat edition.

The two black killers turned and ran west on O Street toward Wisconsin Avenue carrying with them thirty-two cents in loot and a seventy-two-year-old gold watch whose black hands said that it was 6:22 in the morning.

2

THE FUNERALS OF OLD-TIMERS WHO HAVE LUSTED AFTER power, and who may even have bedded her for a while, serve a useful purpose in the District of Columbia. They provide a kind of neutral watering hole where the political animals who inhabit the Washington jungle can gather to eye each other and to mark the absence of other old-timers whose strange alarums and mad excursions once echoed through what's left of the rain forest that stretches along the banks of the Potomac. The old-timers, of course, are those who have lived in Washington for half a dozen years or so.

The President of the United States was such an old-timer. Although not an overly intelligent man, he finally had learned how to walk and chew gum at the same time although there were those who swore he had mastered the trick only after secret midnight practice. Still, he was smart enough to show up at Joseph Gawler's Sons funeral parlor on Wisconsin Avenue where Crawdad Gilmore's body lay, if not in state, at least on public exhibition.

Neither the present tenant of the White House nor his predecessor had been among the six Presidents whom Crawdad Gilmore had served as friend and adviser, which, the current President thought, was certainly not my fault. I wouldn't have minded being friends with the old bastard, if it would have done me any good.

But then the President wouldn't have minded being friends with the seven imps of hell, providing they did him some good. In fact, the President went around trying to be friends with nearly everybody, which was neither good sense nor good politics, and so his new Administration was already in deep trouble not only at home, but also abroad.

The President arrived with his usual entourage of press, White House aides, and Secret Service gunslingers, most of whom chewed gum in slavish imitation of their new boss who had started chewing it in public "just to show 'em I've got spunk," as he told his wife who had replied that "it still looks tacky."

They look fatter this year, the smartest man in Washington decided as he moved through the Secret Service agents to greet the President. I wonder why they look fatter.

"Christ, couldn't they have laid him out in a church at least?" the President snapped after giving the hand of the smartest man in Washington a perfunctory shake.

"He was an agnostic, Mr. President, who finally turned to atheism at ninety-one," the smartest man in Washington said without a smile.

The President glanced at him sharply, just to make sure that he wasn't being kidded, and then said, "Well, let's have a look." He said it in a low voice without moving his lips, another trick he had taught himself after his Press Secretary had informed him that the Knight Newspapers were hiring as their White House correspondent a reporter who had been trained in lip-reading.

Even if he hadn't been President of the United States, he wouldn't have had to stand in line to view the mortal remains of Crawdad Gilmore. There was a small crowd now outside the funeral parlor because of the rumor that the President might show up, but it was a crowd composed mostly of elderly ladies, Social Security pensioners all, each equipped with a paper reticule, usually from Safeway International. No one but the old ladies knew for certain what the reticules contained, although the two most junior Secret Service agents had been posted to keep an eye on them on the off chance that one of the ancients might be a mad bomber with a couple of grenades tucked way underneath the knitting.

The real bulk of Crawdad Gilmore's mourners, if that's what they could be called, had come and gone earlier that day, most of them just before noon soon after the mysterious Washington tom-toms had sent out their signal that an appearance at the funeral home was virtually *de rigueur*. Ten Senators had shown up as had three dozen Congressmen. The dean of the Washington diplomatic corps, His Excellency Dr. Guillermo Sevilla-Sacasa of Nicaragua, who had hung on to the same job since 1943, was among those paying his respects as were the ambassadors from thirteen other countries. The Pentagon, not knowing what else to do, had dispatched a brace of three-star generals accompanied by a Navy captain. Five Cabinet members had come and gone, only one of whom had ever met Crawdad Gilmore and hadn't especially liked him. Enough expensive lawyers to fill a column in the phone book had appeared, looking solemn and sad, as had a large number of out-of-favor economists and nearly four dozen lobbyists of various beliefs and persuasions.

Eleven very old persons, in their eighties and early nineties, came separately, but almost at the same time by chauffeured limousines and cabs, which they kept waiting. They all seemed to have known one another a long time ago, but had lost touch, and now looked faintly surprised and even a little disappointed to discover each other still alive.

And then, of course, there were the Washington wives who arrived in gaggles of two and three. For the most part they were surrogate mourners, representing their husbands, Federal dynamos all, whose impossibly busy schedules prevented them from grieving in person.

And finally, gathered outside with the old ladies and their reticules were the idly curious, the unemployed, the professional funeral-goers, and a surprising number of mostly bearded, middle-aged men who wore their hair rather long, if they had any, taught American history in the two dozen or so universities and colleges in the area, and who, to a man, were fascinated by Crawdad Gilmore's long stroll down the corridors of power.

The President silently counted up to twenty-five as he gazed down at the body of the dead man who lay in the casket, which was the kind that can be opened to display only the upper half of the deceased, or late departed, or corpse, depending on how one feels about the dead.

The President still thought of the dead as good business because his father had owned a chain of funeral parlors in Illinois. He ran a professional eye over the casket and when he was through with his twenty-five-second display of public grief he turned to the smartest man in Washington and said, "Was he broke?"

"No, Mr. President, he wasn't broke."

"That casket. It couldn't have cost more than two or three hundred bucks."

"It didn't," the smartest man in Washington said. "Crawdad wanted to go cheap. It's in his will."

The President shook his head. "Was that his best suit?"

The smartest man in Washington nodded. "He bought it on sale twenty years ago to be buried in." He glanced at the open casket. "He finally got around to wearing it."

"He was a tight old bastard, wasn't he?" the President said, remembering not to move his lips.

"Close, Mr. President. Close."

"They catch who shot him yet?"

"Not yet."

"How much they get?" the President asked. He asked because long ago one of the many self-help books he had read claimed that 99 percent of genius was an infinite capacity for detail and since then he was always asking extraneous, niggling questions that tended to drive others mad.

"Thirty-two cents, Mr. President. I know because that's the amount he had entered in his daybook. He also had fourteen dollars on the bureau in his bedroom. They took his watch, too."

"Good watch?"

"I think so, Mr. President. A gold Hamilton."

"Huh," the President said, which was his final comment on the death of William Makepeace "Crawdad" Gilmore.

The smartest man in Washington was Ancel Easter, a Philadelphia lawyer. That is to say he had been born in Philadelphia fifty-one years ago and reared there in a west side slum from which he had escaped by enlisting in the U.S. Marines on December 8, 1941.

When the Marines tested his intelligence, they refused to believe that a slum kid from Philadelphia could have an IQ of 196. So before throwing him in the brig for cheating they gave him the test again. With practice, Ancel Easter scored a perfect 200 after sitting around doodling with his pencil for a quarter of an hour because he had finished the test early.

He came out of the war unscathed, a twenty-one-year-old major with medals down to here for impossibly brave deeds that at the time simply had seemed the most logical thing to do to keep from getting his ass shot off. He enrolled in the fall of 1945 as a freshman at Harvard, which was happy to get its hands on him in a year when it was being choosy. He could have gone to Yale just as easily, and he might have, except that at thirteen he had read a book called *Stover at Yale.* Dink Stover, he had decided, was a prick and there was just the possibility that all Yale men were pricks. It was an unwarranted prejudice that he never got over, not even after meeting William F. Buckley, Jr., in 1959.

What is loosely termed the Eastern Establishment was waiting for Ancel Easter when he was graduated from Harvard Law School, first in his class and editor of its Review, at the very beginning of the 1950's. A number of old New York law firms made him fat, rich offers. A U.S. Supreme Court Justice wanted him as a clerk. And then there was the offer from Crawdad Gilmore, scrawled on a sheet of his firm's paper: "Dear Mr. Easter, if you want to make a lot of money and have a lot of fun, see me. Sincerely, W. M. Gilmore."

He joined the Gilmore law firm and almost immediately began to make a lot of money. Crawdad Gil-

more's Washington connections went back to the
Hoover Administration when, in 1929, already a multi-
millionaire Wall Street lawyer, he had been asked by
the Great Engineer to join him in the White House as,
"Hell, I don't know, Crawdad, some kind of adviser, I
guess."

But even Crawdad Gilmore's sage advice (which
usually wasn't taken) couldn't stave off the Depression
so he resigned quietly in 1932, and went back into private practice, prospering mightily once again as the
welter of the New Deal's alphabet agencies brought
him rich, but confused and sometimes badly frightened
industrial clients.

It took nearly a full bottle of Scotch and all of his
considerable charm before Franklin Roosevelt could
persuade Crawdad Gilmore to become his Secretary of
Commerce in 1937. "But then I got into a fight with
old man Ickes and quit in thirty-eight," he later told
Ancel Easter. "That's when I swore I'd never work for
the Government ever again."

And he almost didn't, except that the second World
War came along and he spent twenty-six months at a
dollar a year shuttling between London and Washington as one of Franklin Roosevelt's secret emissaries to
Churchill. And there was one other time. It was in
1953 when a bemused Dwight Eisenhower summoned
him to the White House and offered him his pick of
the Cabinet posts with the exception of the State Department. Crawdad Gilmore chose the department that
was then in the most trouble, went back to his law
office, and called in Ancel Easter.

"I told you you were going to have a lot of fun,
didn't I?" he said.

Easter nodded, a wary nod. "That's right."

Gilmore grinned. "Well, the fun begins tomorrow because that's when you start minding the store while I'm away."

So at thirty, Ancel Easter, even then the smartest man in Washington, was jumped over the heads of fourteen senior partners to become, in effect, the most senior partner but one in the firm that was renamed Gilmore, Easter, Timothy and Stern, or GETS, as it was referred to in Washington, a town that dotes on acronyms.

Crawdad Gilmore resigned from the Eisenhower Cabinet in 1955 after a bitter public scrap with the then Secretary of Agriculture, Ezra Taft Benson. Declaring himself publicly to be "a true-blue Democrat now and forevermore," he returned to his law practice to discover that it had doubled under the guidance of Ancel Easter who had gone in for diversification, acquiring such new clients as the International Association of Machinists (AFL-CIO), a major Hollywood studio that was in a constant panic over television, and a small but nicely growing firm called Xerox, which showed promise.

Crawdad Gilmore continued the active practice of law until the day they shot John Kennedy in Dallas. From the first he assumed that it was a "they," because it had all the earmarks of a conspiracy and conspiracy was something he knew considerable about.

It was Ancel Easter who told him that it had happened. Easter walked into his office that grey November afternoon and said, "Kennedy's been shot in Dallas. They think he won't make it—that he'll die."

Crawdad Gilmore nodded and remembered a Massachusetts beach and a skinny, almost gawky kid who ran down it toward him. It had been the now dying

President of the United States, running hard, chasing his older brother. "You've got some fine boys," he had told their father and old Joe had nodded and said in that insufferably self-satisfied way of his, "They'll do, Crawdad. They just might do."

"He's not dead yet?" he asked Ancel Easter.

"No, but it looks bad. You want a radio?"

Crawdad Gilmore shook his head and reached into his pocket. He took out his key ring and removed two keys from it. He slid them across his desk toward Easter. "I'll go home and watch it on television. It'll be on television."

"What're these for?" Easter said, indicating the keys.

Gilmore looked around his office. It was a nice office, almost a splendid one, and suddenly he knew he wasn't going to miss it. "It's all yours," he said. "The whole shebang."

Because he was the smartest man in Washington, Ancel Easter already knew what the old man wanted him to do, but with a good lawyer's cunning caution he sought confirmation. "You want in on it, don't you, whatever it is, and you want me to get you in?"

The old man was putting on his hat. He took another look around the office that he was sure he would never see again. He nodded. "Let them know I'm available," he said. "Squeeze them a little, if you have to."

"All right."

On September 26, 1964, the day before the Warren Commission's report was released, Crawdad Gilmore called on the Chief Justice. "Just for the record," he said. "Your record, Earl, nobody else's. When I signed my name to the report, I signed my name to a piece of shit. You know it's a piece of shit and I know it's a piece of shit, and maybe five years from now or maybe fifty everybody's going to know it's a piece of shit. I just wanted that for the record, Earl. Your record. It'll make me feel better." And with that Crawdad Gilmore turned and walked from the room and never saw the Chief Justice again and never served the United States Government again, except once, when he advised Lyndon Johnson in 1965 to pull out of Vietnam, but only after he was asked what he thought. It was the last time any President ever sought his advice.

After the current President of the United States left the funeral home the number of mourners for Crawdad Gilmore dwindled. Only three or four came each hour but still Ancel Easter stayed on, rising to meet each mourner, introducing himself if they hadn't met, nodding silently at the usually whispered expressions of grief and sorrow and praise for the dead old man.

But Ancel Easter didn't rise when the tall man came in. Instead, he remained seated in the small alcove, not hidden, but not clearly visible because of the dim light. The tall man either didn't see him or decided to ignore him. He walked over to the casket and stood for a moment, gazing down at its occupant.

I don't remember the grey, Ancel Easter thought. I don't remember it being that long either, but still it only looks as if he might have missed a couple of haircuts. Maybe three. What is he now, thirty-four, thirty-five? Probably thirty-five and he's keeping his weight down, or he's missed some meals, but he wouldn't have missed any unless he wanted to. And Christ, was he always that tall? He must be six-four. I don't remember him being that tall although maybe it's those skinny jeans he's wearing. He dresses the way he wants to now,

like it's always Saturday afternoon and nothing's scheduled.

The tall man's jacket was nearly as worn as his
blue jeans. But it had been a good coat to begin with,
even expensive, and its dark grey tweed still advertised
its bespoke tailor although it was too hot for June and
looked as if it might have been slept in or flown in.
Underneath the coat was a blue shirt, its button-down
collar unbuttoned. There was no tie. On his feet were
loafers that looked almost as worn as his coat and just
as comfortable. They were down-at-the-heels loafers,
black, the kind that had been adorned with tassels when
new although the tassels were missing now. Ancel
Easter had the feeling that if he could see their soles,
there would be a hole in one of the loafers, probably
the right one, with maybe a piece of cardboard showing through.

Ancel Easter rose then and walked over to the tall
man. The tall man didn't turn.

"Don't he look natural," Ancel Easter said.

"Don't he," the tall man said, still without turning.
"I was in Madagascar when I heard. I just flew in."

"What the hell's in Madagascar?" Ancel Easter said.

"My boat."

"Oh. I thought they called it Malagasy now."

"They do, or at least some of them do, but I still call
it Madagascar. Somebody shot him? The news was a
little sketchy."

"Somebody shot him and got thirty-two cents and
his gold watch."

"They got the watch, huh?" the tall man said. "You
know something?"

"What?"

"He'd promised me that watch."

"Yeah, well, when's the last time you saw him?"

"Three months ago. Three and a half really. Just before I left. You know how I used to drop by on him every month or so. We'd talk. Or jaw, as he called it. He had some good ones. At first, you know, a long time ago when I was still with the committee, I thought shit, the old man's stretching it now. So I'd check it out. I mean really check it out. I'd turn the Library of Congress loose on it. I could do that then. But when it came back, the report, it'd happened just like he'd said it'd happened, except that he was there, and the only things he'd left out were the things that might've embarrassed somebody, really embarrassed them, even though they were forty-years dead."

"He could keep a confidence," Ancel Easter said. "You know, that's what we might put on his tombstone. 'He Could Keep a Confidence.'"

"We?" the tall man said.

"Who's he got left except you and me and a granddaughter that he hasn't seen in twenty years or heard from in ten? The three of us are in his will."

"I don't need it," the tall man said. "Where's the granddaughter?"

"In Montana," Easter said. "I've been trying to call her, but the phones have been out for a week. It's one of those rural lines. Anyway, there's not going to be any tombstone. That's in his will, too. He wants his ashes scattered on the Mississippi, anywhere south of St. Louis on the Missouri side."

"You want me to do it? I wouldn't mind."

"What about your boat?"

The tall man shrugged. "It's got a crew of six. They can bring it around the Cape and on up."

"Jesus, just like that," Ancel Easter said. "It must

be wonderful to be so rich so young. A crew of six, just imagine it, and they can bring it around the Cape all by themselves and then maybe lie off Cannes for a week until you get back and then you can all go pooping around the Aegean looking for what—sponges?"

"They've got sponges in the Aegean," the tall man said, still looking down at the body of Crawdad Gilmore.

"You know what I mean," Ancel Easter said.

"I said I'd go scatter his ashes. What else is there? The cops'll find who killed him. Or they'll hang it on some dude over on T Street or maybe on some shitfaced kid who's been giving them trouble in Georgetown, and zing, another murder solved."

"He called me," Ancel Easter said.

"When?"

"The night before. He was coming down. I was going to send a car for him."

The tall man turned to look at Easter. Tall as he was, he didn't have to lower his gaze. Ancel Easter was almost six-foot-two. "He was coming down to the office, down to GETS?" he said, spacing his words.

Easter nodded.

"Why?"

"He had something. He said he had something hot."

" 'Hot'? You're sure he said 'hot'?"

Easter nodded again. "He said 'hot.' "

"What else did he say?"

"That's about all. Would you have needed anything more?"

"No, I wouldn't have needed anything more. Except that I wouldn't have waited."

"I'm older," Ancel Easter said. "I've got more patience."

"Sure. You said that's *about* all he said. What does 'about' mean?"

"It means he told me where he got it; not what, but where."

"All right, where?"

"He said he got it in the men's crapper in the Cosmos Club," Ancel Easter said.

3

THE LIMOUSINE TURNED LEFT OFF WISCONSIN AVENUE on to S Street and headed east. It was a seven-passenger Cadillac, dark grey instead of black, the kind with a brougham rear that concealed its passengers from the bleak stares of both the envious and the ecologists. It was $19,000 worth of automobile, with power everything, and it got four or five miles to the gallon in town, maybe seven on the road, and on a full tank it could cruise for all of 211 miles without pulling into a gas station.

Despite its affluence, which is considerable, the streets in Georgetown are no better than anywhere else in Washington, which means that there's at least one good, deep pothole every couple of yards and that front wheel aligning is now the city's sixth major industry. But the fat springs of the Cadillac seemed to fill in the potholes and iron out the bumps as it glided down S Street, used 32nd to switch over to R Street, and continued east past Dumbarton Oaks, Montrose Park, and the Oak Hill Cemetery, which darts quickly downhill to meet Rock Creek Park.

In the rear seat of the Cadillac, the tall man with

greying hair had pulled out a jump seat so that he could cock his feet up on its pale blue mohair.

"You ever worry about the natives stoning this thing?" he said to Ancel Easter.

"Because of the so-called energy crisis?" Easter said.

"There's that."

"We have a couple of oil firms as clients. New clients. I was surprised what you can learn about oil and gas and coal—especially coal—by talking to a smart oil man, and there aren't too many dumb ones. Greedy, yes, and they all lie a lot, but they're not dumb. You know what principle they're operating on now—I mean the real principle, not all that garbage you see on TV about how they're babysitting the 'gators down in Louisiana?"

"I don't know much about oil," the tall man said. "We try not to use the engine much. Just the wind. They're not worried about a shortage of wind, are they?"

"If they could make a buck out of it, they'd tell you there was a shortage of west wind. Plenty of east wind, they'd say, but only a twenty-one-and-a-half-year supply of west wind. Well, anyway, the principle they're operating on is that since Britain is going to be producing as much oil as Kuwait in a few years—you know, out there in the North Sea—and here in the States we're going to be bringing oceans of it down from Alaska by pipe, and the Arabs are going to keep on producing, well, the world's going to be dripping in oil, at least for a while."

"How long?"

Ancel Easter shrugged. "Until the late eighties or early nineties."

"Then what?"

"Steam," Easter said, smiled, and nestled himself more comfortably into his seat. "That's what Detroit and the oil crowd are counting on. Steam. In 1995, you'll drive into a gas station, buy a gallon of oil or maybe a pound or two of specially processed coal that'll fire up the boiler like charcoal, but quicker, and maybe fifteen or twenty gallons of water, and then you're off to your picnic in the country, if there's any country left. And by then the oil crowd will have figured out how to charge you ten cents a gallon for the water."

"Aw, shit," the tall man said.

"So the reason this Cadillac produces no pangs of guilt is because my clients, the oil boys, assure me that the so-called energy crisis is only temporary. You don't think they'd lie to me, do you?"

"It doesn't matter," the tall man said. "You'd ride around in it anyway. If there were only a hundred gallons of gas left in the country, you'd get your hands on ten of them and then use it to ride around in this thing."

"That's because I grew up in a slum," Ancel Easter said. "Sometimes, I think everyone should have grown up in a slum, especially you. It's an enriching, if not ennobling experience."

"You know where I grew up."

"Still, it wasn't a Philadelphia slum."

"West Virginia is a slum with mountains," the tall man said.

The tall man's name was Jake Pope although it could be stretched into Jacob Rutledge Pope III for inclusion in the Green Book, which is as close as Washington now comes to a Social Register. And it actually had appeared there just once a few years back when Pope was newly married, although it had been his wife's social standing, not his, that had got him included in the Green Book, which to this day is still consulted by those who worry lest somebody clever and amusing be invited to dinner.

But Jake Pope didn't feel any need to be included in the Green Book because he had his own rich heritage to sustain him. The Rutledge in Jacob Rutledge Pope III was a legacy from a distant forebear, one Edward Rutledge of South Carolina, who is usually remembered in history books, if at all, as the youngest signer of the Declaration of Independence. He was twenty-seven and, it is said, something of a toper.

Then there was also Jake Pope's sire, Jacob Rutledge Pope, Jr., who hailed from a little place called Glen Jean, down in the southern central part of West Virginia in Fayette County where it's kind of hilly. He was seventeen when he enlisted in the U.S. Navy back in early 1940 and just eighteen when he came back on leave from boot camp and married Simmie Lee Vines, herself just turned sixteen. He was still only eighteen and an ablebodied seaman when, trapped below decks, he went down with the U.S.S. *Oklahoma* at Pearl Harbor without ever laying eyes on either the enemy or his two-month-old son.

Sixteen years later it was generally agreed around Glen Jean that "the Pope boy, he's a wildun now, ain't he?" It was a consensus reached despite the twin facts that Jake Pope was valedictorian of his high school graduating class and that his astonishing good looks had yet to get any girl into serious trouble, although there had been one anxious moment earlier in the spring.

Jake Pope's mother, Simmie Lee, was by then thirty-two and looked fifty-two or even more because she had let herself go and her teeth, never her best feature, had all fallen out, the last one going as she bit into a piece of angel food cake on her thirtieth birthday.

"She spent it all on that boy," was the way the folks around Glen Jean judged it, especially the bachelors who, to a man, had gone courting the Widow Pope, not so much in hopes of sharing her bed, but rather the $10,000 in GI insurance that she had received on the death of her husband.

Simmie Lee had rejected each mumbled proposal because if she got married, she would no longer be a widow, and the Veterans Administration would no longer pay her a widow's pension, which in the 1940's amounted to nearly what her most serious suitors earned in their best month, unless they went up to Wheeling and got themselves jobs in the steel mill.

So Simmie Lee remained a widow, establishing a comfortable, but undemanding liaison with Billy Bolton Hodo, an older man who farmed some, had a fairly good still, and kept his wife locked up in the attic because she was crazy and had been for fifteen years.

For a time things worked out fine for Simmie Lee and her son whom she fed according to the rules set forth in an official U.S. Department of Agriculture diet that she got from the Home Demonstration Agent over in Fayetteville, the county seat. The boy grew like a jimson weed until at thirteen he was six-foot-one and rising.

It was about then that Simmie Lee took up the smoking of Lucky Strike cigarettes and even grew addicted to them. This created a certain amount of friction between her and Billy Bolton Hodo, who didn't much hold with women who smoked cigarettes. A pipe, well, yes, that was all right if you were a woman and past fifty, Billy Bolton thought, but cigarettes were the devil's own invention.

Simmie Lee let him fuss and continued to go through three packs of Lucky Strikes a day until the night she went to sleep smoking one and burned up the mattress. Then she quit as abruptly as she had begun because not only had she burned up the mattress, she had also burned up $5,987, which was what was left from the $10,000 that had been paid on the death of her teenage husband.

The early fifties had started out as pure hard times for Simmie Lee so to keep body and soul together she agreed to start running Billy Bolton Hodo's moonshine over to Charleston where it fetched a better price, part of which she got to keep. Like most youngsters in the South and Southwest, Simmie Lee had learned to drive as soon as her feet could reach the pedals, which in her case was around twelve. Billy Bolton Hodo provided the car that she made her weekly run to Charleston in. It was a 1953 Ford V-8 with a hopped-up engine and overload springs and it could hit 135 miles per hour, should the need arise, which it sometimes did.

Simmie Lee always took the long way around to Charleston, avoiding the main highways and sticking to the back roads that led over to Mossy and up to Kincaid and Handeleye and Marmer. Billy Bolton Hodo paid her $25 a trip and with that and her widow's pension that President Eisenhower got Congress to raise to $100 a month, even though she hadn't voted for him, Simmie Lee managed to scrape by pretty well and send her son through high school.

In fact, it was only two months after he was graduated that Jake Pope was parked about midnight on the side of a back road, the one that led over to Mossy, in Corine Mask's almost brand-new 1956 Chevrolet convertible that her daddy had given her as a graduation present. Jake Pope was trying to get into Corine's pants and he was making good progress when a car without lights screamed by at close to 115 miles per hour. This was a singular enough event to make Jake Pope raise his head from his labors.

"Sweet Christ, there goes Mamma!" he said. "Look at her fly!"

"You sure?" Corine said, sitting up and pulling her sweater down over her bare breasts out of deference to the Widow Pope's fleeting presence.

"I'm sure. It's Thursday, isn't it?"

"Uh-huh."

"Then that was Mamma and she's sure got somebody on her tail," Jake Pope said.

There was a moon that night, a three-quarter moon, which shed enough light to lend a glisten to the winding strip of asphalt that was the road that led over to Mossy. The boy and the girl watched as the Ford disappeared around a curve.

"No brake lights, you notice?" Jake Pope said. "She had Billy Bolton fix it so her brake lights wouldn't show."

"Uh-huh," Corine said.

Jake Pope caught a pair of approaching headlights in the rearview mirror and turned. "Well, look at em come," he said.

Corine turned to look. "That's old J. T. Posey, idn't it?" she said. "I betcha he's got old Humor Hoyt with him."

It was a Plymouth sedan that swept past the parked convertible, twin red lights flashing lewdly from behind its grille, hidden there out of sight so that when not in use nobody, except 92 percent of the adult population of Fayette County, would recognize the car as the property of the Alcohol, Tobacco and Tax Division of the United State Internal Revenue Service.

And Corine Mask had been right, for inside the car behind the wheel was old J. T. Posey with old Humor Hoyt right beside him. They were Federal agents, moonshine warriors, and old J. T. was twenty-seven while old Humor was thirty-one.

Jake Pope started the convertible's engine. "They're not gonna catch Mamma," he said, "but let's go see where they give up."

"Weren't you having fun?" Corine said with a pretty pout.

Jake Pope gave her a grin and her knee a pat, although it was really more of a feel. "We'll have some more fun later," he said. Corine replied with a dirty giggle.

The Federal agents gave up their chase a mile down the road. They gave up when they saw the explosion of gasoline and 185-proof corn whiskey light up the sky nearly three-quarters of a mile away, which was where Simmie Lee Pope, or the car she was driving, failed to make an S curve at 87 miles per hour. It was the car probably, because Simmie Lee had taken that same set of curves at 90 before. Lots of times.

The two Federal agents were the first to arrive and discover that the driver had been burned beyond recognition. But they didn't have to recognize much to know that it was Simmie Lee Pope, dead at thirty-two. Humor Hoyt, who was thirty-one, had gone to school with her and he knew it was Simmie Lee by the way she drove and he tried to say something that would comfort her son who was now standing there at the edge of the gully, whitefaced and trembling, but without tears, staring down at the twisted, smoking wreckage of the 1953 Ford and at the burned thing that had been his mother.

"I went to school with your mamma, Jake," Humor Hoyt said awkwardly. "She sure was a good woman." When the boy didn't respond, Humor Hoyt, Federal agent, tried to think of something else he could say. Something nice. "And you know what else, Jake?" Jake Pope looked at him then, or at least turned his head that way. Humor Hoyt blurted it out. "She was the best goddamn whiskey driver we ever went after."

The next morning at dawn Billy Bolton Hodo came by and found Jake Pope sitting on the steps of his mother's rented house, watching the sun come up. Billy Bolton sat down beside him and together they watched in silence until the sun was an hour up into the sky.

It was then that Billy Bolton took two worn twenties and a fairly new ten from his leather purse, the deep, sack kind with twin clasps, and proffered them to Jake Pope.

"I owed your mamma for last week's drive and also for this un's," he said. Jake Pope nodded and took the money, shoving it into his pocket.

Billy Bolton found a stick and used it to draw an X in the dirt.

"You know, Jake," he said, "I—well, I really liked your mamma."

Jake Pope nodded again.

"I mean I *really* liked her and I think she really liked me. If it hadn't been for my old woman, well—"

"Yeah, I know," Jake Pope said.

Billy Bolton Hodo rose. "Well, I just wanted you to know, Jake. I'm gonna miss Simmie Lee." His voice broke then. "Oh, Lordy God, how I'm gonna miss her!"

He hurried away so that Jake Pope wouldn't see him cry. When he got home, Billy Bolton Hodo took down his shotgun, a ten-gauge pump, went up to the attic, unlocked the door, and fired twice at the woman who was his wife and who had been insane for twenty-five years.

They held two funerals in Glen Jean that week, but they wouldn't let Billy Bolton Hodo go to either of them. Jake Pope went to both and cried at both.

4

THE GREY CADILLAC LIMOUSINE PULLED UP AT THE ENtrance of the apartment building at the corner of 23rd and P Streets, a site once occupied by a Gulf gas station, but now the site of what the architect hoped would look like an eighteenth-century French chateau that just happened to be nine stories high.

The limousine's chauffeur, a tall lean black in his late fifties with closely cropped grey hair and a handsome guard's mustache to match, went around the front of the car and opened the curbside rear door.

The distinguished-looking man with the faintly patriarchal air was Thomas J. Fiquette who had spent twenty years on the Metropolitan Police Vice Squad and retired poor, a resounding testimonial to his honesty, probity, and the iron grip that he had kept on his greed.

Fiquette was now factotum in the Ancel Easter household. It really wasn't a too arduous job because Easter was a bachelor, in fact, Washington's most eligible bachelor if one were to exclude the three unmarried closet queens in the U.S. Senate. Fiquette, himself a widower, occupied two rooms in the rather large house that Ancel Easter maintained in a reasonably tony section of town just down from the French Embassy at the bottom of Kalorama Circle with a view that overlooked Rock Creek Park. The ex-vice squad cop cooked and served and often as not shared the evening meal with Easter. He also supervised the maid, a distant cousin who came in thrice weekly, chauffeured the limousine, did the shopping, served as deacon in his church on Sunday, and about twice or even three times a month brought in some high-class strutters in sets of twos and threes for his employer's amusement, and if he felt up to it, for his own.

Fiquette had worked for Ancel Easter ever since retiring at fifty from the vice squad seven years ago. He had given up smoking at the height of the lung cancer scare ten years before and booze a year later. The only nasty habit he had left was the .38 Smith & Wesson Airweight Chief's Special that he carried around in a hip holster so that its bulge showed hardly at all.

Jake Pope got out of the limousine first, followed by Ancel Easter. "How've you been feeling, Tom?" Pope said to the man who held the door for him.

"Pretty fair, Jake. And you?"

"No complaints."

Ancel Easter paused to look up at the apartment building and shake his head slightly in mild wonderment. "I still don't understand the architectural style any more than I understand your wanting to be a landlord, but it was sure one sweet deal you put together."

"It was Crawdad's idea really," Jake Pope said. "He thought I should have a nice place to live."

Ancel Easter turned to the waiting Fiquette. "I'll be about thirty minutes," he said, glancing at his watch. "Think you can park it here that long?"

"If it looks like they're gonna give me any trouble, I'll put the flags out."

The flags were flown from the front fenders of the Cadillac when Fiquette wanted to park or double-park somewhere he shouldn't. One flag was the Stars and Stripes and the other was the intricately designed cerise, purple and silver banner of a volunteer fire department located just outside of Gadsen, Alabama. Fiquette had run across it somewhere and bought it for a dollar because he liked its looks. With the flags in place and perhaps fluttering a little in a soft breeze, Fiquette could park the Cadillac anywhere because everybody thought it belonged to the President or at least to the Secretary of State. The flags were largely for the benefit of snotty doormen and young cops who didn't know him. The older cops who knew Fiquette, or at least remembered him, wouldn't have given him a ticket if he had been parked halfway up the Capitol steps.

The apartment building's name was engraved on a small, discreet brass plaque that Jake Pope gave a quick rub to with his coat sleeve before entering. The brass plaque said that the building's name was The Simmie-Lee, with a hyphen that had been the engraver's mistake, and Pope was sometimes amused by his tenants' attempt to give the building's name what they hoped was the correct French pronunciation.

The lobby of the apartment was somebody's idea of what the grand hall in a mid-eighteenth-century French chateau should look like providing Monsieur Le Comte had plenty of money and not too much taste. Because the apartment building itself was built on a long, narrow lot, the lobby was long and narrow with a gigantic white marble fireplace that could burn nothing and which was topped by an equally gigantic gilt-edged mirror that had been lifted into place with the use of a small crane.

The lobby's furniture, consisting of a number of chairs and couches and writing desks and one sideboard, was highly polished and of that spindly-legged design that Americans call French Provincial and the French don't call anything at all. Some of it was new and some of it was old and all of it was expensive and almost no one ever sat on any of it.

Inside the elevator Pope punched the button lettered PH which stood for Penthouse. It was one of those high-speed elevators, the fastest that Otis made, and Ancel Easter said what he always said when he rode in it. He said, "Wheee!"

Jake Pope's penthouse consisted of a large combination living room-dining room, a big kitchen, a bath and a half, a master bedroom, a study, and lots of closets. Although there was the flash of chrome here and there, the penthouse would have satisfied few adolescent fantasies, probably because there were too many books and too many paintings and too much old leather and frayed fabric. Actually, the furniture was very much like the clothes that Pope wore: good, expensive stuff and still serviceable, but getting old and worn.

Pope went into the kitchen and started opening cabinet doors. "What do you want to drink, Scotch?" he said.

"And soda, if you've got it."

Pope opened the refrigerator. "I haven't got any soda; how about water?"

"Water's fine," Easter said.

Pope opened and closed a few more cabinet doors. "I don't have any Scotch either. How about bourbon?"

"That's what I wanted all along," Easter said.

"Bourbon and water. And if you don't have any ice, I won't fret."

"I got ice," Pope said.

Easter crossed the living room and looked out through the sheet of glass that formed its west wall. It was the June view, which meant that it was of the trees of Georgetown. A few rooftops were visible here and there, but not many. I wonder if this town has as many trees as it does people, Easter thought and decided to have his secretary check it out when he got back to the office. Ancel Easter liked trees.

When Jake Pope said, "Here," Easter turned and accepted his drink.

"Well?" Pope said.

Easter went back over to the west window for another look at the trees. "Crawdad said he had something hot. 'I've got something hot.' Those were his exact words."

"And you offered to send a car for him," Pope said. "A car that would bring him down to GETS where he hadn't been in what, twelve years?"

"More," Easter said. "More than twelve years. And he agreed. He agreed to come down and he said what he had was hot. So you know what I thought?"

"Probably the same thing that I'd've thought," Pope said.

"I thought he had something important to tell me. I thought he might've found out how the world was going to end, and also when. Something like that."

"That's what I'd've thought."

Easter took a swallow of his drink and turned from the window so that he could look at Pope. "He called me up at home about nine o'clock that night and said he was having some trouble with his bowels. I told him that I was sorry and had he seen a doctor. He said no, that he'd just come back from his walk. You know his walk?"

Jake Pope nodded. "Down O Street to Twenty-sixth over to P, down P to Twenty-third, then back over to O and up past the old folks' nursing home—uh—what's its name—the—uh—"

"Mar-Salle."

"Yeah," Pope said. "The Mar-Salle where all his buddies are. He never went in though."

"No. He just stood outside and looked at it. At ninety-three."

"He'd been looking at it for years," Pope said.

"But he never went in."

"No," Pope said. "He never went in. He'd just look at it and then he'd go on up O Street to Twenty-first and then cut back into Georgetown on Q."

"Past the Cosmos Club," Easter said.

"Yeah, he always went past the Cosmos Club. He had to go down Mass Avenue to get to Q."

"He was a member."

"Of the Cosmos Club."

"That's right."

"Are you?"

Ancel Easter nodded. "Yes."

"Is it fun?"

"Fun?"

"Sure," Pope said. "Isn't that why people join clubs, to have fun? Or maybe I'm thinking of the Gaslight Club or American Legion Post 422. Maybe that's what people join if they want to have fun. People have taken me to the Cosmos Club for lunch and dinner a few times, but I don't think I ever saw anybody having any."

"Fun," Easter said.

"That's right."

"No, that's not the place to go for fun, now that I think of it, which I sure as hell hadn't before. What you get at the Cosmos Club is intellectual stimulation."

"Along with the bad food," Pope said. "I remember the bad food, but I don't remember the other. When I went there somebody was always trying to sell me something and they took me there to make the pitch."

"And you didn't buy," Easter said.

"No, I didn't buy. But that's where Crawdad got it. Something hot, he said."

"Uh-huh," Easter said. "In the men's crapper, as he called it. He said he was having some trouble with his bowels so on his walk that night he decided that maybe he'd stop off and see whether a change of scenery might help him take a crap. So he went in the Cosmos Club, had a drink in the lounge, and then headed for the men's room. You want the details?"

"Sure," Pope said.

Easter sighed, took another swallow of his drink, and sat down in a club chair. "Well, Crawdad told me he didn't sit down on the toilet anymore. He'd come to the conclusion that the reason that most people have trouble with their bowels is that they don't assume the position that God intended them to assume. They sit instead of squatting. So Crawdad the past couple of years had been squatting up on the toilet seat and he told me that it'd worked wonders."

Pope leaned forward. "They checked, didn't they? When they came into the crapper, I mean, they looked under the doors of the stalls to see if anybody was there."

"That's right," Easter said.

"But Crawdad was squatting up there on the toilet seat so they missed him."

"They missed him."

"And that's when he heard it—or overheard it."

"They wouldn't have had to have said much," Easter said. "Not for him to put it together."

"His exact words. What did he say?"

"All right. First he told me about his walk. We can skip that, can't we?"

"Yes."

"Then he told me about his bowels. In detail. I sympathized. Then he told me about the position he assumed on the toilet seat. After that he said, and now I'm trying to quote him exactly."

"All right."

"He said, 'Because of my position on the commode I went undetected. But, Ancel, I believe I have something hot. I firmly believe that I actually overheard two cabalists.' That's when I offered to send the car for him and that's when he agreed."

"And that's all you've got?" Pope said.

"Except that he was shot dead the next morning and robbed of thirty-two cents and a gold watch."

"A coincidence maybe, but you don't much like coincidences, do you?"

"Not much."

" 'Two cabalists,' " Pope said. "Nobody but Crawdad would be that precise, would they? So if there are cabalists, then there's got to be a cabal. A group of secret plotters operating out of the men's crapper at the Cosmos Club. By God, I like it."

"I thought you might."

"Maybe a pair of buck generals, going over the details for next Sunday morning's coup out at the

Pentagon? Or maybe a guy from Ma Bell and a guy from General Motors who're going to take over the Post Office Wednesday noon when everybody's out to lunch and run it at a profit. Maybe it was something like that?"

Ancel Easter held out his empty glass for a refill. "He didn't say."

When Pope returned from the kitchen with two fresh drinks, he said, "But you don't think it was either of those?"

"No, I don't think it was either of those," Easter said, accepting his drink.

"But he didn't tell you what it was," Pope said.

"No. He didn't tell me."

"So you waited around at the funeral home until I showed up."

"That's right."

"How'd you know I'd show up?"

Easter waved his glass a little. "I knew. You owed him a lot. Or thought you did. It adds up to the same thing."

"So you waited for me to show up and now we're sitting here drinking my bourbon and you're about to make your pitch, aren't you?"

Ancel Easter shook his head. It was a well-shaped head, one whose features seemed to have been selected only after a lot of careful planning. It was as if Ancel Easter had decided that he really needed a cleft chin and a widish thin mouth that smiled easily, revealing nice white teeth, but not much gum. Yet he didn't seem to have been that fussy about his nose. It was just a nice, straight nose, not too long or too short, which didn't detract from his eyes. For the eyes were what you really remembered about Ancel Easter. You remembered them because they wouldn't let you forget. His eyes didn't look at you, they seemed to look into you and examine all the nastiness that lay there. They were green eyes, not a cool green, but a dark, hot green that roiled and sparkled a lot as thought what lay beneath them was about to erupt.

Above the eyes were dark thick brows that seemed to have been carefully selected and carefully tended. There was also a high, wide forehead to encase all those brains and it was capped by dark, wavy hair that at fifty-one was just beginning to get some streaks of gray in it, which a lot of young women probably wanted to touch.

Ancel Easter shook the head that he seemed to have designed himself and said, "I'm not going to make you a pitch, Jake. You already know what it is."

This time it was Jake Pope who rose and crossed to the window and looked out at the trees of Georgetown. "Why don't you just go down to the White House and tell dummy about it?"

"Tell him what?" Easter said. "Anyway, I already saw him once today."

"He came to look at Crawdad? No shit. How was he?"

"He smelled like Dentyne."

Jake Pope turned. "You want me to do it, is that it?"

"That's right."

"I've been out of it for six years. I've devoted myself these past six years to being rich. That's a full-time job."

"I know about your being rich."

"Yeah, you do, don't you."

"Well?" Easter said.

Pope's eyes moved around the room as though he

might get lucky and find the answer that he should give lying curled up in a corner. But after a moment he sighed and said, "A couple of weeks. I'll give it a couple of weeks. If I don't turn it by then, you can get somebody else."

"I won't need anybody else."

"Why?"

"Because Crawdad said one other thing. He said that whatever is going to happen will happen on July eleventh. That's a couple of weeks from now, isn't it?"

"A little less," Jake Pope said.

5

THAT SAME AFTERNOON, NOT QUITE HALF A MILE NORTH
and east of the Simmie-Lee apartment building, the
two black killers of Crawdad Gilmore walked into the
Friendly Liquor Store in the 1700 block of Connecticut
Avenue and bought two cans of Coca-Cola from the
store's proprietor, Samuel A. Hermann, fifty-nine.

Samuel Hermann ran the Friendly Liquor Store all
by himself except for his delivery man, Era Booker
Harris, twenty-two, who was out on his bicycle de-
livering a fifth of Smirnoff 80-proof vodka to Miss Jennette Breed, thirty-eight, of the 1800 block on 20th
Street who had awakened only a little while before at
3:20 in the afternoon and needed a drink bad.

Before Samuel Hermann handed the Coca-Colas
over to Crawdad Gilmore's killers he said, "That'll be
fifty-four cents with tax."

The taller of the two killers looked around the store.
"Gimme some of them, too," he said, pointing to a
counter cardboard display that held cellophane sacks
of cashew nuts.

"These here?" Samuel Hermann said.

"Yeah. Them."

44

"Eighty-three cents with tax," Samuel Hermann said and put the sack of nuts on top of the Coca-Colas.

The taller killer started going through his pockets. Samuel Hermann watched, growing bored with the transaction. He made a small impatient gesture. The killer glared at him, then seemed to relax when he produced a wadded-up dollar bill from his left hip pocket. He smoothed it out on the counter and slid it over to Samuel Hermann.

The Friendly Liquor Store's proprietor moved down to the cash register and rang up 83 cents on the soft-drink key. He put the dollar bill into the register and removed 17 cents in change. When he looked up with the change, he found himself looking into the barrel of a Llama Model XV .22 caliber automatic pistol that had been manufactured in Vitoria, Spain, exclusively for export. The pistol was held in the right hand of the shorter of the two killers.

The taller one held a knife. He moved it back and forth in a sideways motion. It's a kitchen knife, Samuel Hermann thought. Like we got at home.

"Come on, mothuh fuckuh, you know what we want," the taller of the two killers said, moving the knife back and forth.

"Please," Samuel Hermann said, stepped back from the cash register as far as he could go, and raised his hands. "Please. Help yourself. It's yours. All of it. Yours."

It was the third time that year that Samuel Hermann had been held up at gunpoint. He didn't keep much money in the cash register anymore. Earlier that afternoon his delivery man, Era Booker Harris, had deposited $350, most of the day's receipts, in the Dupont Circle branch of the Riggs National Bank. Since then business had not been good. In fact, it had been lousy.

Half-pints mostly, Samuel Hermann remembered, and not many of them.

In the cash register now were $29 in bills and $2.23 in coins. Era Booker Harris was carrying another $20 in ones and fives so that he could make change for the $20-bill that was going to be given him by Miss Jennette Breed, who needed a drink bad.

Samuel Hermann made a small gesture with his right hand, indicating the open cash drawer. "Please," he said again. "Take it. Just please don't shoot."

"Shit, man, gimme it," the killer with the knife said.

Samuel Hermann took a hesitant step toward the cash register. Such a little gun, he thought. Like a toy it is. His right hand moved to the cash register, dipped inside, and closed around the grip of the .38 Colt Detective Special which lay there where the fifties and hundreds were supposed to be. The pistol was a birthday gift from his nephew, Morris, who ran a retail clothing store out on Georgia Avenue and packed a Colt Python .357 Magnum on his hip, right out in plain sight. Morris had never been held up.

Samuel Hermann had the pistol almost halfway out of the cash drawer when the knife entered his throat. He felt pain for only a moment because the smaller of the two killers got excited and jerked the trigger of his Spanish-made automatic and shot Samuel Hermann in the left temple. He died standing there behind the cash register.

The two killers watched the dead body fall. They seemed fascinated. Then the taller of the two grabbed a handful of bills from the cash register and stuffed them into his hip pocket. "Git the Cokes," he said.

The smaller killer pocketed his Spanish-made automatic and reached for the Cokes. He handed one to the taller killer. "Doan run," the taller one warned, ripping the top off his Coke. The smaller one nodded, opened his own can, and took a swallow.

They pushed through the door of the Friendly Liquor Store and walked slowly up Connecticut Avenue toward S Street, sipping their Coca-Colas. No one noticed them. When they got to S Street they turned right and ran like hell.

6

AFTER JAKE POPE WAS GRADUATED FROM THE UNIVERSITY of West Virginia in 1961 with a bachelor's degree in English literature he found that there was no great demand for his services. Indeed, there was no demand at all.

It had taken him five years to work his way through the university. He had held all the menial jobs that are usually available to impoverished students in a college town. He had washed dishes, waited tables, driven a cab, bootlegged whiskey, and served as night clerk in a motel that rented its rooms by the hour.

As far as he knew he was the first Pope ever to acquire a college degree in anything. And if it had been another time, or if his mind had been less quick and his spirit less restless, he might have taken his degree and gone back to Glen Jean and maybe have taught school or gone to work for the county or sold Fords or something. Instead, he went to Los Angeles.

He had two motives for going to Los Angeles, neither of them better nor worse than the motives anyone else has for going there. One needs a motive, if not a sound reason, to go to Los Angeles, just as one needs a motive, but not necessarily a sound reason, to commit murder. This is probably because motives don't require good sense, while sound reasons almost always do.

One of his motives for going to Los Angeles was geographical, Los Angeles being almost as far away from West Virginia as he could get without travelling to Pago Pago or Tahiti or some other exotic lotus land that he couldn't afford to get to anyhow.

His second motive for going was even more ephemeral. It was based on various assurances that Los Angeles, or rather its motion picture industry, or rather Hollywood, was crying for astonishingly handsome West Virginia twenty-one-year-olds who happened to stand six-foot-four in their socks.

These assurances had all come from various young ladies, still called coeds back in 1961, who had gone to bed with Jake Pope at one time or another and who thought he was handsome enough to be a film star.

And he was. The USDA diet that Simmie Lee had fed him on had given him a big-boned frame that he needed to carry his height. He had an arresting face because it made you look at it twice to seek out the flaw that you may have missed the first time. But there weren't any flaws. His chin was firm, his mouth was generous, his teeth were perfect, and his slightly acquiline nose complemented his cheekbones and rescued him from being pretty. He had large brown eyes that might have been sad or serious or both, but whose real quality lay in the fact that they were the kind of eyes that would never need glasses. Nor would he ever grow bald because he had a fine mane of slightly wavy hair whose color was that ruddy, reddish brown that some call chestnut.

But despite his good looks and his quick mind,

Jake Pope lacked one ingredient that goes into the composition of most great actors and virtually all bad ones. He lacked vanity. He thought about his looks almost as often as he thought about his toenails. Indeed, he was so dismally lacking in self-consciousness that he might not have recognized himself walking down the street.

So it wasn't any great blow to his vanity or pride when, after getting off the Greyhound bus in Los Angeles, he discovered that nobody in the motion picture industry had heard that he was coming, or cared now that he was there.

Still, he went through the motions. He acquired an agent, a sixty-six-year-old ex-actress who took a motherly interest in him, sent him to an inexpensive diction coach, and occasionally lent him ten dollars, which he always repaid. She even managed to land Jake Pope a few small parts in some rotten television westerns in which he got to speak such lines as "That's not the way I heard it, Carter," and "I'll go," and "Count me in."

To support himself, Jake Pope washed cars in an all-night car wash and later parked them on a lot that belonged to a steak house on La Cienega. After six months of this he decided without rancor or recrimination that he was not really cut out to be either an actor or a parking lot attendant. So he made up his mind to do something else.

He signed up with several employment agencies, wrote a brief résumé and had it multilithed, and started studying the help wanted ads in the *Los Angeles Times*. He had decided that he would not accept a job unless it met a modest two-point criteria. First of all, it would have to pay something and secondly, it would have to be one that didn't bore him into witlessness.

By this time, however, Jake Pope had reached a point in his career, if it could be called that, where $100 a week looked like all the money in the world and anything, even collecting empty Coke bottles, seemed a far more exhilarating occupation than backing cars in and out of empty spaces.

Thus when the ad appeared that Sunday in the help wanted columns of the *Los Angeles Times,* Jake Pope dropped his reply into the mailbox an hour after he read it. The ad itself had a heavy ruled box around it and a flavor all its own:

WANTED!!!

Young Southern gentleman with proper upbringing of good moral character and impeccable references to train for lifetime career in business demanding utmost tact, discretion, and confidentiality. College degree essential. Excellent prospects for advancement. Write LA Times Box 283.

Four days later, Jake Pope received a telephone call. After he said hello, a voice so sweet that it was almost sticky said, "Is this Mr. Pope?", giving Pope two syllables the way that only a Southern girl can do.

"Yes, this is Mr. Pope."

"Mr. Pope, I'm calling for Judge John Whetstone?" She made it a question. She made almost everything she said a question. "You answered our advertisement in the Sunday paper and Judge Whetstone was wondering whether it'd be convenient for you to drop around and see him this afternoon about two?"

"Yes, two would be convenient."

"Oh, isn't that just fine! I'll tell the Judge then that he can spect you about two."

The address she gave him was on Rodeo Drive in

Beverly Hills. It turned out to be a small, fairly new office building whose tenants were mostly lawyers except for something called The Whetstone Organization that occupied the entire fifth floor, which was as high as the building went.

The reception area was just opposite the elevator and from the furniture on the floor and the pictures on the walls it was impossible to tell what the Whetstone Organization did to pay the rent. The furniture was of the Scandinavian variety, mostly oiled walnut upholstered in bright, nubby fabrics. The pictures on the walls were large matted photographs depicting the South as it once had been—or still should be—depending on one's viewpoint. There was a Louisiana bayou shaded by live oaks dripping with Spanish moss. A winding gravelled drive led up between two rows of fine old pecan trees to a white-columned manse. There was even a cotton field being picked by some black field hands whose sweat was out of camera range. A mule dragged an empty wagon and its driver down a lonesome dirt road into a spectacular sunset. A ragamuffin white kid, armed with nothing but some freckles and a cane pole, grinned into the camera as he held up a string of fat catfish.

After he gave his name to the receptionist, a tiny blonde with a crisp smile and flirty blue eyes, Jake Pope sat down in one of the Scandinavian chairs and wondered how long he would have to wait before he found out what it was that the Whetstone Organization wanted with a young Southern gentleman of good moral character.

He didn't have to wait long. The little blonde picked up her phone, dialed a number, and whispered something. Less than a minute later a tall brunette appeared and said, "Mr. Pope? Judge Whetstone will see you now?" She turned her statement into a question and gave his name two syllables so Pope assumed that the brunette was the same woman who had telephoned him. She had a nice slink to her walk and Jake Pope followed it through a door and down a corridor that had ten doors leading off of it, none of them open.

"I'm Mary Sue Hethcox, Mr. Pope, Judge Whetstone's secretary?" the brunette said over her shoulder. She made it yet another Southern question and Pope replied that he was pleased to meet her.

She ushered him into a small office, which was apparently hers because it contained a secretarial desk and an electric typewriter. They then went through yet another door and into the presence of Judge John Whetstone himself. Mary Sue Hethcox withdrew after making the introductions and Pope found himself shaking hands with a medium-sized man in his mid-fifties who had the meanest blue eyes that Pope had ever seen.

The rest of Judge John Whetstone was all thick convivial charm as he pumped Pope's hand. "I'm sure pleased to meet you, son. Now stand back there so I can take a good look at you."

Pope moved back a pace. Whetstone cocked his head to one side and ran his mean blue eyes up and down Jake Pope's frame. Pope decided that those eyes didn't miss much.

"You want me to lift up my skirts and walk across the room?" Pope said.

Judge Whetstone whooped and Pope took it to be a laugh. "How long you been in town, son?"

"Six months."

"Came out here to be an actor?"

"It was in the back of my mind."

"Made the rounds?"

"Most of them."

"Connect?"

"A few times."

"Not enough to eat on though?"

"No," Pope said. "Not enough for that."

"Sit down, son," Whetstone said and Pope sat down on the cool leather of yet another couch that had been made just south of the Arctic Circle. The rest of the furniture in the rather large room was also of Scandinavian design. All but the desk. The desk was a huge oak rolltop with about three dozen little pigeonholes and drawers and recesses, each of them stuffed with important-looking pieces of paper. The desk managed to look awfully old and extremely quaint and terribly busy all at the same time. It was, Pope decided, quite an effective prop, although he wasn't sure he liked it.

Whetstone dragged up one of the chairs close enough so that when he sat down his knees were almost touching Pope's.

"Well, sir, I'll tell you," he said. "I like nice-looking people working with me. There's enough ugliness and stink and corruption in this world. You see it in your living room on TV. Read about it in your papers. Rub elbows with it on the street. So I like to work with people who smell sweet and look pretty, by God, I do. Now do you blame me?"

"What do these sweet-smelling people do who work for you, Mr. Whetstone?"

"*Judge* Whetstone, if you don't mind, sir."

"I don't mind."

"Well, the people who work with me first of all keep their mouths shut and their eyes open. Think you could do that, Mr. Pope?"

"I could try."

"Ever been in jail?"

"No."

"No use lying about it, if you have, because I'll find out."

"I've never been in jail."

"Ever been arrested?"

"A couple of traffic tickets."

"That doesn't count. Not married, are you?"

Pope shook his head. "No."

Whetstone nodded several times as if he found the answer gratifying. He had a big long head with ears like cup handles and putty-colored hair that was going thin on him. Beneath those mean blue eyes was a puffy, turned-up nose with big, black nostrils that sort of stared out at you. When he talked his voice crackled and his thin, pink lips moved angrily as if they wanted to clamp down on something. The rest of his face was a chin with a sharp point that jutted out over a big Adam's apple which kept jumping out from behind his collar when he swallowed. It was an ugly face, Pope decided, but shrewd and smart and all out of illusions.

"Maybe you're wondering why I advertised for somebody from down South?"

Pope nodded. "I wondered."

"Because I'm prejudiced, that's why. I think people from down South have more gumption, better manners, and nicer looks than anybody else in the country."

"Are you from the South?"

"Do I sound like it?"

"Well, no, you don't."

"I'm from Detroit. I wish I was from down there. But I'm not, so I do the next best thing. I hire people to work for me who're from down South. I hire them not just because I happen to think they look nicer and smell sweeter than anybody else, I also hire them because they'll work cheaper—at least for a while. Let me tell you something. When I was about your age I was a rookie cop in Detroit and glad to get the job. But I had ambition so I went to night law school and studied hard and got my degree and then practiced criminal law for a while. Then I got to be a police court judge. And let me tell you this: I got to know more about the criminal mind than anybody else. I mean anybody else in this whole damn country. Now that started me thinking. I asked myself a real crass question. I said, John, how're you going to cash in on all this knowledge? Well, there were two ways. Either I could turn crooked myself or I could do what I did. And what I did was put together the best damned private investigatory agency in Southern California. If you want to go to work for me, I'll pay you a hundred dollars a week."

"That's not much."

"I know. But if you're worth a shit, I'll raise you to a hundred and fifty in six months."

"That's still not much."

"I didn't say it was. But a year from now it could be different. A year from now I got the feeling that you can write your own ticket. You wanta know why?"

"Sure. Why?"

"I make judgments sometimes. Snap judgments. They usually turn out pretty good. I've got a hunch that you've got a real feeling for the criminal mind. I've got even a better hunch that a year from now you're going to be the best investigator I got. What do you say? A hundred a week to start."

"One-twenty-five," Pope said.

"You're hired."

7

THEY THREW DR. DALLAS HUCKS OUT OF THE CAR POOL at 8:15 that morning just after they crossed the Fourteenth Street Bridge. They didn't actually throw him out, of course. He was merely told that from now on he would have to make other arrangements. Since it was Marvin Mousser's car, it was Marvin Mousser who got to do the telling.

"Hey, uh, by the way, Doc."

"Do you always have to start every sentence with 'hey,'?" Dr. Dallas Hucks said.

"I don't start every sentence with 'hey'," Mousser said.

"All right," Dr. Hucks said. "Every other sentence. You start every other sentence with 'hey'. Such as, 'Hey, didja see Flip Wilson last night?' or 'Hey, whadja think of old Dandy yesterday?' Who is Dandy, by the way, Mousser?"

"Don Meredith, for Christ's sake," Mousser said. "Everybody knows Dandy is Don Meredith."

"I didn't until now," Dr. Hucks said. "But then I don't watch television as much as you do, Mousser. How many hours a day would you say that you watch television? Five hours? Six hours?"

"I don't think it's any of your fuckin business how much I watch television. What're you doing, taking a survey?"

"Merely idle curiosity," Dr. Hucks said.

Mousser failed to make the green light and stopped behind a yellow VW. He poked the man who was sitting next to him on the front seat. "Hey, Walt, I think the Doc's taking another survey. This time they've got him working on how many hours a week a guy spends watching TV. Whaddaya think?"

Walter Ditchfield wished that Marvin Mousser wouldn't poke him. He also wished that he weren't the first person that Marvin Mousser picked up each morning. If he weren't the first person to be picked up, then he could sit in the rear of the Chevelle out of poking range. Walter Ditchfield sighed and said, "I think you'd better tell him about the new arrangements."

"I'm trying to," Mousser said. "Hey, Doc, like I was saying—"

"Hey, Doc, like I was saying," Dr. Hucks said. He was a cruel if expert mimic. "You really can't begin a sentence without 'hey,' can you?"

"What are you doing, counting again?" Mousser said. "But shit, I keep forgetting. You're a real hotshot Ph.D., aren't you? Hey, Doc, I almost forgot about that since you haven't reminded me of it in the past fifteen seconds. You're a real hotshot Ph. D. in the Department of Agriculture and a GS-14 on top of that. And here I am just a measly GS-12 and Ditchfield here, he's a 12, and Miley back there, I don't know what Miley is, but—"

"I'm a 13," Miley said from the back seat. "I'll be a 13 until I die."

"Yeah, well, it's like I said," Mousser continued. "Here you are, Doc, a Ph.D. and a GS-14 and all, riding

back and forth to work with a couple of pissant 12's and
a 13, and Jesus, you just don't know how grateful we've
all been just for the opportunity to associate with somebody like you, haven't we, you guys?"

Mousser poked Walter Ditchfield in the ribs again.
Ditchfield clenched his teeth and then unclenched them
just enough to say, "Yeah, I'm real grateful."

"See, Doc, Ditchfield here is grateful and hey,
Miley, you're grateful, aren't you?"

"Sure," Miley said, staring out the window. "I'm
grateful."

"So we're all grateful, Doc. Miley, Ditchfield and
me. I mean, shit, who'd have ever thought a guy like
me who goes home at night and takes a couple of beers
out of the refrigerator and then sits down in front of his
TV set for a few hours—who'd have thought that a guy
like that would ever get to associate with a Ph.D. like
you who goes to concerts and plays and all at night after
you get through counting the chickens for the Department of Agriculture. Hey, Doc, that is what you do over
there, isn't it? You count the chickens before they're
hatched for the Department of Agriculture, don't you?"

"The light's green," Dr. Hucks said. "That means
you can go."

"See what I mean, you guys?" Mousser said. "What
the hell would we ever have done these last six months
without the Doc here? Take you, Ditchfield. Every time
you made a little grammatical error, who could you
count on to correct it? Why, good old Doc. Now you
talk almost as good as I do. And Miley back there.
Miley likes his music. And Miley likes to sing and I
don't care what anybody else says, I think old Miley's
got a pretty good voice."

"Thanks," said Miley, still staring out the window.

"Hey, Doc, what do you think of Miley's voice?"

"I think it's exceptional," Dr. Hucks said.

"Exceptional what?" Mousser said. "Exceptional good or exceptional bad? Well, hell, you don't have to say. But six months ago when there were just the three of us, why we'd let old Miley listen to that country and western station and sing his heart out. Remember that, Ditchfield, when old Miley used to sing all the way to work and all the way back?"

"Yeah, I remember," Ditchfield said. "Why don't you just get it over with?"

"I am. I'm just telling the Doc how grateful we are because now we don't have to listen to Miley sing anymore. Now, if we wanta turn on the radio, we get to turn on WGMS and listen to something that's good for us like maybe Bach and Mozart and all that."

"Mousser," Dr. Hucks said. "I never said you had to turn on WGMS. All I said was that I wasn't going to spend one-and-one-half hours of my life each day listening to somebody try to imitate Hank Snow or Jimmie Dean or whoever it is that Miley was trying—and I repeat, *trying* to imitate."

"Cash," Miley said, not turning from the window. "People tell me I sing a lot like Johnny Cash."

"Hey, Doc, y'hear that?" Mousser said. "You saved us from having to listen to Miley sing like Johnny Cash. That's another reason we're grateful to you. But I don't guess anybody's as grateful to you as I am. I mean you really opened up my horizons."

"Do you actually have something on your mind, Mousser?" Dr. Hucks said. "If you have something on your mind, why don't you just say what it is?"

"That's a good idea," Ditchfield said.

"A hell of a good idea," Miley said, continuing to stare out the window.

"All right," Mousser said. "What I got on my mind is this. Ditchfield and Miley and me, we started this car pool two years ago and up until about six months ago we had another guy riding with us, old man Burney, used to work at Labor, but he retired and so then we got you. And we're grateful for getting you, Doc, because we got to listen to you tell us about all the places you go and all the people you know and all the fancy restaurants you eat in and what somebody said to somebody else at the Cosmos Club last night, whatever the fuck the Cosmos Club is. But I got to thinking."

"You do that occasionally, do you?" Dr. Hucks said. "Think, I mean."

"Oh, yeah," Mousser said, stopping behind the yellow VW again because the traffic was jammed up on the Fourteenth Street Bridge. "I'm really a pretty introspective guy. I got to thinking now why should a guy like the Doc, who's got a Ph.D., and who's a GS-14, and from what he says, a big shot at the Department of Agriculture, why should a guy like that ride in a car pool with three guys who don't wanta do nothing but talk about what they seen on TV last night or try to sing like Johnny Cash or whose grammar may not be too hot, like Ditchfield's here."

"There's nothing wrong with my grammar," Ditchfield said.

"Not now there ain't," Mousser said. "That's because the Doc corrected it. I don't know if he corrected all your grammar, but he sure as shit corrected you from saying more than five words a day."

"I haven't really been that harsh on you, have I, Ditchfield?" Dr. Hucks said.

"I'm okay," Ditchfield said.

"Yeah, old Ditchfield's okay and old Miley back there's okay because he don't sing anymore, he just looks out the window, so it's really just you and me, Doc, who keep the conversation going."

"This is a conversation we're having, is it?" Dr. Hucks said.

"Sure, it's a conversation."

"Sorry. I thought it might be a somewhat rambling monologue."

"Well," Mouser said, "whatever it is, it ain't gonna take much longer."

"Thank God," Dr. Hucks said.

"What I'm saying, Doc, is that a guy like you with all your advantages and your wonderful ways and your sweetheart personality and your Ph.D.—hey, Ditchfield, you know what Ph.D. stands for?"

"Piled higher and deeper," Ditchfield said mechanically.

"That's very good," Dr. Hucks said. "I'll just jot that down, if you don't mind."

Mousser started over again. "You see, Doc," he said, "What I'm trying to say is that before I had the privilege of knowing you and all the wonderful things about you, I was the kinda guy who'd get home from work and maybe open up a couple of beers and plop down in front of the TV and kinda relax, you know what I mean? I didn't think about nothing much. Now you know what I do? I go home and take out a couple of beers, and have maybe a couple of quick shots of the hard stuff, too, and I sit down in front of the TV and start thinking. And you know what I think about? I think about how dull my dipshit job is and how much I really hate my old lady and how the hell did I ever get stuck with two such rotten kids. That's what I think about when I get home and you wanta know why? Because I'm nervous. And you wanta know what makes me nervous? You do, Doc. You make me nervous. So after this morning, you're gonna have to make other arrangements."

"What do you mean, other arrangements?" Dr. Hucks said.

"I mean you're gonna have to find another car pool or drive your own car in or take the bus," Mousser said. "And I don't really give a shit which. All I know is you're not riding in this car anymore. Not after this morning."

"I'm paid up until the end of the month," Dr. Hucks said.

"No you're not," Mousser said. He reached into his pocket and brought out a check. He waved it back and forth with his left hand, steering with his right. The check was green and it had a pink slip attached to it. "Here's your check," Mousser said. "It bounced."

"There's been some mistake," Dr. Hucks said, taking the check. That bitch, he thought. She's been writing them at that liquor store again. She's been driving into the District and writing them at that goddamned liquor store.

"Sure, there's been a mistake," Mousser said. "You wrote me a bum check. That's kind of a mistake."

"I'll write you another one," Dr. Hucks said.

"Don't bother," Mousser said. "Here's where you get out." He pulled the car up at the corner of Fourteenth Street and Independence Avenue. Dr. Hucks continued to sit in the back seat looking at the green check that had the pink slip pasted to it. He made no effort to get out. The car behind honked. Mousser turned around in his seat.

"I said this is where you get out," he said.

Dr. Hucks folded the check and stuck it away in

a pants pocket. "I don't think this is quite fair," he said.

"Get out, will ya?" Mousser said. Ditchfield, sitting in the front seat, looked straight ahead. In the rear, Miley continued to stare out the window at the traffic. The car behind honked again.

"Yes," Dr. Hucks said. "I'm getting out." He pushed the handle on the rear door and got slowly out of the car.

"So long, you fuckin phoney," Mousser said and drove off.

Dr. Hucks watched the car pull out into the Fourteenth Street traffic. I'll have to start driving in, he thought. She'll bitch about that, being stuck with no car. But it'll only be for a couple of weeks, maybe until the eleventh. I'll work something else out after then. It should be easy to work something out after July the eleventh.

8

THE SAME DAY THAT THEY THREW DR. DALLAS HUCKS OUT of the car pool, Jake Pope walked up O Street in George-town until he came to the house with the six wrought-iron steps. It was late morning and the day promised to be incredibly fine and the Georgetown birds were singing about it. There was one mockingbird that Pope thought sounded as though he were trying to drown out everyone else. Pope paused on the top step and tried to find him. He didn't locate the mockingbird, but he did spot a yellow oriole and wondered if he lived around there or was just over from Baltimore on a visit.

He took the key that Ancel Easter had given him and opened the front door. Inside there was a small foyer with a hall leading back to the kitchen. A flight of stairs went up to the second floor. The foyer con-tained an old, straightbacked chair with a cane back and bottom that someone might have sat on once or twice, but briefly, in the past twenty years. There was also a couple of pictures and a magnificent old coatrack. A man's tan raincoat hung from one of the white china spools that stuck out from the coatrack on black metal rods. There were six of the rods, three on each side of an oval mirror. Beneath the mirror two curved wooden arms reached out to embrace a couple of black umbrellas. The tips of the umbrellas rested in deep black iron dishes that Pope assumed were there to catch the water when the umbrellas were wet. He gave the coatrack a pat because he had always admired it and then moved into the living room.

You still like it, he thought, even after all this time. You still like going into other people's homes and poking through their stuff, the really personal stuff like the pills they keep in the medicine cabinet and the balance they keep in their checkbook and, if you're really lucky, a five-year diary kept by somebody who just had to get everything down on paper.

Pope looked around the living room. It was almost camp, he decided, but not quite. The Morris chair was still there in the corner by the window with the 1938 bridge lamp that was positioned just so. It was the only Morris chair he had ever seen, except in pictures, and after he had spent an evening in it once he wondered why they were no longer made. He was convinced that it was the finest chair he had ever sat in.

The rest of the furniture was hodgepodge, the choice of an unfussy man whose wife had been dead for thirty years. There was a dark green couch, a couple of tan wingbacked chairs in front of the fireplace, a wall of books, and a few tables that held lamps that were somewhere between twenty and forty years old. There were also three cane-bottomed chairs that matched the one in the hall. They didn't look as if they had been sat in much either.

On a table by the green couch was a silver box. Pope lifted up its top and looked inside. There were two rubber bands, a ball-point pen, four pennies, and an oversized paper clip.

"The silver's in the dining room," the woman's voice said from behind him. "If that's what you're looking for."

Pope jumped when she spoke, and then turned. She was standing in the entranceway between the living room and the dining room. In her hands she held a dark round metal container, about the size of the kitchen canister that holds tea and usually has a hot, steaming cup of it painted on the side.

"You're not the neighborhood burglar, are you?" she said.

Pope shook his head. "No. I'm not. Are you expecting him?"

A kettle started to whistle. "No. Just curious. You want some coffee?"

"Thanks. I would. I'm Jake Pope. That won't mean anything to you unless you knew the man who used to live here."

"I knew him," she said, "but it still doesn't mean anything to me."

She turned and walked off in the direction of the whistling kettle, still carrying the metal container. Pope watched her go. She was a tall woman, at least six-foot, Pope guessed, and probably twenty-eight or twenty-nine. Maybe even thirty. She wore white slacks that looked like cotton duck and a checked brown shirt whose tail hung out because it was supposed to. She had an oval face that was deeply tanned as though she had spent all year out of doors someplace where the sun never got too hot. Pope liked the way she walked. It wasn't quite a stride, it was too smooth for that, but it was still a long, quick, lively step with a lot of spring to it.

After she disappeared into the kitchen Pope walked over to the wall of books and chose one at random. It was *Green Mansions*. Pope read the first few paragraphs before deciding that it still wasn't for him. He put the book back and turned just as the tall woman came in carrying a tray that held two cups of coffee, sugar, cream, and the dark, round metal container that was about the size of a tea canister.

"It's instant," she said, putting the tray down on a coffee table.

"That's about all I ever drink."

"How do you take it?"

"With a spoonful of sugar."

She put a spoonful of sugar into a cup and handed it to him. "Some people are fussy about coffee," she said. "I'm not. Coffee's either good or it's rotten. There's not much in between."

"I agree," Pope said.

"Well, let's sit down," she said, lowered herself to the green couch, and crossed her legs. Before she reached for her coffee she bent forward, picked up the dark, round metal container from the tray and placed it on a side table underneath a lamp with a fat china base and a tan shade. "I guess you can sit over here, Granddad," she said.

"You're the granddaughter," Pope said.

She nodded. "The errant granddaughter, I'm afraid. Faye Hix, with an *x*."

"And Crawdad's in there," Pope said, nodding at the canister.

"Uh-huh. I picked him up this morning at the funeral home. He doesn't weigh much. I keep apologizing to him every time I put him down someplace. I guess I'm going to sprinkle him into the Mississippi. That's what Ancel Easter says he wanted. I never sprinkled anybody before, have you?"

"No," Pope said. "Never."

"I wonder what it's like, sprinkling somebody's ashes? You suppose it's like emptying the vacuum cleaner?"

"Probably, unless you were close to whoever you're sprinkling."

She shook her head. "I think we were close when we lived here years ago. But then we moved out to the Coast and I never saw him again. I used to write to him when I was a kid though, but I stopped doing that and started sending him Christmas cards. But I don't send anyone Christmas cards anymore—" She stopped and shrugged and took a sip of her coffee. "What about you, did you know him well?"

Pope nodded. "Pretty well. I worked with him once about eight years ago and after that we became friendly. He liked to talk and I liked to listen."

She thought a moment. "He was eighty-six when you worked with him then. I thought he'd retired by then. Are you a lawyer?"

"No, I'm not a lawyer. Your grandfather had retired by then and it was just a private matter that I helped him with."

"Oh." She produced a cigarette from her shirt pocket and lit it with a green throwaway lighter. "You don't say much, do you?" she said, blowing some smoke out and fanning it away with her left hand. "I mean you say things and your sentences parse all right, but so far all I've got is that you're somebody called Jake Pope who's poking around my dead grandfather's house at eleven o'clock of a June morning. So who are you, Jake Pope, and what do you want and would you like me to warm up your coffee?"

Pope grinned at her. "I'd like that, thanks. When you get back I'll lay out my *bona fides.*"

"You make it sound like a threat," she said, gathering up the cups.

When she came back Jake Pope accepted his, took a sip, and said, "Your grandfather was murdered, you know."

Faye Hix nodded.

"I used to be an investigator. I'm not anymore, but Ancel Easter and I thought that since I had some free time, I might spend it looking into your grandfather's murder. Maybe you ought to call him."

"Who?"

"Ancel Easter."

She shrugged. "If your story doesn't click, I'll call him."

"That's about all there is to it. I thought there might be something here that might be helpful."

"Wouldn't the police have already found it?"

"Probably."

"You're just sort of helping them out with their inquiries, as they say in Britain."

Pope nodded. "They do say that there, don't they."

"But usually after they've nabbed the villain."

"You used to live there?"

"For a time," she said. "My husband was British. Or English. I never did get that straight. I think that when they don't like being born there, they say they're British. Or maybe it's the other way around."

"What happened to Mr. Hix?" Pope said.

"Why?"

"You said he was British. What is he now?"

"He's dead," she said. "The poor bastard fell off a horse and broke his neck."

"I'm sorry."

"Don't be. It happened two years ago. He's grown a little dim in my memory. I don't wear the widow's weeds too well."

"What you have on looks nice."

She looked down at her white pants and shirt. "I'm all dressed up. Usually it's blue jeans and boots and one of the late Mr. Hix's old shirts. I run a dude ranch."

"In Montana," Pope said.

"You know Montana?"

"I've been there a few times."

"I'm about thirty miles east of Kalispell."

"You're near Flathead Lake then."

She nodded. "Not too far."

"How's the dude ranch business?"

"Lousy. At least that's how it's been so far this year. We had a blizzard last week. Can you imagine that, a blizzard in June?"

"I've heard it happens out there sometimes."

"That's why I didn't hear about my grandfather. The blizzard knocked out my phone and also most of this month's business. Everybody's canceled out. I'm sorry I missed his funeral."

"Well, it wasn't really a funeral."

"What was it?"

"You might say that they just sort of laid him out in the funeral home and people came by to pay their respects."

"A lot of people?"

"So I understand. The President came."

"No kidding? Was he a friend of my grandfather's?"

"I don't think so."

She sighed or pretended to. "Well, that makes me feel a little better. What did he come for, I mean the President?"

Pope shook his head. "Probably because somebody told him it would be smart politics, whatever that is. This is a funny town."

"But you live here?"

"Part of the time."

She leaned back on the green couch and stared at him curiously, as if trying to understand why anyone would live in Washington, even part of the time. Pope gazed back at her, trying to decide what it was about her he liked best. Perhaps it was the way that she carried her height, he thought, straight up and down, all six feet of her, and to hell with a world that was five-foot-nine. He also liked the way that her carriage thrust out her breasts whose nipples were clearly outlined beneath the thin cotton of her brown shirt. Pope liked that because it gave him notions, which were probably sexist, but which he entertained anyway and enjoyed hugely, operating on the theory that if she hadn't wanted him to admire her breasts and nipples, she would have worn something else.

He liked her face, too. He liked its smooth, even tan and the straw-colored hair that fell to her shoulders. She kept tossing it back carelessly from her forehead, revealing a narrow inch-long white scar that ran up from the corner of her left eye. I'll have to ask her about that scar sometime, Pope thought.

He especially liked her eyes, bold brown eyes that weren't quite enormous, but still oversized and somehow merry as though most of what they saw was worth a laugh. Her nose was straight and probably a shade thin, but not enough to bother about, and her mouth may have been a quarter of an inch too wide, but its width was forgotten when she smiled in that half-wry, half-sad way that she had, which made Pope want to share in whatever it was that could make her smile.

He was thinking about her chin and how its rounded point gave her something of a gamine's look, a big gamine, when she said, "Examining the merchandise?"

"I suppose I was," he said.

"I suppose we both were," she said. "You're awfully tall, aren't you?"

"So are you."

"I've heard about it, but I don't think I ever believed it."

"Believed what?" he said.

"Believed how the housewife hops into bed five minutes after the good-looking siding salesman gets his foot in the door."

"Do you believe it now?"

"I don't know whether I believe it," she said, "but at least I can understand it now. Did you ever sell aluminum siding?"

"No," he said. "I never sold anything. Do you need some?"

"Some what?"

"Some aluminum siding."

"No," she said. "I don't need any."

"How about a dinner?" he said. "Could you use a dinner?"

"Well, yes," she said, "I could use one of those."

"What about seven tonight?"

"Fine."

"Where do I pick you up—here?"

"No," she said. "The Madison."

"Fine."

She cocked her head to the left. "Are you married? Not that it would make any difference."

"No," he said, "I'm not married."

"But you have been?"

"Yes. My wife's dead."

"I'm sorry."

"No need to be," Pope said. "She's been dead awhile and I really didn't get to know her all that well."

9

On January 12, 1964, the second anniversary of his association with the Whetstone Organization as an investigator, Jake Pope was sitting at his desk in his office on the fifth floor of the building on Rodeo Drive in Beverly Hills, trying to decide how the occasion could best be observed. He had almost reached his conclusion when his telephone rang. It was Judge Whetstone and he said what he always said when he wanted to see Pope. He said, "Mr. Pope, I need you."

He continued to sit at his desk after the call, turning over several phrases in his mind. As he did, his eyes wandered around his office. There was nothing in it to show that it was occupied by someone called Jake Pope. There was nothing in it to indicate what kind of business was conducted there if, indeed, there was any business conducted at all.

The surface of the grey metal desk held only a telephone, a dictating machine, and a fluorescent desk lamp. There was a grey metal swivel chair that Pope sat in and two grey chairs in front of the desk that others might sit in. One had arms, the other didn't. There was a dark blue carpet on the floor for a touch of color, but nothing on the walls, not even a calendar. In the corner was a coatrack, also of grey metal. There was one window covered with a grey venetian blind. The slats of the blind were open.

It was an office that contained nothing that would distract its occupant from the work at hand, whatever that work might be. Confessions could be heard in the office, or accusations made, or suspicions voiced, and although each of them might be long remembered, the office wouldn't. But the office was appropriate for something else. It was a place where careful, grim threats could be made and even more important, believed.

Pope said hello to the dark and lithesome Mary Sue Hethcox, Judge Whetstone's secretary, and replied that he was fine when she asked him, "How you today, Mr. Pope?" Pope had long since found out that Judge Whetstone was screwing Mary Sue Hethcox each Tuesday and Thursday night, but it was information that he considered neither useful nor particularly interesting.

"Go right on in?" Mary Sue Hethcox said, still sticking to her Southern rhetoric even after seven years in Los Angeles.

Pope went into Judge Whetstone's office and sat down in a chair near the rolltop desk. The desk was against a wall where it always was and Pope had to wait for Judge Whetstone to swing around. It was just one of the little tricks that the Judge had devised to keep his visitors off balance. Few persons were accustomed to entering offices where there was only the back of a head to greet them.

"The Governor called today," Whetstone said, as casually as he could, his back still to Pope.

"I hope he's well," Pope said.

"Sounded all right."

Whetstone spun around on his high backed swivel chair and gazed at Pope with his mean blue eyes. "New suit?" he said, not quite making it an accusation.

"I bought it six months ago."

"He's made up his mind."

"The Governor?"

"That's right. It's going to be Ransom. James Ransom. You know who he is, don't you?"

"I know who he is."

"Well?"

"Well, what?" Pope said.

"Well, what do you think?"

"Is that why the Governor called, to find out what I think? You should have told him that it's okay with me. That I think old Jim Ransom will make a right fine U.S. Senator. I think he should go ahead and appoint him."

"You do, huh?"

"Shouldn't I?"

"The Governor wants us to take Ransom out behind the barn and snafflehoop him right down to the skin."

"Do what to him?"

"Snafflehoop him. That's what they say down South."

"When do they say that?" Pope said. "I never heard anybody say that."

"When they want to find out everything there is to know about somebody that's what they do to em. Snafflehoop em. Turn em inside out just like you'd turn a bull frog inside out."

"I never did that either," Pope said.

Judge Whetstone frowned. "You sure you're from down South?"

"I'm from West Virginia."

"Well, shit, that's South, isn't it?"

Pope shrugged.

Judge Whetstone shifted his weight and frowned again. He didn't like people to disagree with him, not even silently. "So what do you know about Ransom?"

"Just what I've read in the papers. He's sort of young and nice-looking and he's got a good-looking wife and a couple of kids and he's Speaker of the House of Representatives up in Sacramento. And he's from here in L.A. and I guess he wants to be U.S. Senator. I guess he wants to be that awfully bad."

"Well, he's going to be your baby."

"I want a raise then."

"A raise?" Judge Whetstone shot his eyebrows up. "Did you say a raise?"

"Uh-huh."

"I just gave you a raise."

"That was six months ago."

"How much are you making now a week, two hundred?"

"Two-twenty-five."

"*Two-twenty-five!*" Judge Whetstone looked around his office as if he were afraid of having been overheard. He leaned toward Pope and spoke in a low, confidential tone. "Do you realize, Mr. Pope, that you are making more money, much more, than some of my oldest and most trusted associates who have growing families to support. You realize that, son? Men with families. Little children."

"I'm better than they are. That's the only reason you raised me to two-twenty-five."

Judge Whetstone shook his head. "I don't remember doing that. I must have been suffering from some temporary aberration."

"I want two-fifty."

Judge Whetstone tried to look hurt, but his eyes were too mean to bring it off. "I took you off the street, son, when the seat of your pants was so thin that your butt was about to bust through. Your shoe soles weren't any thicker than this piece of paper." He waved a piece of paper around. "And you didn't know anything, not a thing, except how to park cars and google at girls. And now look at you sitting there with a nice, brand spanking new Sy Devore suit on your back and Johnston and Murphy shoes on your feet and probably a couple of big belts of fine Scotch in your stomach for lunch, and a trade that you can fall back on in any big city in this country, a trade which I personally taught you, which I lost money on teaching you, and now you want to demonstrate your gratitude by demanding—"

Judge Whetstone broke off. He swiveled toward his desk, rummaged through a drawer, and came up with a pistol, a .38 revolver. He extended it to Pope, butt first. "Here," he said. "Take it. Why don't you just take this and hold it to my head and then ask for your raise? Why don't you do that?"

Pope ignored the pistol. "Two-fifty," he said.

"Or?"

Pope shrugged again. "Or nothing. You can put Samuelson on the Ransom thing. He's from Georgia. They ought to know all there is to know about snaffle-hooping down in Georgia."

Without taking his eyes off Pope, Judge Whetstone put the pistol back in a drawer. He didn't shift his gaze even to pick up the telephone and press his intercommunication button. Pope tried not to squirm. It was a hard, cold, mean gaze and Judge Whetstone kept it on him as he spoke into the phone.

"Miss Hethcox," he said, "Please prepare the following memorandum to accounting for my signature. Effective this date the salary of Mr. Jacob Pope will be increased to two hundred fifty dollars per week. Thank you, Miss Hethcox."

He hung up the phone with his mean stare still fixed on Pope. "Mr. Pope, I trust you are now ready to undertake the Ransom assignment."

Pope made himself smile cheerfully although what he still wanted to do was squirm. "I'm ready. Just one question. When I start—uh—snafflehooping Ransom, do you want me to sort of sneak around and do it on the sly or do you want me to snafflehoop him right out in the open?"

"Mr. Ransom is already aware that he will be investigated by this office. He has offered his full co-operation. Now, Mr. Pope, I'm going to try to impress upon you the importance of this assignment. I don't know whether I'll succeed, but still I'm going to try."

"All right."

"When I spoke to the Governor today, he was quite frank with me. Even blunt. As you may know, he's a plain-speaking man."

"So I've heard."

"He pointed out the gravity of the situation. He said, 'This is the first time I've ever appointed anybody a United States Senator, Judge, and I don't want to find out six months from now that I made somebody Senator who was once a cocksucker or a Communist because if I do, it'll be your ass.' I think I'm quoting him exactly because it wasn't terribly difficult to remember."

"No," Pope said. "It wouldn't be."

"So, Mr. Pope, our investigation of Mr. Ransom will be in your hands and I don't want you to fuck it up because if you do, son, it's going to be your ass. Think you can keep that in mind?"

"I'll try," Pope said.

James Ransom was young, only thirty-seven, which is quite young for a U.S. Senator and he looked even younger than that. He looked about twenty-nine and Pope wondered how that would go over in the Senate where he understood that they didn't put much stock in the youth will be served notion.

They were sitting in Ransom's office on Santa Monica Boulevard where he practiced law when he wasn't up in Sacramento serving as Speaker of the state's House of Representatives. It was an extremely well furnished office and Pope decided that Ransom was making a lot of money out of his law practice and had spent some of it on a decorator. Either that or his wife had taste.

Ransom had a tousled look about him, mostly because of the way he combed his longish blond hair. Pope also thought he might as well have had "made in California" stamped on his forehead because he was of that lean, rangy, white-smiling design that the state has been turning out by the thousands in both male and female models since the early thirties.

"How old are you, Jake?" Ransom said, slipping into a chummy first-name relationship although they had met only three minutes before. It was another hallmark of California, Pope thought. Southern California anyway.

"Twenty-four," he said.

"I was expecting somebody perhaps a little older."

"They're probably expecting the same thing in the Senate."

"Ouch," Ransom said and smiled his wide winning smile which, Pope thought, was terribly white and terribly sincere.

"And you're going to look for any skeletons I might have in my closet?" Ransom said.

"I'm going to be looking," Pope said evenly, "for the nigger in the woodpile."

He watched for Ransom's reaction. It was there. A slight frown clouded up the sunny look. His mouth compressed itself into a harder line. His eyes got colder. "You use racial epithets a lot, Jake?" he said softly.

"Only when I'm working," Pope said.

Ransom wasn't dumb. Understanding spread across his face. "How'd I do?" he said.

"You passed," Pope said.

Ransom nodded. "Interesting. So you're not just looking for who I'm screwing or how much I'm embezzling or what the take is under the table. You're looking for it all, aren't you?"

"As much as I can find in the time I've got."

"I'm not sure whether I like it," Ransom said.

"I wouldn't," Pope said.

"But if I want to be appointed Senator, I have to cooperate."

"So I understand."

"So once again I compromise my what, beliefs, principles? Is principles too grand a word?"

"I wouldn't know."

"I compromise my principles in order to achieve the larger goal and thus again the end justifies the means, wouldn't you say?"

"If you become Senator, it won't be the last compromise you'll make. The real question is, how bad do you want to be Senator."

"Bad. Real bad."

Pope nodded. "Then let's get started."

"All right. What do I do?"

"Just answer my questions."

"Honestly?" Ransom said and smiled.

"That'll help. Okay, first off, women."

"Now? None."

"Before?" Pope said.

"All of them?"

"All of them," Pope said, taking an elaborate glance at his watch. "Have we got time?"

Ransom grinned again. He glanced at his own watch. "I think I ought to be able to finish by lunch," he said. "But just barely."

There had been a lot of women in Ransom's life, Pope learned, but no boys, and the women were the kind that wouldn't bother him now because most of them were married, or remarried, and apparently none of them held any animosity toward the Senator-designate. In fact, most of them, Pope later learned, wouldn't mind hopping in bed with Ransom again, if things could be worked out.

As for politics, Ransom had been a registered Republican until he was twenty-three, but Pope felt that he probably would be forgiven for that.

"Insanity," Pope said.

It was late in the afternoon and Ransom was growing tired. "What about it?"

"It run in your family?"

"No."

"You sure?"

"Positive."

"How about incest? You ever fuck one of your sisters or maybe a good-looking aunt?"

"For Christ's sake, Jake!"

"Well, did you?"

"No. Did you?"

"That's all we ever used to fuck down in West Virginia," Pope said. "Kinfolk."

"How much longer?"

"Until I'm through," Pope said.

"When will that be?"

Pope shrugged. "Midnight. Maybe later."

"Then I'd better call my wife and tell her I won't be coming home."

"That's right," Pope said. "You'd better."

By two o'clock the next morning, Pope had learned that there was no real reason why James Ransom shouldn't be appointed U.S. Senator to fill out the term of the one who had dropped dead a week before at fifty-three from a heart attack on the 16th hole of Burning Tree near Washington.

Ransom was lying on his couch now with his hands behind his head and Pope was seated behind the desk with his feet up on it. "Pills," Pope said.

"What pills?"

"What pills do you take?"

"Aspirin. Sometimes."

"That's all? No prescribed medication?"

"No."

"You're sure?"

"I'm sure."

"Dope."

"Marijuana," Ransom said.

"When and how much?"

"Ten or eleven years ago in Tijuana. I tried it. That's all."

"That's all?"

"That's all."

"No hard stuff? No heroin, cocaine, anything like that?"

"No. Never."

Pope yawned and stretched. "Okay," he said, "Let's knock it off. We start again at nine tomorrow."

"Sweet Jesus," Ransom said, sitting up. "How much longer tomorrow?"

"You'll be home for dinner."

"Then you'll be through?"

"I'll be through with you."

"Then?"

"Then I'll know what you think about yourself," Pope said. "After that I'll find out what everybody thinks about you."

Ransom was having a cup of coffee at his desk when Pope came in at nine the next morning. "Morning," Ransom said, not trying to keep the grumpiness out of his voice. "Coffee?"

Pope shook his head. "Let's go," he said.

"Go where?"

Pope looked at his watch. "The banks open at nine don't they?"

"That's right."

"And it's now two minutes after nine."

"So?"

"So you've got a safety deposit box and I want to see what's inside it."

Five days later Pope walked into Ransom's office carrying a briefcase.

"You've been busy, I hear," Ransom said.

"Fairly."

"I keep getting calls from people I haven't even thought of in years. They say you've been talking to them. Asking them questions."

"That's right."

"They say you've been asking some pretty shitty ones."

"Those are the best kind."

"Well, what did you find out?"

"You mean about you?"

"Yeah. About me."

"You pass. Except for one thing."

"What?"

Pope opened his briefcase and brought out a sheaf of papers. "Here're your income tax returns," he said. "I won't need them anymore." He handed the forms to Ransom. "And here's your personal financial statement, the one that you want to hand out to the press. It won't do."

"What do you mean, it won't do? It's all down there in black and white. It's what I'm worth and where I got it from. I don't have anything to hide."

"Huh," Pope said.

"What does huh mean?"

Pope leaned over and ran his finger down the second page of Ransom's financial statement. He tapped one of the lines with his forefinger. "This won't do."

Ransom read it and looked up at Pope. "What the fuck you talking about? That's a sweet deal. It's probably the best investment I've got."

"Who put you on to it?" Pope said.

"The Governor did. He's got a hundred thousand in it himself."

"A hundred thousand in olive oil," Pope said. "And you've got fifty thousand in it."

"That's right."

"And you really want to be Senator?"

"Hell, yes, I want to be Senator."

"Well, if you want to be Senator, then you'd better make two phone calls this morning. The first one'll be to your broker. The second one will be to the Governor. And your message to both will be the same. It'll be, 'Get out of olive oil.'"

"But it's been paying off like a slot machine."

"You're a pretty smart lawyer, aren't you?" Pope said.

"I try."

"And you'd like to be United States Senator and have people think that you're a pretty smart Senator, wouldn't you, not some dumb, easy mark who got fleeced for fifty thousand bucks by some sharpies?"

"You know something, Jake," Ransom said. "You know something about the olive oil."

"Two words should spell it out for you, if you're as smart as I think you are. If you're not, then you shouldn't be Senator anyway."

"Two words?"

"Two words."

"You're going to tell me what they are, aren't you, Jake? You're going to tell me because you're a nice guy and because you wouldn't like to see a cleancut young family man like me not become Senator."

"They begin with a P," Pope said.

"My fucking career is on the line and he wants to play twenty questions. P. I don't know what begins with P. Tell me the magic words, Jake."

Pope was grinning. "P as in Ponzi and P as in pyramid."

"Oh, shit." Ransom slumped back in his chair and

threw a yellow pencil across the room. He looked up at Pope. "This isn't just some tricky little test you're putting me through, is it?"

"No. Did you check it out?"

"The olive oil?"

"That's right."

"Christ, I didn't have to check it out. The Governor got me in and then they started sending me four-color reports and fancy brochures and God knows what else. Hell, even my broker got in on it. You're sure?"

"There isn't any olive oil. Not a tankful, not a gallon, not a quart, not even enough to wet down a salad. It's the same old pyramid con. They promise you thirty or forty percent profits and they pay out from what they take in from new suckers. It's all going to go tits up in about two or three weeks. If you want to cash out now, you probably can. You and the Governor and maybe your broker."

"His name was Charles, wasn't it? Charles Ponzi."

"Right."

Ransom started to reach for the telephone, but he stopped and looked at Pope. "You're good, aren't you?"

Pope grinned again. "Yeah. I'm pretty good."

"You know, I'm only going to be Senator for two years and then I'll be up for reelection again. In fact, I'm going to be running flat out from the moment I'm sworn in."

"I know."

"So I'm going to have to make some noise while I'm in Washington. Stir things up. Go after some baddies."

"Got anyone in mind?" Pope said.

"How about the malefactors of great wealth?"

"Malefactors are always good. Nobody likes them much anyhow."

"Jake, I think you'd better come to Washington with me."

"All right," Pope said. "How much?"

"We'll work it out," the Senator-designate said and reached for the phone to call the Governor and tell him that he'd better get out of olive oil.

10

THE HOMICIDE DETECTIVE WAS IMPRESSED WITH ANCEL Easter's office. Most people were. It was the same office that Crawdad Gilmore had once occupied and it was almost as large as the squad room that the detective worked out of down on Indiana Avenue Northwest.

The detective was twenty-nine years old and white and as formal as he knew how to be. He always became formal in the presence of authority or wealth or what he thought of as sticky situations. These were situations in which raw emotions simmered and sometimes boiled over into violence or rage or grief or hate or even remorse. He had learned that by adopting an air of cool, even icy formality he could remain detached and remember what was said and done, which was very useful in his line of work.

The detective's name was Hugo Worthy and he had been with the Metropolitan Police Department for eight years, the last six of them in Homicide. He lived in Cheverly, Maryland, in a three-bedroom house with his wife, Mary Anne, and two children, Donna, five, and Steven, three. He made nearly $18,000 a year because he arrested a lot of people and this meant a lot of time in court, which was usually overtime. Yet on most days he was broke, or nearly so, drove a four-year-old Impala sedan, and spent a good deal of his free moments trying to figure out how he could afford to divorce his wife and move in with a twenty-three-year-old ballet dancer who was out of work most of the time.

Just then Detective Worthy was wondering who the tall man was with the greying hair who sprawled in an easy chair near Ancel Easter's desk and looked as though he wanted to put his feet up on it.

The tall guy's been in it, Worthy thought. You can always tell a guy who's been in it. The guy behind the desk, Easter, like Easter egg, he hasn't been in it although he's been close, but then most lawyers have been close and some of them have even been in it, but not the way the guy in the chair and me have. Funny how you can always tell a guy who's been in it. It never wears off.

Ancel Easter decided that he had better introduce Detective Worthy to Jake Pope. It might defrost him a little, Easter thought. I never knew that homicide was such an icily formal business, but then you haven't had just a hell of a lot of experience with homicide.

"Detective Worthy, Jacob Pope. Mr. Pope is an associate of mine who also was a friend of Mr. Gilmore's. He's as interested as I am in anything you can tell us about what developments there've been."

Worthy nodded at Jake Pope who nodded back. "Are you an attorney, Mr. Pope?" Worthy said.

"No, I'm not."

"Your face is sort of familiar. I thought I might've seen you around."

"No," Pope said. "I don't think so."

"You didn't used to be with the narcotics people,

did you?" Worthy said, politely but persistently, determined to find out when Pope had been in it.

"Mr. Pope was formerly a Senate committee investigator, Mr. Worthy," Easter said.

Like that, huh, Worthy thought. Well, that still makes him a member of the club although being a Senate investigator must be awful nice clean work. But I bet what he did before he got to be a Senate investigator wasn't so nice and clean. I bet he got his hands in it a few times. Funny how you can always tell.

"You're not with the committee anymore, Mr. Pope?" Worthy said because he was curious and because he had found that his curiosity often paid off, sometimes with unexpected dividends.

"No," Pope said. "Not anymore. Not for some time, in fact."

"Mr. Pope's in—uh—the real estate business now," Ancel Easter said, giving Pope a label because the detective seemed to want him to have one.

Worthy nodded as if satisfied. "As you know, I've been asked to keep you up to date on the Gilmore case."

Easter nodded once, gravely. The Gilmore case, he thought. Crawdad would have liked that. He would have had something pungent to say about being turned into the Gilmore case.

"It's very good of you to take the time," Easter said. "I'm grateful."

Don't be grateful to me, Worthy thought. Be grateful to the mayor or the chief or whoever it was you called. With an office like this in a building like this it wouldn't be anybody farther down the line than the mayor or the chief. You wouldn't know anybody farther down the line than that.

"Well, there has been a development," Worthy said. "Yesterday at approximately three thirty-five P.M., a person or persons unknown effected an entry into the Friendly Liquor Store in the Seventeen hundred block of Connecticut Avenue."

"Effected an entry?" Pope said.

"Yeah, they went in. Or he went in."

"I see," Pope said.

"There wasn't anybody else in the store but the owner, Samuel A. Hermann, a male Caucasian, fifty-nine years old. Hermann was stabbed once in the throat and shot once in the left temple. His body was discovered by his delivery man, Era Booker Harris, who summoned the police."

"Harris summoned them?" Pope said.

"Yeah, he called nine-one-one."

"I see," Pope said.

"Well, we got a report this morning that the ballistics check on the slug that helped killed Hermann matched the two slugs that were taken from the body of William M. Gilmore. But we haven't got anything else. Nobody saw anything."

"How much did they get?" Pope said.

"From Hermann?"

Pope nodded.

"Close as we can figure, about fifteen dollars. Maybe twenty. Anyhow, that's what the delivery man thought and he'd made a bank deposit for Hermann earlier. He didn't think it could've been any more'n fifteen or twenty dollars."

"What about the watch?" Pope said.

"What watch?"

"The watch they took from Gilmore along with the thirty-two cents."

"Oh, yeah. We've been checking the pawnshops, but so far, no watch."

"Well, what do you think, Mr. Worthy?" Ancel

Easter said. "Have you come up with any theories about who might have killed Mr. Gilmore?"

"Well, you can come up with all sorts of theories," Worthy said, "but I've been in Homicide six years now and I wouldn't give you two cents for all the theories I've come up with in six years. You can come up with a fact like we came up with today—like the gun that killed Gilmore is probably the same gun that killed, or helped kill, Hermann because he also got stabbed like I told you. Well, that's a fact—or almost one. It won't be a fact until we get our hands on the gun and run it through some more ballistics tests. But it's almost a fact. So with that fact you might come up with the theory that whoever shot and killed Gilmore also shot and killed Hermann. That's a pretty nice theory, wouldn't you say?"

"I'd be tempted to go along with it," Easter said.

"So would I," Worthy said. "Except that in this town that gun—it's a twenty-two automatic by the way—except like I was saying in this town that gun could've changed hands four times since it killed Gilmore. It might've been thrown away and found. It might've been sold. It might've been borrowed. It maybe even could've been stolen from whoever shot Gilmore with it. Guns change hands in this town awful fast."

"But you're operating on the theory that whoever killed Gilmore also killed—uh—what's his name, Hermann?" Pope said. "That's the theory you're operating on until you come up with something better."

"Yeah, that's right."

"But no witnesses. Three-thirty in the afternoon on Connecticut Avenue and nobody saw anything. Anybody hear anything, like a shot?"

"It's June," Worthy said. "They've all got their doors closed and their air conditioning on and it was a twenty-two."

"Long or short?" Pope said.

"Long."

There was a silence. Pope had no more questions. Worthy wasn't at all sure whether he would answer any more and was wondering how he was going to get out of it if any more were asked when Easter said, "Well, thanks for coming by, Mr. Worthy. I'm deeply obliged."

Worthy rose. "If anything else develops, we'll let you know. Either me or my partner."

"Thanks very much," Easter said, also rising. Jake Pope got up, too. Worthy nodded at him and said, "Mr. Pope." He started to turn and nod his good-bye to Easter when Pope said, "You keep up with what's going on in town, don't you?"

"I try," Worthy said.

"What's going on July eleventh?"

Worthy thought a moment. "Not a thing."

"Does it ring a bell?"

"It's a week after the Fourth of July," Worthy said, "but that's not much of a bell, is it?"

"No," Pope said, "it isn't."

After Worthy had gone, Easter turned to Pope and said, "Well, what do you think?"

Pope shrugged. "He was being polite. Who'd you lean on to make them send somebody down?"

"I called the mayor."

"Does he know what July eleventh means?"

"I didn't ask."

"I don't think it means anything."

"Nothing?"

"Nothing that you'd take a day off from work for."

"Does it have to mean something like that?"

"I don't know what it has to mean."

"You didn't find anything in Crawdad's house?"

"His granddaughter," Pope said.

"So you said. What'd you think of her?"

"She's tall, isn't she?"

"Uh-huh, she's tall. Anything else?"

"I'm having dinner with her tonight."

"Well," Easter said. "Did you ask her what July eleventh means?"

"I asked her but she didn't know. Is she broke?"

"No, she's not broke. Why?"

"She said her dude ranch wasn't doing too well. I just thought she might be broke."

"Well, she isn't. What if she were?"

"Well, if she were broke, she might have snuck into town and shot her grandfather dead and then inherited all his money so she wouldn't be broke anymore."

"Why didn't you tell Detective Worthy about your granddaughter theory?"

"Detective Worthy wasn't too keen on theories. He said he wouldn't give two cents for his own."

"How much do you think he might have given for yours?"

"Less," Pope said. "Much less."

11

THE BUS TO FAIRFAX, VIRGINIA, WAS CROWDED THAT EVE-
ning and Dr. Dallas Hucks had to stand for nearly an
hour before getting a seat. The day had turned hot,
reaching 93 at 4 P.M., and the air conditioning in the
bus had broken down. There was an accident on Lee
Highway, a four-car pileup, and the bus got stuck·for
twenty minutes before the police and the tow trucks
arrived to sort things out. Dr. Hucks had to stand up all
during that, too.

When he got off the bus in Fairfax, he had to walk
eight blocks in the 93-degree heat to his house and by
the time he arrived it was well past 6 o'clock. He had
left his office at 4:30.

Dr. Hucks had bought his house nine years before
and he now liked to tell anyone who would listen that
it was the smartest investment he had ever made. Actually, it was a development house, a squatty three-bedroom affair with vaguely Colonial lines. It looked
squatty because instead of going up to its full two
stories it went down into the ground so that the lawn
came up level with the first floor windowsills. But the
architect, if indeed there had been one, had still insisted

on running up some short white round pillars to support the wide gable above the front door. Everyone but Dr. Hucks agreed that the pillars looked awful.

Dr. Hucks lived in the house with his wife, Amelia, who had been named for the flier who went down in the Pacific Ocean in 1937. The Huckses had no children, although three years ago they had had a cat, but the cat had run away after six days and Amelia still dreamed about it sometimes. She told her psychiatrist about these dreams, but never her husband.

The Huckses had been married twelve years before while Dr. Hucks was studying for his doctoral degree in agricultural economics at Oklahoma State University in Stillwater. His thesis had been concerned with *The Death of the Brannan Plan*, which was a controversial system of production payments that had been proposed by a former Secretary of Agriculture, Mr. Charles F. Brannan, during the Truman Administration. Dr. Hucks's thesis argued forcefully that the Brannan Plan had been hatched at a midnight meeting in the offices of the CIO and had been wisely struck down by the American Farm Bureau Federation, the U.S. Chamber of Commerce, the National Association of Manufacturers, and the American Legion. Three years later Dr. Hucks's thesis, somewhat edited, was published by the University of Oklahoma Press under the title, *Who Killed the Brannan Plan?* Two thousand copies were printed and 632 copies were sold, mostly to libraries.

Civilian employees of the United States Government, unless they work for the State Department, are classified by Government Service grades that range from one to eighteen. Grades fifteen through eighteen are known as supergrades. They are roughly equivalent to the army rank of general officer, a GS-15 earning approximately as much as a brigadier general.

As a GS-14, Dr. Dallas Hucks earned $24,247 a year and enjoyed the approximate rank of colonel in the army of Washington's civilian employees. But while a GS-14 might be a minor potentate in Denver, in Washington, D.C.—as is the sad case in most headquarters towns—there is a surplus of rank and GS-14's are as plentiful and as common as redbugs in Georgia.

So while a GS-14 in Denver might command anywhere from forty to a hundred loyal civilian troops of various rank, a GS-14 in Washington, D.C., might rule over a shriveled empire that consists of only a handful of subordinates or, as in Dr. Dallas Hucks's case, just two, his secretary and a GS-7, one Wendell Taunton, who wore a mad, silvertipped Afro, clothes so extremely stylish that they virtually beggared description, and who, to supplement his income, enthusiastically ran the numbers concession out of his office in the south wing of the Department of Agriculture.

Dr. Hucks had tried twice to get Wendell Taunton fired, but had failed. This past year he had tried for the third time to have him transferred, also without success. So for the last six months Dr. Hucks had not spoken to Taunton, a fact that Taunton, an unfettered soul, was totally unaware of.

The Huckses had been married when he was twenty-four and she was twenty and a senior at Oklahoma State, majoring in home economics. After receiving his doctoral degree Hucks had taught for two years at Texas A&M in College Station before the Civil Service sent word that there was a position awaiting him with the U.S. Department of Agriculture in Washington. The

Civil Service had sent the word only after it received a hard, mean nudge from a Republican U.S. Senator who happened to agree with Dr. Hucks's rightist economic theories.

Dr. Hucks was as conservative in his domestic life as he was in his economic theories. He refused to permit Amelia to work because her job, as he explained it to her, was the most noble of all, that of serving as a homemaker for him, for the children to be, and incidentally, for herself.

After trying rather diligently but unsuccessfully for three years to have a child, they learned that Amelia had a tipped womb and most probably could never conceive. Dr. Hucks adamantly refused to consider adoption. Nor would he permit Amelia to find a job.

As a concession, however, he bought the house in Fairfax one afternoon and presented it to Amelia as a surprise. She walked through it, upstairs and downstairs, without saying a word. Then she sat down on the bare floor in the living room and bawled for an hour because she hated the house.

Nevertheless, the Huckses moved into it and to demonstrate his further devotion, Dr. Hucks gave his wife carte blanche to furnish it. At first, Amelia wasn't much interested in what went into the house. But then she discovered that she liked buying things. In fact, she learned that buying something—it didn't much matter what—made her feel better. So she began buying things just to give herself a lift, but when she found that the lift didn't last as long as it had at first, she increased her spending and at the end of two months Dr. Hucks discovered that his wife had on order nearly $11,000 worth of new furniture. The night that he found out he was in hock for $11,000 was the same night that Dr. Hucks beat his wife for the first time. After that, he beat her on a more or less regular basis.

When he let himself into his house that night after his agonizing bus ride, he put his briefcase down, picked up the mail where Amelia had left it, saw that it was nothing but advertisements and bills, put it back down, and went into the living room where Amelia was watching a black and white film on television.

"When do we eat?" Dr. Hucks said.

"When we always eat," she said. "At six-thirty."

Dr. Hucks sat down and looked at the film for a moment. He saw that it was an old Abbott and Costello film. He had never liked Abbott and Costello.

"I have to have the car tomorrow," he said.

She shook her head, not looking at him. "I have to go to group tomorrow."

"Amelia," he said. "I have to go to work tomorrow. I need the car."

"Well, how do you expect me to get to group?"

"Take a bus."

"It's all the way out in Silver Spring. In Maryland. I can't take a bus out there."

"Skip it then."

"Skip group?" She sounded horrified.

"I don't think it would hurt you to skip it. I can't see that it's doing you any good anyway. What good is it doing you?"

"It's doing me good," she said, still looking at Abbott and Costello.

"All you do is go out there and sit around in a circle and tell each other how much you hate your husbands. Isn't that what you do in group therapy?"

"No, that's not what we do. You don't understand."

"What don't I understand?"

"Why don't you go fix yourself a drink?" she said. "You look hot."

"I am hot, Amelia. I had to take the bus home. The bus broke down. So did its air conditioning. When I got off the bus I had to walk eight blocks in ninety-three-degree weather. I'm not going to do that tomorrow, Amelia. That's why I'll need the car."

"I have to go to group," she said.

Dr. Hucks moved over to the television set and switched it off. "You can skip it tomorrow."

She looked up at him. "No," she said firmly, "I can't skip it."

"Why?" he said. "Why can't you skip it?"

"Because it ruins the—the continuity, that's why."

Dr. Hucks shook his head and disappeared into the kitchen. He came back with a tall gin and tonic. He didn't ask his wife if she wanted one. He took a swallow of his drink and sat down in his favorite chair. "Tell me, Amelia, I'm really interested. You've been going to this psychiatrist, Dr. Whatshisface—"

"Dr. Gantt," she said. "You know what his name is."

"Yes, Dr. Gantt. You've been going to Gantt once a week now for three years and to your group therapy once a week for a year and for the life of me, I can't see what good it's done. You're still as nutty as ever."

"I'm not nutty," she said, looking away.

"Nervous, then. You're still as nervous as ever. What good has it done, will you tell me that? What does Gantt say? He must give you a progress report every now and then."

"He says we're getting in touch with our feelings," she said, not quite whispering it.

"Who—you and the other members of the group?"

"That's right."

"In touch with your feelings." Dr. Hucks said the words slowly as if he liked not only their sound, but also their taste. "Isn't that pretty? It's what I would call a most felicitous phrase. You know what a felicitous phrase is, Amelia? Never mind. What else does the good doctor have to say about group therapy, I mean in general?"

"Nothing."

"He must say something."

Amelia was twisting her hands now. She always twisted her hands while undergoing her husband's interrogations. "He—he says that it's like family. That we—we share our experiences and feelings and that helps to provide—uh—what he calls illumination."

"Sharing and illumination," Dr. Hucks said. "That's beautiful. That's really beautiful. Now, Amelia, I'm going to share something with you and maybe you can illuminate something for me. All right?"

"I'd better go fix dinner," she said.

"No, stay right there," Dr. Hucks said, taking another swallow of his drink. "The newsy little item that I'm going to share with you is that I had a check bounce on me today. Maybe you can throw some illumination on how that happened."

"I don't know."

"'Did you write some checks at that liquor store?"

"No."

"Don't lie to me, goddamn it."

"Maybe I wrote one, but it wasn't at the liquor store."

"I told you not to write any checks. Why did you do what I told you not to do?"

"I—I had to buy something."

"You had to buy something. You're back on that,

are you? Three years of psychiatry and you're back on that. You had to buy something. What'd you have to buy, Amelia?"

"I don't remember."

"Something to make you feel a little better, isn't that right?"

"I guess so."

"How much did it cost, this something that made you feel a little better."

"It was just a picture."

"Just a picture. Well, how much did just a picture cost, Amelia?"

"Two hundred dollars." She whispered the sum.

"Two hundred dollars," Dr. Hucks said slowly.

"I saw it in one of those galleries on O Street and I bought it."

"Was it a pretty picture, Amelia?" Dr. Hucks said. "Tell me, was it a pretty picture?"

"It wasn't pretty. It was, well, it was—oh, what difference does it make?"

"It makes a lot of difference, Amelia. Because you wrote a check without telling me, I overdrew at the bank. I wrote a bum check. I may have written more than one bum check. But I know I've written at least one because the person I wrote it to gave it back to me. And now I no longer have a ride in the car pool because they don't like people to ride in car pools who write bum checks. And so because I no longer have a ride in the car pool, I'm going to start taking the car to work."

"How am I going to get to group?"

"That's your problem, Amelia. Tell me," he said, looking around the living room, "where is your pretty little picture?"

"In the garage. Behind the snow tires. It's not fair."

"Behind the snow tires. Well. What a clever place to hide something. No one would ever think of looking there until next October, would they? What's not fair, Amelia?"

"Your taking the car and going every place and I never go anywhere."

"You never go anywhere. Why Amelia, my fair, you are constantly going somewhere. On Tuesdays you go and visit with the good Dr. Gantt. On Thursdays you attend—is that the right word? Yes, well, you attend group therapy. That's about sixty dollars a week worth of going somewhere."

"The insurance pays for it. It pays for most of it anyhow. That's not fair to say it costs that much. I never go anywhere where people are. You're always going somewhere."

"With all due modesty, Amelia, that's because I am considered something of a scholar and because I am respected for what I know and for what I have written."

"You don't know so much," she said. "You don't know so damn much."

"What do you mean, Amelia?" Dr. Hucks said, finishing his drink.

"If those people who invite you out knew how much you lost in the stock market, they wouldn't think you're so smart. If they knew you had to sell my car just to pay the bills, they wouldn't always be inviting you to places like the Cosmos Club."

"I only went to the Cosmos Club once, Amelia."

"Well, I didn't go. And now I can't even go to group. It's not fair. It's not fair, damn you."

"Tell me something, Amelia. Why are you really

going to see a psychiatrist and to group therapy? I'm really very interested. Why do *you* think you're going? Your real reason, not somebody else's."

Amelia starting twisting her hands together even faster than before. She looked as if she were trying to wash them of some grime that would never quite come off. "I'm—I'm—" She stopped.

"Yes?" her husband said, trying not very successfully to look patient and understanding.

"I'm trying to find out who I am," she said, rushing the words together.

"Trying to find out who you are," Dr. Hucks said, separating the words as though for individual examination. "Why, that's really quite simple, Amelia. You're my wife."

"If—if—" She stopped.

"Yes."

"If—if I'm your wife, then why don't you ever fuck me?" It started as a mild inquiry, but ended as a yell.

Dr. Hucks rose, strode across the room, and struck his wife very hard on the left side of her face just below her ear. "Don't ever talk to me like that again," he said and then proceeded to beat her.

After he was through beating his wife, Dr. Hucks left her huddled on the sofa, went into the kitchen, fixed himself a sandwich, took a bottle of beer from the refrigerator, and retired to the room that he called his study because it had a desk in it.

He ate the sandwich, drank the beer, licked his fingers carefully, and then unlocked the bottom drawer of the desk. From it he removed a tan folder, opened it, and once more went carefully over his notes on the plan that would make him $100,000 on July 11.

12

Jake Pope put on a tie for the occasion. He had three of them, he noticed, two wide fat ones and one narrow skinny one, and he couldn't remember buying any of them.

You dressed better when you were making three hundred bucks a week, he told himself. In a bureau drawer he found that he had six shirts, all blue, all button-down, all from Brooks Brothers. That makes it easy, he thought, and put one of them on. He examined his three ties and selected the one that didn't have any grease spots. Pope was mildly pleased that the tie didn't have any spots on it because he regarded himself as possibly the world's messiest eater.

It wasn't that his table manners weren't good. They were standard American table manners, maybe a little Southern, that had been drilled into him by Simmie Lee Pope from the time he was old enough to sit up at the table. Keep your left hand in your lap except when you're cutting up your meat. Never cut up your salad. Always leave a little on your plate to show that you're not really hungry. Just a little, though; no need to waste anything either.

Out of habit, Jake Pope still followed all these dictates and more. But something always happened. The steak slipped off his fork, the soup spilled out of his spoon, the lettuce writhed and suddenly leaped into his lap. That's where all your ties went, he told himself, they sailed out with the gravy tide.

As he knotted the tie Pope wondered whether parents still taught their children table manners. It wasn't any of his business, but he had noticed that a lot of the young now attacked their food as though it were alive and had to be stabbed to death. Maybe that's some more middle-class baggage that went overboard in the sixties, he thought, table manners. He grimaced at himself in the mirror, combed his hair with his fingers, left his apartment, and went down to the basement garage to find out whether the battery would turn his engine over.

Pope still liked cars. He liked to look at them and to drive them fast and to read about them, especially the ones that they didn't make anymore. He didn't think that he would like to own them now, but at least he would have liked to have driven a Cord and a Duesenberg and a Pierce Arrow and a Bugatti and a prewar Lincoln Continental and maybe one of the big old drophead Bentleys. It's part of your heritage, he told himself. All hillbillies are car crazy.

In the basement garage he kicked the front tire of the one he owned. It was a dusty 1969 brown 911 Porsche that he had bought new one afternoon, paying cash for it, and then almost died of remorse as he drove it home because it had cost so much and because he didn't really deserve it anyway. The remorse lasted until he forced himself to realize that he could easily afford a dozen of them, if a dozen of them conceivably were needed. Jake Pope had had a difficult time becoming accustomed to the fact that he was rich.

The Porsche had been sitting untouched in the basement garage for more than three months, but its engine caught after the fourth try. Pope let it idle while he checked the gauges. There was more than half a tank of gas. The oil pressure looked all right. The temperature was beginning to creep up to where it should be. As long as it runs, Pope thought, backed out of the parking slot, and headed for the garage exit.

Faye Hix was staying at the Madison Hotel on Fifteenth Street. Pope gave its doorman, whom he knew slightly, a dollar to let him park his car where he shouldn't. He remembered that the doorman was a graduate of Howard University and had started out in the hotel as an assistant auditor. But after he caught on to how much the doormen were making he had applied for the first vacancy. That had been four years ago. The doorman now had a house in Chevy Chase, sent his children to private schools, drove a Stingray to work, and kept a thirty-two-foot cruiser at a marina down in Solomons, Maryland.

Faye Hix was ready. She was sitting in a chair in the lobby just to the left of the hotel entrance and rose when she saw Pope. She was wearing a tan dress with a brown bag and brown shoes whose heels gave her another inch of height. She smiled at Pope. "My God, you're prompt."

He smiled back. "It's one of my three virtues."

"What're the other two?"

"Thrift and continence."

"I think I'll go back up to my room."

"Don't," he said. "I'm really a profligate with abnormal sexual appetites."

"That's better."

Outside, the doorman helped Faye Hix into the car and gave Pope a wink of frank approval. Pope winked back at him and got into the car.

"I knew you'd have something sporty," she said.

"It gets twenty-six miles to the gallon. Think of it as a conservation measure."

"I'll try,' she said.

The restaurant was one of those French places on K Street west of Connecticut. The space it occupied had once housed a men's clothing store that had gone out of business three years ago when its owner died. After a couple of slow months the restaurant had caught on and now it was jammed for lunch and reservations were needed for dinner. Pope had a reservation and the maitre d', who was also one of the owners, led them to their table and seated them with a Gallic flourish.

"It's nice," Faye said, looking around. "I'm glad it's French. I don't get much French food in Montana."

"The food used to be good here," Pope said. "I hope it still is. What would you like to drink?"

"A Scotch, I guess."

"With water?"

"Water's fine."

The waiter came with the menus and Pope ordered the drinks. Faye began studying a menu.

"Christ," she said.

"What?"

"The prices."

"You're not supposed to read the prices."

"They jump out at you."

"They do kind of."

"Well, I'm going to have something real Frenchy. Can we afford it?"

"I think so."

"Snails. I'll have the snails."

"That's French all right," Pope said.

"And the veal. The French know what to do with veal."

"You just made up my mind for me," Pope said. He ordered when the waiter brought the drinks. After he had left, Pope said, "Are you very fussy about food?"

"No. Not very. Are you?"

"No. Sometimes I think I could get by just fine on peanut butter and jelly sandwiches."

"They're good," she said. "I eat a lot of peanut butter and jelly sandwiches. Grape jelly. I think I grew up on them. I think my whole generation grew up on them. Funny."

"What?"

"My generation. Our generation. Did they ever get around to calling us anything?"

"No," Pope said, "and now it's getting too late."

"What'd they call the one that came along during the fifties, the silent generation?"

"Actually there were two of them. There was the silent generation and then there was the beat generation. Kerouac and that bunch."

"He's dead, isn't he?" she said.

"Kerouac?"

"Yes."

"Yeah, he's dead. The drink got him, I hear."

"They're mining the fifties now," she said.

"For what?"

"For nostalgia. Do you feel nostalgic about the fifties?"

"Christ, no."

"When were you born?"

"In 1940," he said.

"Then you ought to feel nostalgic about them."

"I don't feel anything about the fifties. If I feel nostalgic for anything, it's for World War Two."

"You're not old enough to remember World War Two."

"I can remember VJ day," he said. "I can remember that."

"I was born a week after VJ day."

"I think I would have got along swell in World War Two," Pope said. "I think I would have been very big in the black market in Europe. Something like that."

"You have a criminal bent?" she said.

"Your grandfather thought so. He thought I had a fine criminal mind that only an unfortunate set of circumstances kept me from using—and out of jail."

"How'd you meet him?"

"Through my wife. He and Ancel Easter were sort of my wife's guardians."

"Sort of?"

"Her parents died in a plane crash when she was fifteen and Crawdad was executor of their estate. Well, there wasn't anyone else so he roped Easter into it and together they sort of raised her. I do mean sort of."

"What was she like?"

"A little wild."

"Was she pretty?"

"Very pretty."

"Where'd you meet her?"

"At a party. It was a farewell party for ex-Senator Ransom of California. I used to work for him. In fact, he brought me to Washington to help him stir things up. Well, we stirred things up all right. In fact, Ransom stirred things up so much that the oil crowd raised a

five-million-dollar kitty to make sure that he didn't
come back to the Senate. That was in 1966. His campaign, I mean. He lost and the farewell party was in
1967. I met her at that party and we ran off and got
married the next day."

"The next day?"

"I think it was the next day. It was a little drunk
out. We got married in Las Vegas. January tenth, 1967.
We came back to Washington on January seventeenth.
On January eighteenth she wrapped her Maserati around
a tree in Rock Creek Park. It killed her. On January
nineteenth, or maybe it was the twentieth, I met Crawdad who informed me that I stood to inherit something
like nineteen million dollars."

"You're not making it up, are you?"

"No."

"Nineteen million."

"Give or take a few hundred thousand."

"What'd it do to you?"

"At first it scared me. I thought if you had nineteen
million you had to do something. You know, make deci-
sions, buy and sell, issue orders, things like that. But
then I found out that you didn't have to do anything.
That there were people who knew all about those things
and that they worked for you. So I didn't do anything."

"Didn't you spend some?"

Pope shook his head. "I was working for a special
Senate subcommittee then as investigator. I just kept on
working. I think now that I kept on working because
that was something that I knew how to do. I sure as
hell didn't know anything about the care and feeding of
nineteen million dollars."

"But you learned," she said.

"Yeah, I learned. Crawdad helped. So did Ancel

Easter after they decided that I wasn't some sort of con man who had filed down the tie rods on her car."

"Did they really think that?"

"I don't guess they really did. But they hired a guy here in Washington to run a check on me. I don't blame them. I would've done the same thing."

"So you just went on being an investigator for the Senate. What'd you investigate?"

"Usually people or corporations who made too much money doing something that they shouldn't. I got to be pretty good at it."

"But you finally quit?"

Pope nodded. "I quit when your grandfather called me one day and asked me to come see him. He was semi-retired by then. By that I mean he didn't go down to an office. In fact, he hadn't been down to an office since the day John Kennedy was shot. But he still worked out of his house. You saw his study there. Well, he wanted me to look into something for him because, as he said, it was my kind of nastiness. Or he thought it was. So I did."

"What was it?"

"Crawdad still had a few clients. This one was the niece of an old friend of his. She had some money, not a tremendous amount, but still it was quite a chunk. Also, she wasn't quite bright. You know, really dim, and Crawdad looked after her money for her. Well, she had married this guy, he was just an ordinary guy, a GS-14, who worked for the Government, and they had gone out to dinner one night and when they came out to get into their car they were abducted. The husband said that they had been abducted by two black guys with two big guns. They robbed them and then tied the husband up in the back seat and raped the woman and killed her. Choked her to death. Well, the husband was beaten up pretty bad so everyone said what a rotten shame it was that you couldn't even go out to dinner anymore without having a couple of spades shove pistols in your face. Everybody but Crawdad."

"Ah," Faye said. "Granddad was suspicious."

"Very. So he asked me to look into it."

"Why was he suspicious?"

"Because, as he said, 'Although I was very fond of Margaret, Jake, nobody would marry a woman who was that dumb and that ugly except for her money.' And Crawdad had it fixed so that nobody could get their hands on the money, not even the husband, unless, of course, she died."

"Weren't the police suspicious?"

"No. Not very. Not enough, anyhow. After all, the guy was beaten up pretty badly himself and had to spend two weeks in a hospital. He was still in shock when they finally found him. And then, too, nobody really wants to believe in monsters."

"Monsters?"

"The husband and wife were driven out on a deserted farm road not too far from Herndon. That's in Virginia. The wife was raped repeatedly not over ten feet from the car where her husband was tied up. She must have screamed. He must have heard it. He must have heard all of it. Now what kind of a guy would pay two other guys to rape and strangle his wife after they beat and tied him up and left him in the back seat of his car with the windows down so that he could hear what a good job they were doing on his wife?"

"A monster," she said.

"Yeah, well, he didn't look like a monster. He seemed to be just an ordinary guy who held down an ordinary government job. He belonged to a couple of civic clubs. He bowled every Tuesday night. They didn't have any children so he was even a Big Brother. You know, he took some fatherless ghetto kid to football games."

"But he wasn't an ordinary guy?" she said.

Pope shook his head. "That's the point. He was. No police record. He didn't hit the bottle. He didn't gamble. He was what is known as a solid citizen."

"But he did it?"

"Uh-huh. He did it."

"And you caught him?"

"I didn't catch him. I just came up with some evidence."

"How?"

"Well, first of all I burgled his office. I'm a very good burglar by the way. I sort of like it. Crawdad used to tell me that I'd've made a hell of a jewel thief. You know, the kind that works the Plaza in a dinner jacket with a monocle stuck in his left eye."

"You'd look good with a monocle."

"Sure. Well, anyhow, I burgled his office and found some correspondence. The guy had incorporated. He called his company Fairweather Resorts, Inc. There wasn't a dime in it, but there was all this correspondence about motels that he was dickering for. He never bought any, he just dickered for them by mail."

"What's so wrong with that?"

"Nothing. The Government might not have liked it because he was doing it all on Government time. His address was a post office box. But in his latest batch of correspondence there was this firm offer he'd made for a motel down in Florida. A hundred-thousand-dollar offer. Well, he was worth about three thousand dollars on a good day."

"But the wife had money?"

"That's right, but she wouldn't let him have any of it."

"Why?"

"Maybe she figured that if he ever got his hands on it, he'd leave her. That's what Crawdad thought anyhow. She wasn't bright, but she was bright enough to figure that out."

"So you had your motive?" she said.

"Yeah, I had my motive."

"How'd you prove it?"

"I looked up the ghetto kid, the one he used to take to ball games. It was just a hunch. The kid had a real brother who was one mean dude who'd spent a few years in Lorton for deadly assault. The dude had a friend that he palled around with who was just as mean as he was. Well, both of them had blossomed out with sudden signs of new prosperity although I doubt that either of them had ever worked a day in their lives. I found out from the ghetto kid—he was a real nice kid, by the way—that he had introduced his real brother to his Big Brother, the dead woman's husband. So I started checking out the husband from another angle."

"What angle?"

"Whether he had borrowed any money recently. I found out that he had borrowed nine thousand dollars on his life insurance, four thousand from his bank, and another two thousand from his credit union. And he didn't have a cent of it left."

"So what happened then?"

"You sure you're really interested in all this?"

"Good God, don't stop now," she said. "Not when you're about to pounce."

"Well, I didn't exactly pounce. What I should have done was to go see Crawdad. But I didn't. I went to see the husband instead at his home. I thought if I laid it out for him, what I'd found, he'd go down to the cops and tell all. I almost had him cold and besides, he wasn't a hard case. He was just an ordinary guy."

"What did he do?" she said.

"Well, first of all he cried. He cried for about fifteen minutes and then he admitted everything. He had hired the two dudes to kill his wife for fifteen thousand. But he didn't think they'd rape her—or so he said. Also, he was glad that I'd found out because he just couldn't live with it anymore. I suggested that maybe he'd better put on his coat and we'd go downtown and he could tell the homicide boys all about it. He said that was a good idea, but that he'd better go wash his face first. I said all right and he went into the bathroom and blew his brains out."

"How awful. How really terrible."

"Yeah. It was. But that wasn't the end of it. The cops got into it then, of course, and they weren't very polite. They seemed to think I'd screwed things up."

"But they weren't going after the husband."

"They were working on it. They said."

"But they got the two men who killed the woman."

"No. They didn't. They're still walking around loose the last I heard."

"But the money that the husband paid and what he told you."

"He didn't tell anyone else. Just me and that wasn't enough. The two dudes had an alibi for the night that the woman was killed. It was a half-assed alibi, but still good enough."

"What did Granddad think about all this?"

"He was philosophical about it all. One of the culprits had been punished, he said. I think he said culprit. And he also gave me some advice, which I took. He advised me to stop being an investigator and to start doing something else. So I did."

"What?"

"I started being rich."

13

AT 12:30 THE FOLLOWING DAY FAYE HIX CALLED ROOM service at the Madison Hotel and ordered what she thought of as a hangover breakfast even though she hadn't had that much to drink. A hangover breakfast consisted of black coffee, orange juice, and rye toast. It would also be her lunch, she decided.

She moved over to the mirror, opened her robe, and slipped it halfway down her body. She examined herself in the mirror. No marks, she thought, and no bruises and he certainly wasn't all that gentle. The word vigorous came to her mind. A vigorous lover. You were fucked with vigor last night. And this morning. And if you have anything to say about it, you will fuck with vigor again tonight.

Faye Hix drew her robe around her again. Vigor was a Kennedy word, she remembered. John Kennedy had used vigor a lot—or the mimics who came along had imitated his using it because of the way he said it. She tried to remember the way Jake Pope talked. He had an interesting voice, she thought, because it still had flavor to it—an occasional drawn-out vowel, a softened *r*, just enough to make you know that he had come from somewhere else where he had once done other things. And God, we did talk, she thought. She smiled at the round, dark metal container on her bureau. She even gave it a pat. "He must not have bored you either, Granddad," she said.

While Faye Hix was waiting for her breakfast, the former United States Congressman sat patiently at the banquette table five floors below and watched the Madison's Montpelier Room fill up for lunch. The Montpelier Room was one of Washington's more expensive restaurants and the persons who filled it up looked expensive. The men were mostly thickbodied and grey and in their late forties or mid-fifties and they all seemed to have arrived at where they were going in life five years before and were well pleased with the trip.

The women who lunched at the Montpelier Room appeared to be of two types. First, there were the older ones who came in the company of other women their own age and who looked as if they could well be the wives of the thickbodied men in their grey and blue suits. The older women, after carefully noting what each other wore, turned their attention to the other type of women in the room, the daughters who the thickbodied men had decided to take to lunch.

Except that they weren't their daughters, of course. The thickbodied men wouldn't have been that attentive to their daughters. They wouldn't have hastened to light their daughters' cigarettes or insisted that they try a bottle of thirty-five-dollar wine. The women who were young enough to be the thickbodied men's daughters cast appraising eyes around the Montpelier Room, slipped off their shoes to dig their toes into the carpet, inspected the chandeliers, decided on steak for lunch because then they wouldn't have to worry about dinner, and gazed coolly back at the bleak stares that came from the tables of the women who were old enough to be the thickbodied men's wives.

The former Congressman who sat at the banquette table in the northeast corner of the Montpelier Room was forty-nine years old and thinking about sex. He was thinking about the night before and the blond girl who had raised her head from between his thighs and said, "This isn't doing much good, honey. You wanta try something else?"

He hadn't wanted to try anything else. He had sat on the edge of the bed, naked, and watched her dress. "Don't worry about it, honey," she had told him. "It happens to lots of guys."

"It does, huh?" he had said.

"It even happens to young guys. It goes away. I bet next time I'll be able to chin myself on it."

"Sure," he said. "Next time."

"You've still got my number, don't you, sugar?"

"I've got it."

"Maybe next time I'll bring a friend. Maybe that's what you need. Guys your age sometimes need a little variety. How does that sound?"

"It sounds just fine," the former Congressman had said, knowing that he would never call her again. Still, he might take her prescription for a little variety and try two of them. He had never done that, although he'd had fantasies about it and the fantasies had been fine. What had she said? Guys my age need a little variety. Well, maybe she's right. Maybe I'll try it tonight, but not with her. I'll try it with a couple of new ones and if that doesn't work, then I'll see a doctor.

There must be a cure for it. They've got a cure for everything else now.

The former Congressman was from Omaha, Nebraska. His name was Kyle Tarr and he had served three terms in Congress before he had lost the primary election four years back to a younger, more aggressive candidate who had had some excellent advice on how to use television spots. Former Congressman Tarr knew that it was television that had cost him the election. It was not just that his opponent was younger, far better-looking, and had used television as though it was a medium designed exclusively for him. That wasn't what had beat him. What beat you, he often told himself, was when you went on television and tried to match him spot for spot. He came on looking like Gregory Peck and sounding like Lincoln and you came on looking like Tubby Tarr, the Used Car Salesman. The voters chose Gregory Peck and Lincoln. Who wouldn't?

After his political defeat, Tarr had gone back to his Omaha real estate business determined to get rich quick by whatever convenient means came to hand. He let the word get around that his prestige as an ex-Congressman was up for sale if it were needed to shore up the foundations of an otherwise shaky deal. He was quickly approached by a small syndicate that wanted to put together a string of parking lots. There was a little trouble with zoning. Tarr agreed to front for the syndicate. This didn't have much effect although the three discreet bribes that he parceled out did wonders. Tarr made what he thought of as a few bucks and had been casting around for something else when he was approached by the two men from Chicago.

The two men had a business proposition, they said. To make it work, they needed somebody who knew his way around Washington, who was smart, who could keep his mouth shut, and who wanted to make a lot of money. According to a mutual friend of theirs, Tarr was just the man. Tarr had replied that he was always interested in making a lot of money and how much did they think of as a lot? They said they thought that maybe half a million dollars was a lot. Tarr had said that it was a hell of a lot and the two men had agreed.

"Especially, if it's made legally," Tarr had said. "How much would I have to put up?"

"Maybe a hundred thousand."

Tarr had remained silent for a moment. "Then it's not legal, is it?"

The two men had said nothing. One of them had looked at his hand and had rubbed his palm as if he were trying to smooth out all of the wrinkles in it. He had still been looking at his hand when he spoke. "Would you like to hear the rest of it?"

Tarr had thought about it for a moment and decided that there was no harm in listening. It didn't cost a dime to listen.

"Yeah," he had said, "I'd like to hear the rest of it."

"If you hear the rest of it, you're in," the man who had been smoothing his palm said.

"Wait a minute. I don't go into any deal without first knowing what it's all about."

"It's about your making half a million dollars."

"Anybody could walk in off the street and say, hey, Tarr, give me a hundred thousand bucks and I'll make you half a million. But that doesn't mean I'd put up the hundred thousand bucks unless I got maybe a couple of more details."

"I'll give you a detail," the man had said.

"All right."

"Fulvio Varvesi," the man had said. "He sends his regards."

Tarr's eyebrows had gone up to show that he appreciated the name. "This one of Fulvio's deals?" he had said, unable to keep the awe from crawling into his voice.

The two men had looked at each other. They were both in their early thirties and they both wore dark suits with white shirts and quiet ties. Both were a little under six feet. One was blond and the other was dark and neither of them needed to see a barber. Both had eyes that gave off those direct gazes that aren't quite stares and which usually belong to people who seldom forget a face and don't have too much trouble with names. Both had the quick, impatient moves of men in a hurry, but they kept the impatience out of their voices from which all traces of regional accent had been erased. They looked fit, competent, and hard-muscled and as if they knew all there was to know about doing what they did. They could have been from the bank or the insurance company or the FBI. Or they could have been two astronauts just back from the moon. Instead, they were from Chicago and worked for Fulvio Varvesi and did whatever he told them to do.

"You know Mr. Varvesi, don't you?" the blond man had said.

Tarr had shook his head. "Well, I don't exactly know him. I've talked to him on the phone."

"Mr. Varvesi contributed twenty-five thousand dollars to your last campaign."

"I called him up and thanked him. We had quite a nice little talk."

"Yes. Mr. Varvesi remembers that. He also seems

to remember that his contribution was in cash and that you didn't get around to reporting it. He thought you might have simply forgotten and that perhaps we should bring it to your attention."

Tarr had looked at the two men, first at the one with the dark hair and then at the blond. They had looked back at him with their forget-nothing eyes. "Well, no, I hadn't forgotten it," Tarr had said.

"But you didn't report it."

"No," Tarr had said, "I didn't report it."

"Well, there's really no problem, of course. I mean, if you're interested in Mr. Varvesi's proposal, there's no problem."

Tarr had sighed. "I'm interested."

"What we said before still goes," the blond man had said. "If you hear the proposal, you're in."

"I put up one hundred thousand and I make half a million, is that the pitch?" Tarr had said.

"Roughly. Yes."

"And this is one of Fulvio's deals?"

"Yes."

"All right," Tarr had said. "I'm in."

The man that Tarr had been waiting for at the banquette table in the Montpelier Room wore bangs. His hair was grey, almost silver, and his barber had combed it straight forward in razored layers and then trimmed it off in carefully ragged bangs that lay just so not quite halfway down his forehead.

As the man followed the maitre d' to Tarr's table, heads turned to look at him. He was worth a look. Like most of the rest of the men in the room, he was middle-aged, probably somewhere in his fifties, but there all resemblance stopped. He was tall and slender almost to the point of being thin. He had a dancer's walk that moved his hips and legs but not his shoulders. It was a walk that just escaped being a swish.

And while the rest of the thickbodied men in the room dressed to resemble good grey marsh hens, the tall man who glided after the maitre d' dressed like a bird of brilliant plumage. He wore a jacket that had been tailored out of carefully aged denim. Around his neck was a piece of scarlet silk that did for his necktie. It plunged down into the open neck of a cream-colored shirt made from raw silk. He didn't wear a belt. Belts were out and besides he really didn't need one. He let his nipped-in waistline hold up his slacks which were made out of a glorious red, white and blue plaid. The slacks may have been a little tight around the crotch or he may have had them cut that way just to show off. On his feet were black loafers with the gold bridle thing across them which let you know that he had bought them at Gucci's.

You could tell from his face that he didn't at all mind the stares that he got as he crossed the room. Beneath the silver bangs were gleaming blue eyes that had a look of sly mischief about them. He had a straight, longish nose that probably was good for poking into other people's business. As he neared Tarr's table he switched on a white, wide smile that showed a lot of capped teeth and a good jawline that was just beginning to develop the trace of a sag.

It was a face that was refusing to grow old because the man who owned it refused to feel old. It was also a face that looked as if it knew all the gossip in town and wasn't particularly surprised by any of it. It was the face of someone who had few morals and even fewer scruples, and who was too realistic to become a cynic because cynics didn't have enough fun.

The face belonged to Noah deGraffenreid, who,

when anyone asked, described himself as an antiques dealer. He did indeed spend some time in a shop called deGraffenreid's Antiques on Wisconsin Avenue on the northern edge of Georgetown, but it wasn't how he made his living. He was also a high-class fence, a thief, a usurer, if not a loan shark, and a fixer, which in Washington can mean almost anything. In previous lives he had been a foreign service officer, an infantry captain, a college instructor, a radio actor in soap operas, a lobbyist, and one lean year, a riding academy instructor.

Kyle Tarr decided that he would have to shake hands with deGraffenreid. He didn't want to, because he thought deGraffenreid was a fairy, which he wasn't, and Tarr didn't like to shake hands with fairies because he was afraid somebody might see him and think that he was a fairy, too. He didn't mind deGraffenreid himself; he just didn't like to be seen shaking hands with him.

But there was no way to get out of it because deGraffenreid was standing there with his hand stuck out. Tarr rose awkwardly, as far as the banquette table would let him, and gave deGraffenreid's hand a brief shake.

"I'm just a tiny bit late," deGraffenreid said, sliding on to the seat beside Tarr.

Jesus Christ, now he's got to sit by me, Tarr thought. "That's okay," he said. "I went ahead and ordered a drink."

"Oh, I do want one of those," deGraffenreid told the waiter, pointing to Tarr's Bloody Mary. "But not too much Tabasco now and do be a good lad and see if they'll put a celery stick in it."

DeGraffenreid, Tarr decided, couldn't order a glass of water without telling somebody how far to turn the tap.

"Well, I must say I was surprised to hear from you again so soon," deGraffenreid said, evening up the silver.

"How come we always have to meet out in front of God and everybody?" Tarr said. "Haven't you ever heard of a hotel room?"

"I conduct all of my business in public, Tarr, baby," which was what deGraffenreid called Tarr when he didn't call him Congressman, which was what he knew that Tarr really liked. "It gives everything I do an aura of respectability." He smiled and waved at a middle-aged woman across the room who nodded and smiled back. "There's Mrs. Hardegree, the old bitch, and doesn't she look nice?" Without waiting for Tarr to answer, he said, "Well, Congressman, what does bring you back to Washington, homesick for the Hill?"

"Not quite," Tarr said.

"Well?"

Tarr waited for the waiter to serve deGraffenreid's Bloody Mary. It had a celery stick, he noticed.

"There's been a change," Tarr said.

DeGraffenreid took a sip of his drink first. Then he said, "Oh? What kind of a change? Big or little?"

"Big, I'd say."

"Well, let's have it," deGraffenreid said, patting his stomach. "Then we can order a nice lunch and maybe my tummy will stop making strange noises at me."

"It's about this guy you got lined up," Tarr said. "The Ph.D."

"You mean the good Dr. Hucks?"

"Yeah, Dallas Hucks. Well, my friends out in the Midwest have been thinking about him."

"Your friends who shall remain nameless."

"It's better that way."

"Oh, I quite agree. All I need for liaison is you, Tarr, baby."

"You don't really have to call me that, do you? I got called that all through grade school and it really isn't very funny."

"I'm sorry, Congresman. It was only a sign of affection. Now what have your friends out in the Midwest been thinking about our Dr. Hucks?"

"Well, they've—" Tarr took another swallow of his drink, a large swallow. "Christ, I never did anything like this before."

"Like what?"

"Well, let me start from the beginning. When you approached Hucks, you made him an offer of one hundred thousand dollars, right?"

"First I located him," deGraffenreid said. "That was really my most important job, selecting him from all of the scores of persons who possibly would have been eligible candidates."

"First you found him—"

"And then I cultivated him, much as one cultivates a sick geranium. It was, I hope you understand, a terribly delicate task requiring the utmost in diplomacy."

"First you found him, then you cultivated him, and then you made him the proposition."

"In the Cosmos Club, can you imagine?" de Graffenreid said. "He was most impressed by the Cosmos Club, young Dr. Hucks was. I even hinted that there was the possibility of his becoming a member. I thought for a moment he might lick my hand."

"We all know how wonderful you are, Noah," Tarr said.

"I just don't like anyone to forget."

"You do a good job."

"So what's on your mind, Tarr, baby? You seem to be having a most difficult time getting it out."

"Well, this guy Dallas Hucks. You're pretty sure he hasn't told his wife about the proposition?"

"I am almost positive he has not. I warned him not to."

"Yeah, well, would he be the kind of a guy to keep a diary and leave it lying around?"

"Again, I can say that I'm almost positive that he is not."

"Uh-huh. And you don't think he'd leave one of those letters that you hear about lying around?"

"What kind of letters?"

"You know, the kind that have 'To be opened only in the event of my death' typed on the envelope they come in."

DeGraffenreid smiled at Tarr, but it wasn't a pleasant smile. DeGraffenreid hadn't meant it to be. "I don't honestly think that Dr. Hucks is concerned about the imminence of his death, Tarr, baby. Should he be?"

Tarr was uncomfortable. He squirmed. He tried to cross his legs but the table was too low or his thighs were too fat and he couldn't do it. This shouldn't be my job, he thought. Somebody else should be doing this. He didn't look at deGraffenreid when he spoke. He looked at the ice in his Bloody Mary instead.

"My friends were thinking that after we got the information that we need from Hucks then he really wouldn't be needed anymore, would he?"

DeGraffenreid was enjoying Tarr's discomfort. "Needed or wanted?"

"Well, both."

"Well, certainly after he has completed his assigned task, he would no longer be needed. So the question is, would he be wanted?"

"My associates say he wouldn't be wanted either," Tarr said, still examining the ice in his glass. "Not after he did what he was supposed to do."

"Your friends would rather like him to go away, I take it?"

Tarr nodded. "Yeah, they'd like that. They mentioned something about an accident maybe."

"Well, accidents do happen, even to the most careful of us," deGraffenreid said.

"They'd sort of like to make sure that this accident does happen."

"I see. Is there a going rate for accidents?"

"Well, in this particular case they think it oughta be worth about twenty thousand."

"In advance?"

"Half in advance," Tarr said. "They also don't want to have anyone else brought in on it."

"I understand," deGraffenreid said. "They'd like personal service."

"Yeah, very personal."

"Well, I think that could be arranged. Do they have particular preference as to time?"

"Uh-huh. They'd like it to happen on the same day that you get the stuff from Hucks."

"That would be July eleventh."

"July eleventh."

"All right," deGraffenreid said. "I see no great difficulty there. Well, July eleventh seems destined to become quite a big day for all of us, wouldn't you say, Congressman?"

"Yeah," Tarr said. "A real big day."

14

JAKE POPE SAT AT HIS DESK IN THE ROOM THAT HE USED as a study and looked at the list of names that had been typed out on two sheets of paper. The list had been given to him by Ancel Easter. It contained the names of those members of the Cosmos Club who had dined there the night before Crawdad Gilmore had been killed. It also contained the names of those who had been guests of members. Seventy-four members had eaten their dinner at the club. They had been joined by 125 guests.

"It was like getting state secrets," Easter had told Pope when he handed over the list earlier in the day.

"What did you tell them?"

"That a rather prominent person who'd had dinner there that night became awfully ill and was thinking of suing them. I told them that I thought I could talk him out of it if I could check with some of the other guests who had also eaten there, but hadn't become ill. I made it a little fancier than that, of course."

"I think I got sick the last time I ate there," Pope said.

"You probably have a delicate palate. You think the list will do any good?"

"It's a start," Pope said. "I have to assume that who-ever Crawdad overheard that night is on the list."

"Well, you can eliminate about a third of the people who are on it," Easter said.

"Why?"

"Crawdad said he did his eavesdropping in the men's room, didn't he?"

"So you said."

"Well, a third of the people on that list are women."

Pope shifted in his chair and read through the list again. He recognized some of the names because they were the names of persons who were prominent in a mild sort of way and got their names in the papers once or twice a year. Nobody big though, Pope decided. No four-star generals. No admirals. Not even an Under Sec-retary of State. There was one Senator on the list, but Pope knew from his own time with the Senate that the old man ate at the Cosmos Club almost every night, almost always alone, and always at the same corner table.

Pope picked up the District of Columbia phone book, looked up a number, and dialed it. When a man's voice answered, "Associated Press," Pope asked to speak to a reporter he knew. When the reporter came on the phone, Pope identified himself.

"Ah, my one millionaire friend," the reporter said. "What're the rich folks up to, Jake?"

"Staying rich."

"And the poor stay poor."

"God intended it that way, Sam."

"In his infinite wisdom. What can I do for you?"

"You guys keep a list of stories that are coming up that you have to cover, don't you?"

"We do indeed. We pride ourselves on keeping abreast of our times. I think we have the apocalypse scheduled for 1997."

"What about July eleventh?"

"This year?"

"This year."

"Hold on a second."

When he came back on the phone, he said, "You're talking about Washington, aren't you?"

"That's right."

"July eleventh is a very dull day."

"How about the President? Is he making a public appearance?"

"Nothing scheduled."

"What about visiting firemen? Any premiers, presidents, or benevolent dictators scheduled to show up?"

"Nope. It's too hot in July. They like to come in April when it's cool and the cherry blossoms are out."

"What about Congress?"

"It'll be in session, but that's about all."

"The Supreme Court?"

"They've done gone home to rest up for three months."

"Nothing else, huh?"

"Well, let's see. Now here's a real dandy. The Department of Agriculture will release this year's official wheat crop estimate at five P.M. Does that stir the blood?"

"Not really. Is that all?"

"That's absolutely all we've got budgeted. Would it be amiss of me to ask why you're so interested in July eleventh, me being in the reporting business and all?"

"Somebody told me something big was going to happen, but they didn't tell me what."

"How about where and why?"

"They didn't mention that either. Just when."

"Something nasty, I hope?"

"Maybe."

"Well, it could be that somebody's dog'll get run over. From what July eleventh looks like now, even that could make a front page or two."

"Sam, you've been most helpful."

"No, I haven't, but I tried."

"What about lunch sometime real soon?"

"Sounds good. You're buying, of course."

"I always buy now that I'm rich. Atonement, you know."

"God bless you, Jake Pope, you're a Christian."

"Pray for me, Sam."

The reporter said that he would and then said good-bye.

Pope made thirty-two other telephone calls that afternoon. He called the administrative assistants of three Senators whom he thought of as knowledgeable types. He called a syndicated columnist whom he had once done some favors for. He called five lobbyists who prided themselves on knowing what went on in Washington. He called a private detective who had grown so rich from various real estate deals that he only took two or three cases a year now and only if they really interested him. He called nine criminal lawyers, five of them expensive and four of them cheap. He called two agents he knew at the Federal Bureau of Investigation. He called a reporter at UPI. He talked to the president of a labor union. He called a girl who worked for Ralph

Nader. He called an assistant U.S. District Attorney. He called three reporters on the *Washington Post* and two on the *Star-News*. He called a bail bondsman. And finally, he called Faye Hix in her room in the Madison Hotel.

After they said hello, Pope said, "Where would you like to eat tonight, or do you say dine?"

"I say eat," Faye said. "We don't hold with fancy airs in Montana."

"I know a pretty fair steak house."

"I don't like steak," she said. "I can eat steak at home. When I go out I like to eat something that somebody's fussed over."

"I know an Italian place. The Italians fuss over their food a lot."

"Fine," she said. "We'll have some fussy Italian food."

"I'll pick you up at seven."

"Can you make it six-thirty?" she said. "I had one of those starvation lunches and I don't think I can hold out till seven."

Pope said that he would be there at six-thirty, said good-bye, hung up the telephone, and then went back to the list of names of those who had dined at the Cosmos Club the night before Crawdad Gilmore had been killed. He crossed out all the women's names on the list. Then he drew connecting lines between the names of the members and the names of those who had been their guests that night. Real progress, he told himself. You draw an awfully straight line for freehand.

He kept returning to one name because it was familiar to him and because he was a little surprised that the man was a member of the Cosmos Club. He followed the line he had drawn from the man's name to the guest that he had had for dinner that night. The guest's name meant nothing.

Pope picked up the phone again and called Ancel Easter.

"I've been working," Pope said.

"Any progress?"

"None. I called thirty-two people and all of them agreed that as far as they knew July eleventh will probably be the dullest day of the year. Thirteen of them pointed out that it was a week after the Fourth of July."

"That was helpful," Easter said.

"I've been going over this list you gave me."

"And?"

"You're not too exclusive, are you?"

"We admit to membership only those who're prominent in the arts and sciences, whatever that means. I really don't go there much. As you say, it's kind of stuffy."

"You know Noah deGraffenreid?"

"The name's familiar."

"He has an antiques shop on Wisconsin."

"Yeah, I think I met him once. Tall, thin guy who dresses like he thinks he's always in Palm Springs."

"He still dresses that way, huh?" Pope said.

"The last time I saw him he did."

"When was that?"

"I don't really remember. You know him?"

"His name came up in an investigation I was once on."

"What kind of an investigation?"

"We were looking into loansharking practices as they exist in these United States. We got a tip that deGraffenreid might be practicing it in a small way."

"What'd you find out?"

"Another guy handled it. He said that deGraffen-reid was more of a usurer than a loan shark."

"What's the difference?"

"Not much. I think a loan shark will bust you up with a baseball bat if you miss your payments. A usurer just hounds you to death. They both charge about the same amount of interest."

"What happened?"

"To deGraffenreid? Nothing. I think he was just getting started. It was about eight years ago, as I remember. The guy who was in on it also turned up a couple of other rumors about him."

"Unsavory, no doubt."

"Yeah. The word was that he's a pretty high-class fence. And the other rumor we got is that he's not above backing a truck up to somebody's house and carting out the family heirlooms—especially if the family happens to be down in Florida at the time."

"Just rumor though?"

"That's right. Just rumor."

"What'd you do about it?"

"Well, you know how those things are. You think you're going to pass it on to the cops, but something happens and you never get around to it."

"What do you want me to do," Easter said, "bring all that to the membership committee's attention?"

"That's for your conscience to decide."

"DeGraffenreid needn't worry then."

"I would like to know how long he's been a member."

"Okay," Easter said. "I'll call you back in a few minutes."

It was seven minutes later when Pope's phone rang.

It was Easter. "He's been a member for ten years. He used to be an actor."

"Where?"

"In Chicago in the early forties. He was in *Our Gal Sunday*. You ever listen to *Our Gal Sunday?* It was on radio."

"I'm afraid I missed it," Pope said.

"It was probably before your time. Well, after that he went into the Army where he got to be captain and then he went into the State Department for a while. He even wrote a book. It was called *How Not to Buy Antiques.* I think I heard of that. It was sort of a best-seller, wasn't it?"

"For a while, I think," Pope said.

"Well, maybe that's how he got to be a member. People have qualified for membership on far less. I think there're some down there who've never read a book, let alone written one. You think deGraffenreid might be our boy?"

"I have no idea," Pope said.

"What about his guests? Did he have any guests that night?"

"He had one," Pope said and read off the name of the man who had been deGraffenreid's guest. "It doesn't mean anything to me; does it to you?"

"Not a thing," Easter said.

"I think I'll check him out."

"Let me know if you turn something."

"Don't worry," Pope said.

For a few more moments Pope stared at the list of names. Then he sighed and picked up the District of Columbia telephone book again. When he didn't find what he was looking for he turned to the Maryland and Virgina sections. In the Virginia section he ran his finger down the page until he came to the name he wanted. He wrote the number down on a pad.

"Become a private detective," he said to himself in a voice that he coarsened and deepened. "Earn big money in your spare time."

He dialed the number and when a woman said hello, he said, "Lemme talk to your husband, lady." He used his new harsh voice.

"He's not here," the woman said.

"Well, where is he?"

"He's—he's at work. Who is this?"

Pope made his tone confidential. "You sure he hasn't skipped town, lady?"

"He's at work, I said. Who is this?"

"Look, lady, this is O'Brien at the Metropolitan Collection Agency. You know why I'm calling, don't you?"

"I have no idea why you're calling."

"I'm calling, lady, because your husband don't pay his bills. He owes four hundred and twenty-six dollars, that's why I'm calling. You'd better let me talk to him."

"He's not here, I told you. He's at work."

"Where's he work, lady?"

"At the—at the Department of Agriculture."

"You got his number?"

"I'm not going to talk to you anymore. I don't have to give you his number." The woman hung up the phone.

Pope put his own phone down. He took a fresh sheet of paper and wrote Department of Agriculture on it. Next he wrote down the name of Noah deGraffenreid. The last name he wrote was that of Dallas Hucks. He looked at them for a while and then he drew a line that connected all three names and formed a triangle.

Pope stared at the names and the triangle he had drawn for a long time. It has a rather interesting design, he told himself, but does it have any meaning? Sure it does, he thought, it's a triangle and he kept on staring at it until it was time to go pick up Faye Hix.

15

PETER BERRY, TWENTY-THREE, DECIDED TO USE THE ALLEY because it was a little closer. Peter Berry's hair was brownish blond and fell to his shoulders. It had been his turn to go to the Stone Soup where he had picked up the groceries. The Stone Soup was a cooperative market on upper 18th Street that was trying to do something about the high price of groceries. The Stone Soup felt that chain food stores were a rip-off. The Stone Soup also had a lot of other ideas about what was wrong with the country and the economy and, for that matter, the world and the people who bought their food there, like Peter Berry, all pretty much agreed with what the Stone Soup thought.

Peter Berry was a member of an eight-person commune that dwelt in a house on R Street just off 17th. If one broke it down by sex, which members of the commune didn't like to do, there were five women and three men living in the house. There were also six cats, two dogs, and a three-month-old baby that belonged to Wilma Peppers, nineteen. Wilma didn't know who the baby's father was and didn't really care. The baby's name was Shawn. Not Sean, but Shawn. That's how Wilma was.

Peter Berry had just spent $59.24 at the Stone Soup, which wasn't bad considering that it would feed eight persons, a baby, six cats, and two dogs for almost a week. The members of the commune, which didn't call itself anything, took turns going to the Stone Soup. They carried the groceries home in a red metal wagon that had American Flyer written in cream on its sides in sans-serif italics. On the back of the wagon was a faded old bumper sticker that said, Impeach Nixon.

Peter Berry had dropped out of the University of Chicago in his second year. He had come to Washington two years before with the idea of going to work for some organization that was doing something meaningful. Instead, he had gone to work as a deck attendant in the Library of Congress. He helped locate books that the members of Congress ordered. Many members of Congress, he discovered, read nothing but westerns and detective stories and Peter Berry was a bit disillusioned.

However, he liked living in the commune, mostly because nobody hassled him. Peter Berry didn't like being hassled. He was well into Greek now and nobody at the commune hassled him about it. They all thought that his being into Greek was pretty wonderful.

The alley that Peter Berry turned down was between R and S Streets. By going down the alley he could go in the back door of the commune's house and save almost half a block. The north side of the alley was lined with garages. On the south side were the back yards of the houses on R Street. The commune had turned its back yard into a vegetable garden. However, the vegetables weren't doing too well, especially the tomatoes. The bugs were getting the tomatoes. They should have been sprayed, but the members of the commune didn't believe in insecticides. It was a real problem.

Peter Berry noticed the two blacks who stepped out of the open garage. He didn't think anything about them. He just kept on walking down the alley pulling his red wagon. When he got abreast of the blacks, the shorter one reached inside his shirt and pulled out a small automatic pistol.

"Ah, come on, man," Peter Berry said. "I haven't got any bread."

"Git his money," the shorter black said to the taller one. Peter Berry saw that the taller black held a knife. It was a kitchen knife, he noticed.

"Man, all I've got is seventy-six cents," Peter Berry said. "Look, if you're hungry and want some groceries, help yourself."

Peter Berry turned toward the red wagon. The smaller black shot him in the back with the .22 automatic pistol that had been made in Spain. Peter Berry fell, moaned, and then tried to get up. The smaller black shot him again, this time in the head. The taller black knelt down and quickly went through his pockets.

"He ain't got no money. All he got is seventy-six cents."

"Let's take his groceries. We can sell em."

"Shit, I ain't gonna pull no wagon down no street. You crazy, man?"

"What he got in theah?"

The shorter black looked in a sack. "He got oranges. You want a orange?"

"Yeah, gimme a orange."

The shorter black took out two oranges. He gave one to the taller black. They walked slowly off down the alley, leaving behind them a string of orange peels, a red wagon full of groceries, and a twenty-three-year-old dead man called Peter Berry who was well into Greek.

16

YOU COULD SEE LAKE MICHIGAN FROM WHERE THE TWO men stood near the door in the large paneled room. The paneling was of real walnut and had cost a tidy fortune. So had the three paintings that hung on three of the walls. The fourth wall was all glass and through it the two men stared out at the lake. They could have examined the paintings which were by Dubuffet, Gromaire, and Kuniyushi, but they didn't. They had already seen them and they didn't much like them so they looked at the lake and at the back of the chair.

The chair was tallbacked and it could swivel and it was covered in pale brown suede. It was behind a large desk that had been carved out of another expensive piece of walnut. The desk had nothing on its surface but a 21-inch-high Kief bronze. There was a thick, rich tobacco-brown carpet on the floor. There were also three other upholstered chairs in the room and a long couch. These were grouped around a low glass-topped table. The glass was thick and cut in a free form shape that vaguely resembled a flat peanut. The base of the table was cleverly formed out of a big chunk of highly polished driftwood.

The two men continued to stand and stare out at the lake. From sixty-two stories up it looked blue and sparkling and even inviting. From behind the back of the suede-covered chair came a sound. It was a man's voice and it managed to combine a grunt and a sigh with a moan. Then the voice said, "That was good, honey. That was damned good. I liked that."

A woman's voice said, "So did I. You know, you're wonderful, just wonderful."

The chair swiveled around. Fulvio Varvesi stood up so that he could pull up his shorts and pants, tuck in his shirttail, buckle his belt, and close his zipper. A young woman rose from where she had been kneeling. She was Marie Exum and nineteen years old and quite pretty in a brittle sort of way. She was also naked. The two men who stood near the door watched as she put on a pair of blue slacks and a pink shirt. She learned over and kissed Fulvio Varvesi on the top of his head. "Be sure to call me, sug," she said.

Fulvio Varvesi lifted a hand and waved it in dismissal. Marie Exum moved around the desk and crossed the room. She went past the two men without a look. She left, closing the door behind her.

"How did you like that?" Fulvio Varvesi said.

The man who had blond hair said, "Looked like it'd be all right."

"Best damned cocksucker in Chicago," Varvesi said. "Maybe the best in the world. Who knows?"

"I talked to Tarr," the blond man said. "In Washington."

Varvesi nodded. "Let's sit over here," he said and rose. He wasn't very tall, just a fraction over five-nine. He was slightly built with small delicate bones that looked as if they would snap easily. His hair was brown and wavy and long enough to cover up most of his ears. His face was round and childishly smooth with deeply sunk brown eyes that were covered by gold-framed glasses that kept sliding down his thin nose. Beneath the nose was a small mouth with pink lips that looked pouty and wet. The voice that came out of the little mouth was surprisingly deep, almost a bass baritone. There were no lines in Fulvio Varvesi's face. Not one. But then he was only twenty-six years old.

The three men sat around the low glass table. There were no ashtrays in the room. Varvesi didn't smoke. He didn't drink either. His indulgences were carefully under control and limited to sex, art, and money. He felt that there really wasn't quite enough of any of them.

The Varvesi family fortune had been founded by Giancarlo Varvesi who had arrived in Chicago as an infant in 1902 in the arms of his mother. She had been greeted at the end of her long trip from Naples with the news that her husband, Paolo Varvesi, had died the week before in a construction accident. Giancarlo grew up to become a petty thief until by accident he discovered that he had a real talent for firearms, especially the sawed-off shotgun. As a very young man he had offered these talents to Al Capone in the mid-twenties and thereafter when the newspapers ran headlines something like GANG GUNS ROAR AGAIN ON CHICAGO'S SOUTH SIDE it could be assumed that Giancarlo was once more hard at work.

But where his associates had frittered away their money on large cars, flashy women, splendid clothes, and strong drink, Giancarlo had carefully husbanded his. He married a brilliant, if uneducated woman, a genius really, who shared his parsimonious nature. Together they quietly assembled a small real estate empire that consisted mostly of one- and two-family dwellings. In 1931 Giancarlo retired from killing people to devote himself to the management of his property. The Chicago police, although they could never prove it, privately estimated that Giancarlo Varvesi had dispatched thirty-nine persons during his fortunately brief career, but the Chicago police have been known to exaggerate.

Only one son was born to Giancarlo Varvesi and his wife. The son was born in 1927 at the height of Giancarlo's prowess with the shotgun and he was named Franco. The son grew up in comfortable surroundings and even went to Northwestern University. After brief service in the Army he met and married a young woman in 1948 and in keeping with the luck of the Varvesi men, she turned out to be a genius with an IQ of 173 as measured by the Stanford-Binet test.

The son was no dummy either, so when his father died in bed in 1949 of a ruptured appendix, mistakenly self-diagnosed as acid indigestion, Franco took over the family business. He was just twenty-two. With the aid, encouragement, and guidance of his mother, the genius, and his wife, who was just a little bit smarter than the mother, Franco sold off most of the real estate holdings and started building shopping centers all over the Midwest. He had made another fortune for the family, this time a huge one, by the time that he was twenty-five and his son, Fulvio, was three.

It was then that Franco and his wife and his mother discovered that there was yet another genius in the Varvesi family. Fulvio, although not too sturdy as a child, could draw better than most twelve-year-olds when he was three. They promptly hired him a tutor. By four he could read as well as most ninth-graders.

By seven he was nearly through with high school or rather, its equivalent. By twelve he knew more than most college graduates, but had just discovered that he liked to hurt things. Cats, dogs, bugs, birds—things like that. By thirteen he had discovered sex and also that it was even more enjoyable if he could hurt his partner, in this instance a thirty-two-year-old woman who was tutoring him in the farther limits of mathematics for which he had developed a pronounced flair. It had worked out all right though because the woman liked to be hurt.

Fulvio Varvesi never went to school a day in his life. College, of course, would have been a redundancy so when Fulvio turned seventeen his father, Franco, took him into the family business. By twenty-one, Fulvio was running the business and Franco, then forty-four, retired to the Italian Riviera, taking with him for company those two strangely compatible geniuses, his mother and his wife.

The first thing that Fulvio did at twenty-one when he was in full control of the family fortune was to build himself a sixty-two-story skyscraper in Chicago and name it the Varvesi Building, reserving the two top floors for both his residence and the company offices. From there he directed not only his extensive real estate holdings, but also other diverse interests that by now included oil, gas, shipping, mining, milling, and by the time he was twenty-two, politics. Fulvio Varvesi had begun collecting politicians at twenty-two in the same careful discriminating way that he had begun collecting art at seventeen. He bought early and he bought cheap. He specialized in helping to finance the campaigns of ambitious young men who wanted to jump from the county courthouse to the state capital or from the state capital to the capitol in Washington. He was extremely selective in those he aided and his aid was remembered, appreciated and, of course, reciprocated.

Fulvio still liked to hurt things, but mostly people now, mostly girls, and he had absolutely no compunction about eliminating someone who stood in his way. He had them murdered although he didn't call it murder. He called it having them twepped, a phrase he had borrow from accounts of the CIA's activities in Southeast Asia. The CIA, according to these accounts, had once issued orders that certain persons whom it didn't much care for should be Terminated With Extreme Prejudice, which usually meant that they should be shoved out of a helicopter or pushed over the side of a boat or just shot. The acronymn for all this terminating with extreme prejudice was TWEP, which amused Fulvio who adopted it as his own. By the time he was twenty-six he had had thirteen persons twepped, which was still far below the record of thirty-nine that had been set by Grandfather Giancarlo Varvesi with his sawed-off shotgun back in the 1920's when he was just about Fulvio's present age.

"You said you talked to Tarr," Varvesi said.

The blond man nodded. He called himself Ralph Hayes, but in Los Angeles he had been known as Marvin Dansby and the police wouldn't have minded talking to him about a drug dealer called Frank Bell who had been found shot to death in his brand new 1969 Mercedes coupe in the parking lot at Los Angeles International Airport.

But all that had happened more than six years ago and the police were no longer looking for Marvin Dansby as diligently as they once had. Still, Ralph Hayes didn't get to Los Angeles anymore. He didn't even get to California, although he had once toyed with the idea of going back in 1973, to San Francisco, which would have been his tenth wedding anniversary. He often wondered what his wife was doing in San Francisco now, whether she had divorced him and remarried, and whether she still saw any of the people whom they had once gone to school with in Berkeley. He had worn a beard then and his hair had been down to his shoulders. Now he no longer wore a beard and his hair was cut short and he wore dark suits with white shirts and dull ties. At Berkeley he had been majoring in economics until he had dropped out to start dealing full-time, mostly in LSD and marijuana.

Hayes, as he almost always now thought of himself, had worked for Fulvio Varvesi for four years. He made approximately $48,000 a year and his new wife thought it was wonderful that he had such an important job with such an important firm at only thirty-three even though he had failed to get his degree at the University of Texas, which is where he lied to her that he had gone to school. During his four years with Varvesi, Ralph Hayes had shot and killed four men who, his employer decided, had needed killing. He had subcontracted out—as Hayes thought of it—the deaths of two others.

"What did Tarr say?" Varvesi asked.

"He said he's got everything fixed with the antiques dealer, deGraffenreid."

"How much?" Varvesi asked.

"Twenty thousand."

Varvesi pushed out his lower lip and nodded. "That's not bad for an accident," he said. "Tarr told him an accident, didn't he?"

Hayes nodded. "An accident."

"Okay. That takes care of the guy in the department. What's his name again?"

"Hucks," the dark man said. "Dr. Dallas Hucks."

"Yeah, Hucks," Varvesi said. "What about our friend Tarr?"

Ralph Hayes looked at the dark man who smiled. The dark man was a year older than Ralph Hayes, which made him thirty-four, and his real name was Elefteris Spiliotacopoulos, although he had called himself Jack Sperry ever since he had run away from home in Newark, New Jersey, when he was fourteen. He hadn't run far, only to Manhattan where he had found that he could support himself by letting older men pick him up and pay him for the use of his body, which more than one hard-breathing middle-aged man from the Midwest had told him looked just like that of a Greek god.

At sixteen Jack Sperry had met a Times Square grifter who specialized in fake birth certificates and high school transcripts. They had cost $250 each and Sperry had ordered a set, making a down payment of $50 in cash and $50 in trade, which had consisted of letting the grifter have his way with him for two nights running. When Sperry had gone back to pick up his faked documents, he had insisted on inspecting them closely. After satisfying himself that they were adequate, he carefully put them down on a table, reached into his pocket, took out a six-inch switchblade, and cut the grifter's throat, making sure not to get any blood on the faked documents.

The next day he had enlisted in the United States Army where he spent eight years, three of them with the Special Forces in Vietnam. He had spent the final year of his enlistment in 1965 as a sergeant at Fort

Bragg, North Carolina, teaching unarmed killing to recruits. His officers considered him to be the most gifted instructor they had ever had.

After his discharge, Jack Sperry drifted to Chicago where he worked as an instructor in a fat factory for three years. The fat factory was a health club that sold year-long memberships on time. The club discounted its paper to a finance company. Its fat members usually turned up for one or two sessions, discovered that it was hard work, and quit. This enabled the health club to oversell its facilities by as much as 1500 percent. Those who quit still had to make their installments, but the health club let the finance company worry about that. Those who did stick it out came under the merciless direction of Sperry who received a small bonus for each member who gave up and quit.

In 1967 Sperry tired of the fat factory and went to work for a karate school in Chicago where he met an awkward eighteen-year-old student called Fulvio Varvesi whose lack of coordination made him virtually hopeless. But what Varvesi lacked in coordination, he almost made up for in enthusiasm.

During a break one afternoon Sperry had asked Varvesi why he had enrolled in the course. Varvesi had stared back at him. "I want to hurt somebody," he had said.

"He bigger than you?"

"That's right. He's bigger than I am."

"Forget it."

"Why?"

"You just haven't got it, kid. As far as you're concerned, karate's just a nice way to get some exercise. My advice to you is stay away from guys who're bigger'n you."

"I thought I was doing all right."

"Well, you're not. Not if you're thinking of using it seriously."

Varvesi had looked at Sperry. "He's not bigger than you are though, is he?"

"I wouldn't know. I never met the guy."

"Would you like to?" Varvesi had said. "For a thousand dollars. Cash."

"What would I do after I met him?"

"Hurt him. And let me watch."

Sperry had shaken his head. "And then the cops could go down and ask him how come he's in the hospital. No, thanks."

"Not if you hurt him badly enough."

"If I hurt him bad enough he'd be dead."

"Yes, he would, wouldn't he," Varvesi had said.

"For a thousand bucks? Still no, thanks.

"For five thousand?"

Sperry had stared at Varvesi for a moment. "You're rich enough not to be kidding, aren't you, sonny?"

"I'm rich enough and I don't like being called sonny."

"Five thousand still isn't a hell of a lot of money for doing what you want done."

Varvesi had smiled. "Make it seventy-five hundred. I shan't haggle, Mr. Sperry."

It was the first time that anybody had ever asked Jack Sperry to kill somebody for money and it was also the first time anybody had ever used "shan't" in a conversation with him.

The man Sperry killed for $7500 was a pimp, one Willie Bice, who had made the mistake of objecting to the way that Varvesi had marked up one of his clients. He had not only objected, he had also slapped

Varvesi around a little. Willie Bice had been a big man and Sperry had killed him methodically in a Loop alley, using nothing but his hands while Fulvio Varvesi had watched.

When it was over they had walked out of the alley and Varvesi had said, "How would you like to go to work for me?"

"Doing what? This?"

"No, not this. I think I need what might be called an assistant."

"How old are you, sonny?"

"I don't like being called sonny. I told you that."

"How old are you, *Mister* Varvesi?"

"I'm eighteen."

"And you need an assistant?"

"That's right."

"How much are you paying?"

"Oh, fifteen thousand dollars a year to start."

Jack Sperry was barely making $8,000 a year at the karate school then in 1967. "I shan't haggle, Mr. Varvesi," he had said, enjoying his own use of "shan't" for the first time. "You got yourself an assistant."

Jack Sperry now made $50,000 a year, was married to the former Nita Christodoulides, was the father of two sons and a daughter, had been responsible for seven of the thirteen persons that Fulvio Varvesi had ordered twepped, and considered his immediate prospects to be bright, if not dazzling.

He now smiled when Ralph Hayes looked at him because the look was a question about something that he knew how to do. "You'd like something to happen to Tarr, right?" he said.

Varvesi nodded impatiently. "He's the only link there is to us. Without him, there's no link. None."

"What about deGraffenreid?"

"He doesn't know about us so he can stay. And now that we know who he is, we might be able to make use of him later." Varvesi looked at Ralph Hayes. "Make sense?"

Hayes nodded. "Makes sense."

"Okay," Sperry said. "When do you want the Congressman taken care of?"

"At the same time that this guy Hucks is taken care of," Varvesi said.

"On or around July eleventh then," Sperry said.

"That's right," Varvesi said, "July eleventh."

17

THAT NIGHT IN WASHINGTON THEY LAY IN JAKE POPE'S bed and looked at the ceiling. There had been no hurry to their lovemaking and it had lasted nearly forty-five minutes, although neither had timed it, and now they lay there remembering what they had done and how they had felt while they were doing it. They also made their inevitable comparisons and decided that they had never made love quite so well before with anyone else and maybe they should let each other in on the big news.

What should you tell her? Jake Pope thought. That you're the best fuck I ever had in my life, honey? Or should you work on it and come up with some well-polished phrase whose obvious sincerity is gracefully ameliorated by its wit. To hell with it, he decided, turned toward Faye Hix, and smiled.

"You're the best fuck I ever had in my life, honey, and I was just lying here wondering how I should tell you."

She smiled back although it was more of a grin than a smile. "You certainly can turn a phrase."

"I worked on it for a while."

159

"We are good together, aren't we? Awfully good."

"That's because we're so tall."

"Did you ever go to bed with anyone taller than I am?" she said, propping herself up on one elbow.

"No, but I wanted to though."

"How tall?"

"Real tall."

"Well, how much taller, damn it?"

This time he grinned at her. "Tall enough to fuck, suck, and kick on the shins at the same time."

She hit him in the face with a pillow. He laughed and tossed it on the floor. "You're not one of those, are you?" she said.

"One of those what?"

"One of those professional down homey country boys. If you turn out to be one of those, I'm going to put on my pants and go home."

"That's an old joke."

"I know. It's an old down homey joke. See, it's catching."

"But seldom fatal," he said. "It's only rural Americanus acute. Maybe you caught it up there in Montana. On the ranch."

"It's a dude ranch."

"Who runs it while you're away?"

"The foreman."

"Ah. The foreman."

"You've got it all figured out, don't you?" she said.

"Sure."

"He's tall and lean, isn't he?"

"A little like Gary Cooper."

"Craggy features, right?" she said.

"Right."

"Doesn't waste words either?"

"Tight-lipped."

"But underneath it all he seethes with lust."

Jake Pope thought about it. "Yeah, I think he might seethe a little."

"Well, his name is Marvin Pemberton and he's forty-four and his wife, Shirley, is forty and they've got these three kids and Marvin grew up on a ranch but studied to be an accountant and helps me out with the books, but he gets these awful fits of depression sometimes because at forty-four he's only a dude ranch foreman and he thinks maybe he should have stayed with accounting, so once a week he goes in to see this female psychologist in Kalispell who's set up shop there, God knows why, and Shirley, that's Marvin's wife, is worried about Marvin talking about them to a female, and the three kids hate living on a ranch and want to move to Great Falls and all five of the Pembertons like to come to me and tell me all about their troubles and Jesus, Jake, I'm sorry I'm not a latter-day Lady Chatterley."

"Not even close, huh?"

"Not even close."

"How'd you ever get stuck with it?"

"The ranch? My husband. He inherited it from an uncle."

"What did he do before that?"

"He was charming. He was charming in advertising for a while. Then he was charming in television. And after that in public relations. We lived in San Francisco and London and New York. He was charming in all those places, but he was never ever really good at any of it, not in the professional sense anyway, and when the people who'd hired him found out that he wasn't very good, just charming, they let him go. He had six jobs in the four years that we were married. The ranch was a Godsend. He did ride well and he learned to hunt and a dude ranch is one place where charm pays off. So we made a living and after he broke his neck, I went on making a living."

"Could you sell it?"

"The ranch? It's got a fat mortgage. There wouldn't be much left. But now I guess I could. I saw Ancel Easter today. He tells me I'm going to be rich, not rich like you, but sort of ordinary rich. Granddad was very generous in his will. How is it being rich, Jake?"

"I won't lie to you. It's not bad."

"Even if you didn't do anything to—well, earn it?"

"That might bother you for a while, but you get over it. It takes about a week."

"It took you longer."

"I'm very sensitive."

"Sure you are. What'd you do after you finally quit being an investigator? Play around?"

"Not really. I decided that since I was so rich I should find out if I should do something in business and get even richer. Crawdad helped me. So did Ancel Easter. I built this place although somebody else decorated the lobby."

"Some girl you knew."

"She was a nice girl; she just didn't have much taste."

"Well, I'm glad to find out it wasn't yours. It had me a little worried."

"Is it that bad?"

"Almost."

"I must be used to it. Well, then after that I dabbled—I think that's the word I want—I dabbled in the stock market, but found out that I don't have that kind of mind. Then I went into my playboy period, I think you would call it, and discovered sailing. So that's what I do now. I have a ketch and this crew of six and we sort of sail around."

"That's all you do?"

"That's about all."

"What's a ketch, a kind of a yacht?"

"Kind of."

"Mixed crew."

"You mean male and female?"

"Uh-huh."

"It's mixed."

"Tell me about your crew."

"You sound like I did when you mentioned the foreman."

"Well?"

"Well, there's this doctor and his wife. The wife's a biologist. That's two. Then there's the economist and his girl friend, she's a systems analyst, believe it or not."

"Oh, I believe it."

"That's four. Then there's this guy who used to be with the Brookings Institution and his wife. Before he was with Brookings he was with the State Department. He's sort of a philosopher. His wife's some kind of management specialist. That makes six. They're all on a year's sabbatical."

"Who keeps you warm at night?"

"Nobody."

"It sounds like a very heavy crowd."

"It is that."

"And you just sail around?"

"We stop off here and there."

"Where were you when you heard that Granddad died and you flew back?"

"Majunga."

"Where's that?"

"Madagascar."

"What's in Madagascar?"

"Not much really. There might be a plywood factory there next year though if everything checks out."

She sat up then. "You bastard. It'll be your money, too, won't it? That's why you've got all those brains aboard, isn't it? You were feeding me all that crap about how you're the playboy of the Indian Ocean—"

"You even know where it is, don't you?"

"I know where Madagascar is. Anyway, you were feeding me this world-weary line of yours and all the time you're some kind of international do-gooder."

"No, not really. I'm still an investigator. That's what I'm good at. We pick out a place, make some feasibility studies, find out what its resources are, what some of its problems are, and then figure out how to put something together that'll be viable. We use that word a lot, viable. So Madagascar might have a new plywood factory. Some people there will have jobs that they didn't have before. The balance of payments might get a little better, but not a hell of a lot, not enough to matter, and I'll either make a few bucks or lose a few bucks or break even. But in the meantime we've all learned a lot about Madagascar, made some new friends and probably some enemies, the doctor's learned a little more about tropical diseases, which is his specialty, and then we sail off into the sunset not knowing what adventures tomorrow might bring."

"Bullshit," she said. "It can't be all that casual with the high-domed crowd you're running with. I'll bet they've got every step planned down to the last detail."

"They are a little that way," Pope said.

"And you're bankrolling it all."

He shook his head. "No, they're paying me for the use of the boat. Not a lot, but enough. They put up the expertise; I put up the risk capital. If I lose, I won't really notice it and a lot of their theories will be shot to hell. If it works—which I doubt—then they think it might work in a lot of other places. And they also think they can get it funded. Maybe they're right."

"Jesus Christ, it's the Jake Pope foundation."

"You don't approve, huh?"

"I think it's tremendous. I just don't see how you made the jump."

"From where to what?"

"From Madagascar plywood to Washington homicide."

"It's like I told you, I'm an investigator. I like looking into things. I don't know why I do, but I do and I'm good at it. I'm curious. I don't know what makes people curious. Maybe they're born that way or maybe they somehow get that way. I'm not sure. But finding out who shot a ninety-three-year-old man standing on his doorstep in Washington isn't too much different from finding out whether Madagascar really needs a new plywood factory. You'll get lied to along the way in both investigations. But then I'm not really trying to find out who killed your grandfather. I'm trying to find out what it was that he wanted to tell Ancel Easter. Maybe the two are connected. I don't know. But your grandfather wanted to tell somebody something because he thought it was important. He didn't get a chance to because somebody killed him. Anyway, he thought that whatever he'd found out should be stopped. So if he thought it should be stopped, it probably should. If I find out what it is, maybe it can be stopped. Or maybe it will be too late. I don't know that either. But I'm going to try to find out because I'm curious and because Ancel Easter asked me to and because Crawdad thought it was important. There may be some other reasons, but I can't think what they are."

"There's one you haven't mentioned," she said.

"Oh. What?"

"That you're a decent sort and there're not a lot of those around anymore for some reason. I've looked."

"Decent sort," he said. "You know, I rather like it. Here lies Jake Pope, Decent Sort. Or better yet: Jake Pope, thirty-four, well-known decent sort, announced today that—"

"Hey," she said.

"What?"

"I've been thinking."

"About what?"

"Those females you've got on board."

"What about them?"

"They're pretty smart, aren't they?"

"High-domed, as you said."

"Well-liberated?"

"Extremely."

"Can any of them cook?"

"They try."

"Who do I talk to about signing on as cook?"

"Turn over this way," Pope said, "and I'll help you fill out your application."

18

ANCEL EASTER LOOKED DOWN AT THE FACE OF THE DEAD
young man with the naked body and turned away. "No,"
he said. "No connection."

Hugo Worthy, the homicide detective who was still
trying to figure out how he could leave his wife and
move in with the twenty-three-year-old ballet dancer,
nodded and shrugged. "I didn't think so. But thanks
anyway for coming down on short notice."

"What was his name?" Easter said. "I saw it in this
morning's paper, but I've forgotten."

"Peter Berry."

"He was young, wasn't he?"

"Twenty-three."

Easter shook his head. "Seventy years difference."

"Sorry?"

"I was just thinking. He was twenty-three. Crawdad Gilmore was ninety-three and you say the same
gun probably shot both of them. There should be a
moral there some place."

Worthy shook his head. "I'm not looking for a
moral. I'm looking for who killed them. Those clowns
who write the editorials for the *Post* will come up with

your moral first thing in the morning. They're awfully good at coming up with a moral."

"You mean their gun law position."

Worthy changed the subject. "They've got some pretty good coffee upstairs. You want a cup?"

"I would at that," Easter said and took another look around the room. "I've never been over here before."

"Who goes to morgues?" Worthy said and led the way to the stairs.

It was a small windowless room with three tables and some chairs and a large electric coffee urn. The coffee urn bore a sign that said: "All Coffee Fifteen Cents a Cup. This Means You!!!" The fifteen cents had been scratched out and a felt pen had been used to raise the price to twenty cents. A cigar box lay next to the urn. Worthy tossed two quarters into it, swore when he saw that there was no change, and reached for two paper cups. When he had filled the cups he carried them over to the table where Easter sat.

"There's some cream and sugar over there, if you want it," he said.

Easter shook his head. "Just black." He took a sip of his coffee and said, "What do you think about a gun law?"

"You wanta know whether I'm for one or against one, don't you?"

"That's right."

"You're for one, aren't you?"

"Yes. I'm for one."

"You go along with the *Post*."

Easter smiled. "I prefer to think, Mr. Worthy, that the *Post* goes along with me."

Worthy thought about that for a moment, looking

at Easter. Then he nodded. "Uh-huh, I can see what you mean. You can say that, can't you? I mean there're probably fifty people in this town who could say that and have it mean anything and I guess you're one of them. Don't get me wrong. I'm not being smartass. I'm just stating a fact. I say it's a fact because of the way they told me to keep you up to date on this thing. I checked that out. It came straight out of the mayor's office."

"I do appreciate your cooperation," Easter said and took another sip of his coffee. He's lost some of that icy formality that he had in my office, he thought. When the surroundings are familiar he seems to relax. This morgue to him is familiar surroundings. Well, why shouldn't it be? This is where they keep his source material.

"You still didn't tell me what you think about a gun law," Easter said.

"It wouldn't put me out of a job," Worthy said. "I'm for it. Homicide's funny, you know. There're not too many really premeditated murders. I'm talking about the kind where a guy goes out and gets himself a gun because he's going to shoot his wife with it come a week from next Thursday. You don't get too many of those. And a gun law wouldn't make much difference there anyway because if the guy had really made up his mind to get rid of his wife, well, hell, if he couldn't get hold of a gun, he'd use a knife or a brick or whatever else was handy."

"What you're saying is that a gun law wouldn't help prevent a carefully planned murder."

Worthy nodded again and drank some of his coffee. He reached into the pocket of his jacket and produced a

package of filter-tipped Camels and offered them to
Easter. Easter shook his head. The detective lit his
cigarette with an old Zippo lighter.

"That's right," Worthy said. "A guy who's going to
kill somebody is going to kill somebody and a gun law
isn't going to stop him. If he's hell-bent on using a gun
to do it, then he's going to get himself a gun. And if a
buck can be made out of it, there's going to be somebody around who'll sell him one. A gun law wouldn't
have stopped the Kennedys from being killed. Or
King or what's his name from Alabama, Wallace, it
wouldn't've stopped him from getting shot."

"I don't think anybody much argues that anymore."

"You'd be surprised," Worthy said. "But let me tell
you the kind of homicide it would stop. You take the
guy who says he keeps a gun around the house for
protection. All right?"

"All right."

"Well, he's read about people who've been sitting
around in their living room watching TV and somebody'll bust in on them and rape the wife and shoot
the dog and make off with the TV set and all the cash
that's lying around. So this guy says to himself, by God,
that's never gonna happen to me. Okay?"

"Okay."

"So this guy gets himself a handgun. And he gets
himself some ammo. And maybe he goes out and plunks
away at some tin cans or some bottles and maybe he
hits them a few times and maybe he doesn't, but he
thinks he knows how to shoot. And the funny thing
is, he does. He really does. You just point the gun and
pull the trigger and, hell, the things works. Right?"

"Right."

"You married?"

Easter shook his head. "No, I'm not married."

"Well, this guy I'm making up is married. He goes to work every morning. Maybe his wife goes to work, too. Or maybe she stays home with the kids. It doesn't matter. Anyway, they get along pretty good. Maybe they have some fights and maybe he slaps her around a little, but what the hell, that happens. But this one Sunday night rolls around."

"Why Sunday night?"

"You got me, but Sunday nights are good for this sort of thing."

"Really?"

"Yeah. They're calling them Saturday Night Specials. Cheap handguns, I mean. If they were halfway smart, they'd call em Sunday Night Specials."

"That's an interesting point."

"Yeah, it is, kind of. Well, it's Sunday night and this guy's been with his wife all day and somehow the argument gets started. Maybe it's about money. A lotta times it's about money. Or maybe it's about some fox she thinks he's been balling. Or maybe it's about the kids' teeth. Who knows what married people'll argue about? Well, he's had a few drinks and she's had a few drinks. Then they have a few more drinks and then it all starts to come out, all the things that they've been keeping bottled up, all the real rotten things that they've never gotten around to telling each other before, and something clicks in the guy's mind. He remembers he's got a gun. Well, that's his ace. The gun's gonna solve the argument. So he takes it out from under his shirts or wherever he keeps it and points it at her. Well, since she's also had a few drinks, like I said, she makes a mistake. She makes some wise-ass remark.

Maybe she says you haven't got the nerve, or maybe she says go ahead and shoot, you sonofabitch, I'd be better off dead, or maybe she says something real nasty like the length of the two-inch barrel on the gun reminds her of the size of his cock. I've heard that one about six or seven times now. Well, the guy plays his ace. He pulls the trigger. Sure enough the gun goes off and she falls down dead just like on TV except it isn't like on TV because on TV they don't show all the mess. On TV it always looks like the maid's just been in. And on TV they don't show the blood much although in the movies they're getting better about that, showing the blood, I mean. They're doing that pretty good now. So after he's shot her, this guy I've made up, that's when we come in and this guy tells us that he didn't mean to shoot her, that he was just showing her the gun and it went off and that it was an accident, and we say, sure, why don't you tell us about it."

"What if there had been no gun in the house?" Easter asked after he swallowed the last of his coffee.

"Maybe she'd've lost a couple of teeth or maybe she'd've gone to work the next day with a black eye. Or maybe he'd've put her in the hospital with internal injuries or he might even've stabbed her a couple of times, but she'd still've been breathing. You want another cup?"

"Yes, I think I would. It is good coffee, isn't it?"

"I don't know how they do it, but the morgue makes the best cup of coffee in town."

"Let me buy this time," Easter said and picked up Worthy's cup before he could object. He put a dollar bill in the cigar box and took out fifty cents in change. While he was filling the cups, Easter said, "How would a gun law have prevented what you've just described?"

"It wouldn't've," Worthy said. "It wouldn't do any good at all if the guy already has a gun in the house. I mean, you pass a law that makes it worth five years in jail and a five-thousand-dollar fine to keep a handgun in the house and people are still gonna keep handguns in their house. I mean the ones who've already got em will. They got some pretty tough laws about people smoking dope, but half the country smokes dope now. Well, maybe a third anyway. What a law could do is make it hard to get hold of a handgun. I'm all for that. I don't think anybody should be allowed to buy one unless they got a damned good reason and there aren't many of those. And if they do come up with a reason, then the Government oughta run a ballistics check on the gun and keep it on file."

"What about the guns that are already in circulation?"

"Heirlooms," Worthy said and shook his hand. "You can pass all the laws you want to, but there'll still be a lotta guns floating around. They'll be handed down father to son, uncle to nephew, brother to brother. Heirlooms." The thought of it made Worthy's face grow gloomy. "But no law's gonna help me find who killed your friend and the old guy who ran the liquor store and that young kid down there."

"No leads, huh?"

"Not a one."

Easter moved his coffee cup slightly. "But you've come up with a new theory?"

"Oh, yeah. My partner and I've come up with a new theory. You haven't met my partner, have you?"

"No."

"Well, we've come up with sort of a new theory. Winos."

"Why winos?"

"Because otherwise, it doesn't make any sense."

"I mean why the plural. Why not just one?"

"The liquor store guy. He was shot *and* stabbed. There's gotta be at least two of them."

"I see."

"Well, off of your friend Gilmore they got thirty-two cents and a gold watch, as near as we can figure it. Off of old man Hermann, the guy with the liquor store, they got fourteen, maybe fifteen dollars. Off of the kid downstairs they got exactly seventy-six cents."

"How did you get the exact amount?"

"The kid lived with seven other people over on R Street in one of those commune things. You know, they all split the rent and the groceries and everybody balls everybody else, I guess. There used to be a lot of em around. Communes, I mean. There're not too many left now. It seems they've sort of gone out of style. Well, anyway, this one over on R Street is still going and it was the kid's time to go get the groceries. He was flat-ass broke. Not a penny. So everybody anted up for groceries and when he goes to the store he has exactly sixty bucks. The groceries cost fifty-nine twenty-four. When we found him he didn't have a dime."

"Senseless," Easter said. "Absolutely senseless."

"Yeah. That's why we're thinking winos. The only thing a wino wants is a jug. They don't think much beyond that. So maybe they found the gun and figured they could use it to score just enough for a few bottles. But it's just a theory. Most winos, if they find a gun, would try to sell it, not use it. But whoever's using this one isn't getting rich."

"No," Easter said. "They're not."

"The kid worked in the Library of Congress."

"I see."

"Those people he lived with said he was studying Greek at night."

"Greek?"

"Yeah. Greek. Ancient Greek."

"That's rather unusual this day and age, isn't it?" Easter said, feeling suddenly old and stuffy.

"Yeah, I guess so, but he didn't get shot because he was studying Greek."

"No."

"He got shot for what he had in his pockets."

"Seventy-six cents, you said."

"That's not very much to get killed for, is it?" Worthy said.

"No," Easter said, "that's not very much at all."

19

JAKE POPE BEAT THE GARBAGE TRUCK BY SEVEN MINUTES. It was still two blocks away when he stopped his Porsche in front of Dr. Dallas Hucks's stubby-columned house in Fairfax, Virginia.

The Huckses had put out two green plastic bags of garbage. Pope got out of the Porsche, walked around it, opened the curbside door, put one bag of garbage in the Porsche's small back seat and one in the front seat. He didn't look around to see whether anyone was watching. He walked around the car, got behind the wheel, waited two minutes, and then drove off.

Pope had used the telephone earlier that day to discover what he could about Dr. Dallas Hucks. Pretending to be with the Washington Credit Bureau, Incorporated, he had learned from the personnel office at the United States Department of Agriculture that Hucks was indeed gainfully employed there in the programming and planning section of the Secretary of Agriculture's office. His official title was Assistant to the Assistant Deputy Director for Programming and Planning. His grade was GS-14. He had been employed by the department for nine years. He was thirty-six years old. He lived in Fairfax, Virginia, at the address that Pope already had. He was married. His wife's name was Amelia. That was when Pope stopped asking questions of the woman in personnel. He knew that to ask more would be to step outside his assumed role as a bored credit bureau employee. He thanked her and hung up.

Pope looked at the notes he had made. Then he looked at the triangle he had drawn the previous night just before he had gone to meet Faye Hix. It still has three sides, he thought. That hasn't changed. What you hoped was that it had turned into a four-sided triangle. But it hasn't. And its three points are still formed by our old friend Noah deGraffenreid, Georgetown's finest fence; our new friend, Dr. Dallas Hucks who is Assistant to the Assistant Deputy Director for Programming and Planning, whatever that is, and the U.S. Department of Agriculture, for whom the good Dr. Hucks does whatever it is that he does. And on July 11th something is going to happen.

He picked up the phone and called Ancel Easter. When Easter came on Pope said, "Busy?"

"I just got back from the morgue. There's another one. I was going to call you."

"Any connection with Crawdad?"

"No. It was a kid. Twenty-three, I think. He lived in a commune and was studying Greek. On his own."

"That same detective on it, what was his name, Worthy?"

"Yes. Worthy. He's on it."

"The kid, was he shot?"

"Twice. They haven't run the tests yet but they're pretty sure it was the same gun. A twenty-two."

"When did it happen?"

"Late yesterday afternoon. The kid's name was Peter Berry. That mean anything to you?"

"No."

"Well, he lived in a commune and he was bringing the week's groceries home and they shot him in an alley between R and S. They got seventy-six cents."

"What does Worthy think?"

"Winos, maybe. No other leads."

"That's three now."

"Yes," Easter said. "Three. Have you come up with anything?"

"I don't know. But I need a quick credit check. Can you get me one or are your clients all so rich that you never stoop to such things?"

"You'd be surprised by how often we're stooping nowadays."

"Who're you using?"

"Let me think. Johnson Mercantile, I believe is the name of the outfit."

"Yeah," Pope said. "I've heard of them. How soon can you get it?"

"I'll get a speed check. It's all done by phone. I can probably have it for you this afternoon early. Whose credit are we checking?"

"Dr. Dallas Hucks, deGraffenreid's friend."

"Ah. Anything positive? Or should I say anything negative?"

"Neither. I'm just curious."

"I have to be out of the office this afternoon, but when the report comes in I'll have my secretary call you. Will you be home?"

"It all depends," Pope said.

"On what?"

"On what time they pick up the garbage in Fairfax."

It took Pope two calls to find out what time Dr. Dallas Hucks's garbage would be picked up that day. He called the city of Fairfax first and learned that the county was responsible for Dr. Hucks's garbage. Fairfax County's refuse department, after some delay, informed Pope that as near as they could figure, Dr. Hucks's garbage would be picked up that day between three and five o'clock.

Pope thanked the refuse department, hung up the phone, and looked at his watch. It was a little after noon. He decided that he was hungry and went into his kitchen. He made himself a bacon and egg sandwich, poking at the yellow of the egg until it broke and fried hard so that it didn't run. By the time the egg and the bacon were ready the whole wheat bread had popped up out of the toaster. Pope smeared the bread with mayonnaise, added some lettuce, and put the sandwich on a plate. He poured himself a glass of milk and carried his lunch into the living room. Just as he was about to take his first bite, the phone rang.

Pope picked up the phone and said hello.

"Mr. Pope?"

"Yes."

"This is Mrs. Marlon, Mr. Easter's secretary."

"Yes, Mrs. Marlon."

"I have the speed credit report you wanted on a Dr. Dallas Hucks."

"That's very quick."

"Well, it seems that Dr. Hucks's file is quite active."

"You mean there're a lot of people who're interested in whether he can pay his bills."

"That's right. The Johnson Mercantile people sent it over by messenger. If you'd like, I can have the messenger bring it on over to you."

"That would be most helpful," Pope said, told Mrs. Marlon good-bye, hung up the phone, and went back to his sandwich. By the time that he had finished it, rinsed the plate and glass, washed and put away the frying pan, and made himself a cup of instant coffee, the messenger was knocking at his door. Pope signed for the envelope, tipped the messenger a dollar, and got a surprised "Thank you."

The Johnson Mercantile company's letterhead boasted that it had the entire ninth floor of a building on Thirteenth Street Northwest in downtown Washington. It also claimed to have "more than eighty outside trunk-line telephones, not private wires." After giving its address, phone number, and a few plugs for its services, it offered the observation that "Home Ownership Indicates Family Stability." Below this trenchant comment, which Pope decided not to argue with, was a list of the abbreviations that the firm used in its credit reports. Ch-mtg was a chattel mortgage. Clrd was cleared. Fo was formerly. WNCA was Would Not Credit Again. Et ux was and wife. Et vir was and husband. Jdgt was judgment.

The report itself was a page-and-a-half of single-spaced, much abbreviated information to the effect that Dr. Dallas Hucks owed everybody in town. His assets, except for the house that he owned in Fairfax, were summed up by the report in a single line: "Household goods, bank account." However, the bank account, according to the report, was usually in the low three figures. As for the house, it had a $10,000 second mortgage on it which meant that Dr. Hucks's equity was not what it should have been.

He owed for his car, a 1973 Impala. He also owed the Hecht Company, Woodward & Lothrop, Sears, and a Washington credit service called Central Charge. He owed his lawyer and his dentist and his doctor. He was behind in his utility bills. He owed the phone company. The State of Virginia was suing him for back income taxes. Another suit had been filed by the Gulf Oil Company. And yet another, by American Express. In fact, there were seven such suits either pending or already decided. After each suit that had already been through the courts, the credit company had entered the notation "jdgt for plff", which Pope interpreted to mean judgment for the plaintiff.

Not counting the two mortgages on the house, Pope estimated that Dallas Hucks and his wife, Amelia, owed close to $22,000. He needs money, Pope thought, quite a bit of money. People who need money sometimes go see Noah deGraffenreid, the friendly Georgetown usurer. He wondered how much interest deGraffenreid was charging now. He used to charge 50 percent, but he's probably gone up. Everyone else has. So you have the fact that Dr. Dallas Hucks owes a lot of money. You also have the fact that on the night before Crawdad was killed, Hucks had dinner with deGraffenreid at the Cosmos Club. The only thing wrong with your facts is that deGraffenreid would never take a loan shark victim to dinner. Not unless he wanted something else. The question is, what does deGraffenreid want from Dallas Hucks? Or maybe you turn it around and ask what does Dr. Hucks have to sell?

Pope was still wondering about it when he left his

apartment, took the elevator down to the basement, got in his car, drove down M Street through Georgetown, turned left over the Francis Scott Key Bridge, turned right on to the George Washington Parkway and took it all the way to 495, the beltway that circles Washington. He headed south on the beltway and turned west on Route 50. Five miles later he turned right, got lost twice, and finally found Merrimac Drive, the street that Dr. Dallas Hucks lived on.

It was a curving street and the houses all looked very much alike. They were all pseudo-Colonial and all of them were white although some had blue shutters while others had green ones. Most of them had basketball nets above their garage doors. Ninety percent of them had a car in the driveway, which probably meant, Pope decided, that they were two-car families. A few of the houses had power boats parked alongside the garages on trailers. Nearly all of the houses had a bicycle or two parked outside. Pope also noted three motorcycles and four campers.

Dr. Dallas Hucks's house had blue shutters. The garage door was closed, so Pope couldn't tell whether the Huckses were a two-car family although he did know that they still owed $2,175 to the General Motors Acceptance Corporation on their 1973 Impala. There was no basketball net above the garage door, however, and no camper or power boat, and no bicycles. The lawn needed mowing. A couple of small elm trees, not more than ten years old, looked as if they were dying. Pope thought the house looked unlived in.

He reached up and adjusted his rearview mirror. The Dempster Dumpster garbage truck was down at the end of the block. Pope got out and put the two plastic garbage bags in the Porsche. After he got back in the car, he waited. Nothing happened. No one came flying out of the front door screaming, "Stop, thief! He's stealing my garbage!" No curtain moved. Pope waited some more and when nothing happened he started the engine and drove off.

Back in the apartment, Pope spread newspapers on his kitchen floor. He dumped the contents of one of the plastic bags on to the newspapers. He looked at it for a moment. A newspaper wrapped around something wet and greasy reminded Pope of a telephone call that he had made. He left the garbage in his kitchen and went into the bedroom that he used as a study. Once more he looked through his notes. Then he picked up the phone and dialed a number that he had written down.

When the Associated Press reporter came on the phone, he sounded in a hurry. "What can I do for you, Jake?" he said.

"You mentioned something about the Department of Agriculture issuing a crop report on July eleventh."

"Yeah, we decided that's the real big news for that day, unless the President sneezes."

"I'm sort of interested in it."

"Jake?"

"Yes."

"Why are you interested in a crop report?"

"I'm thinking of buying a farm."

"Jake?"

"Yes."

"Why do you lie to me?"

"Habit, I guess. No kidding, who would I call down there to find out more about it?"

"At Agriculture?"

"Yeah."

"Let's see here, I have to look it up. The guy's name

is Bill—uh—Bill Bailey. I'm not kidding. Old Bill Bailey."

"What's his number?"

The AP reporter rattled the number off. "Now, you owe me two lunches, don't you?" he said.

"Jesus," Pope said, "I thought it was three."

After saying good-bye to the AP reporter, Pope sat at his desk looking at the number. Well, you're back at it, aren't you? he thought. You're back doing what you do best, which is lying to people and stealing garbage. And in a little while there'll be a real treat. You'll get to paw through the garbage and see what it is that Dallas and Amelia Hucks throw away. It's such an intimate way to get to know people and if you're lucky, you should be through by teatime and then you can have a very large bourbon and water as your reward for having sifted through the garbage so nicely.

Pope noticed that he was talking to himself aloud. Another wonderful trait, he thought. Lonely people talk to themselves. At first they do it only in the privacy of their homes. Then they start doing it on the street. More and more people are doing it nowadays, he thought. You can scarcely walk down a block without spotting two or three who're deep into conversation with themselves. I wonder if Mr. Bill Bailey ever talks to himself? More important, I wonder if he will talk to me?

Pope dialed the number that the AP reporter had given him and when the woman answered and said, "Mr. Bailey's office," Pope asked if he might speak to Mr. Bailey and the woman wanted to know if she might tell Mr. Bailey who was calling.

"Leo Aaron with the *Denver Post*," Pope said.

"This is Bailey," a man's voice said.

"Yeah," Pope said. "This is Leo Aaron with the *Denver Post*. I'm sort of new on the job and I've got a query here about your crop report that comes out July eleventh, isn't it?"

"That's right. July eleventh."

"That's when you come out with your new estimate on what the wheat crop will be, right?"

"That's right. Corn and soybean acreage, too, for that matter."

"I'm trying to get an angle on the story. I remember hearing something about the security measures you use to keep the report buttoned up. Could you give me a rundown on that?"

"Well, it's all a little hokey, but we still go into lockup conditions around here."

"What do you mean, lockup?"

"We make it sort of like Fort Knox around here that day because that's when all the predictions or estimates of the crop are in from the states."

"How are they sent in?"

"Well, they're coded first of all and then they're sent in in what we call red-X envelopes. All these envelopes are deposited in a locked box."

"What's the box look like?" Pope said.

"It's just like a mailbox that you see on the corner," Bailey said. "Except that it's got two locks. One of the keys is held by the Secretary of Agriculture's office and the other by the head of the Crop Reporting Board."

"All this security is for what, to keep speculators from making a killing in the commodity market?"

"That's right."

"What else do you do?"

"Hell, we seal off the blinds. The phones are cut off. The whole basement section is sealed off, in fact. Nobody gets in or out. There's even a GSA guard with a gun although I'm not sure if he knows how to use it."

"And the reports are sent in from the states, is that right?"

"That's right."

"Are they accurate?"

"We've got a pretty good track record."

"So if somebody had this information before it's released," Pope said, "they could go into the market and have a pretty good idea of whether to go long or short?"

"You know much about the commodity market?"

"Not much. Hardly anything."

"Well, it's not quite that simple. It would all depend on what the report said. If the report would estimate an unexpected twenty or thirty percent drop or increase in the wheat crop, for instance, then there would be some action. But if there weren't anything dramatic, there wouldn't be much action."

"Uh-huh," Pope said. "So what actually happens on July eleventh?"

Bailey sighed over the phone. "Well, like I said it's all kind of hokey. The whole place is sealed off. Phones are cut. The guards are posted. Then at five o'clock in the morning—"

"Five o'clock?"

"That's right. Five o'clock. A representative of the Secretary of Agriculture's office accompanied by three representatives from the Crop Reporting Board go down into the basement where the sealed off area is. They're accompanied by an armed guard, like I said. They take the red-X envelopes out of the box—"

"The mailbox with two locks?" Pope said.

"That's right. Two locks."

"Who'd you say has the keys?"

"One key is held by the Secretary of Agriculture's

representative. The other key is kept by the crop report-ing service."

"Then what?"

"Then the contents of the envelopes which, as I said, are in code are decoded behind locked doors. This is the information in which there's a lot of speculative interest."

"I see."

"Well, the information is decoded and then it's interpreted by the specialists. After that it comes out as a press release at exactly three P.M."

"So everybody gets it at the same time?" Pope said.

"That's right."

"How many envelopes in the box?"

"Forty-four."

"From forty-four of the states."

"Right."

"What are the key speculative states?"

"Let's see. Illinois, Indiana, Kansas, Missouri, Ne-braska, Oklahoma, Ohio, Texas. That's it. Sorry, no Colorado."

"I'll make out," Pope said. "Is all this security for real or is it just ceremony, like the changing of the guard at Buckingham Palace?"

"It's for real all right, but like I said, it's also sort of hokey."

"Have there ever been any leaks?"

"Not yet."

"Okay," Pope said. "I've got enough here to tell 'em in Denver what kind of story it would make. If they want it, I'll get back to you."

"Fine," Bailey said.

"Oh, yeah, one more thing. The guy who comes

down from the Secretary of Agriculture's office. The one who has one of the keys to the locked box. You have his name and where he's from?"

"I don't think he's from Denver."

"I wouldn't be so lucky," Pope said.

"They keep changing them. Let's see. Oh, yeah, here it is. He's from Oklahoma originally, if that's any help."

"That's not quite in our Rocky Mountain Empire," Pope said. "But what's his name anyway?"

"His name," Bill Bailey said, "is Dr. Dallas Hucks."

20

JAKE POPE FOUND THAT DALLAS AND AMELIA HUCKS threw a lot of their bills out with the garbage. He sat crosslegged on his kitchen floor and picked gingerly through the pile of junk mail, old bills, used Kleenex, celery tops, chicken bones, tin cans, empty bottles, detergent boxes, light bulbs, panty hose, and the rest of the things that are thrown away because they have been used up or worn out.

From the discarded meat labels, Pope learned that the Huckses ate a lot of hamburger, three or four times a week at least. They also ate a lot of spaghetti and macaroni. Many of the bills had *final notice* stamped on them in red ink. Pope put these to one side. He also segregated the empty beer cans and liquor bottles, but decided that there weren't enough to matter. Five empty Schlitz beer cans, one empty Almaden Mountain Red burgundy wine bottle, and an empty fifth of Gordon's gin didn't add up to alcoholism or even heavy drinking.

Pope turned to the pile of bills and started going through them. It makes sense, he thought. Why keep old bills that you're not going to pay anyhow? The people you owe will always send more. They won't forget.

One of the bills interested Pope. It was the only one that was directed to Amelia Hucks herself. It was dated June 1 and it was from Perry G. Gantt, MD, PA and it had "please" written across the bottom of it in green ink. Dr. Gantt had offices in Silver Spring, Maryland, and he was billing Amelia Hucks not only for May, but also for April and March. Dr. Gantt hadn't bothered to itemize his April and March charges but they amounted to $480. For May, however, he offered a breakdown. For four sessions of individual psychotherapy, he was charging Amelia Hucks $40 a session for a total of $160. For four sessions of group psychotherapy at $20 a session he was charging $80. Total, $240. Grand total for all three months, $720. It was under the grand total that the word "please" had been written in green ink.

Pope sat on his kitchen floor in the middle of the piles of carefully segregated garbage and studied the bill that Amelia Hucks had thrown away. Then he gathered up the garbage that he had dumped onto the newspapers and put it all back into the two green plastic bags. He rolled the newspapers up and put them into a separate bag. Taking the medical bill that he had salvaged from the Huckses' garbage he went into the room that he used as a den and sat down at his desk.

He looked at a small desk calendar and then at the dates that were on the bill that Amelia Hucks had received from Dr. Gantt. All of her private sessions of individual psychotherapy fell on Tuesdays. All of her group sessions fell on Thursdays.

Pope reached for the District of Columbia section

of the telephone book and looked up a number. He dialed it and it rang twice before a woman's voice answered with, "Doctors' office."

"Dr. Forslund, please," Pope said.

"May I ask who's calling?"

"Jake Pope."

"Dr. Forslund is with a patient. May I have him call you?"

"This is an emergency," Pope said. "Just tell him that Jake Pope is calling and that it's extremely urgent."

"One moment," the woman said.

It was almost two minutes before a man's voice came on the phone, asking, "What the fuck kind of emergency have you got, Pope?"

"Hello, Will," Pope said. "How're things in the CIA?"

"Don't you ever forget anything?"

"I've never mentioned it to a soul. After all, who'd really be interested in the fact that Dr. Will Forslund, prominent Washington heart specialist, is actually on the CIA's payroll and is used to—well, let's see. Who's the last one they flew you out to operate on? The guy in Cambodia, wasn't it? The one who died on the table."

"You talk far too much."

"I know. There's a guy I owe a lunch to down at AP. In fact, I owe him a couple of lunches now because he's been helpful. You wouldn't mind if I mentioned your name, would you? I mean, Christ, Will, you've got a hell of a story to tell. All about how you're on a constant standby basis for our friends out in Langley and how they've sent you to—"

"You're a slimy sort, Pope. Did anyone ever tell you that?"

"Often. I just try to live with it. The reason I'm

calling, Will, is that I need some help. Some professional help."

"You've got trouble?" Dr. Forslund sounded pleased.

"Not the kind that you can do anything about. I wouldn't let you go after a splinter."

"Jake?"

"Yes."

"I don't like you very much, Jake."

"I know."

"You're blackmailing me again, do you realize that?"

"I haven't told you what I wanted yet."

"Regardless of what you want, it's going to be blackmail again. Just because a few years ago you stumbled across a perfectly legitimate arrangement that I have to help out in emergencies when there's need for a skilled specialist—"

Pope interrupted. "Oh, you're skilled all right, Will. The way I understand it and, as you say, I just stumbled across it, but from what I stumbled across, there could be six other doctors standing around, but because you're so slick with the scalpel not one of them could tell just what it really was that caused the patient to stop breathing all of a sudden."

"That's not true. That's not true at all."

"Of course it's not true, Will. And that's what I thought you'd like to explain to the AP guy. You know, why it's not true that the CIA sends you out to operate on heads of state and other assorted dignitaries that they don't much care for and who happen to be suffering from a heart condition and need an operation that—"

"What do you want?"

"I need a psychiatrist."

"That's the first thing you've ever said to me that makes sense."

"I need a particular psychiatrist and I want you to refer me to him."

There was a silence on the phone while Dr. Forslund thought about it. Finally he said, "Jake."

"Yes."

"If I do this, I don't want to hear from you again. Ever."

"All right."

"No more cute threats."

"I didn't think they were so cute," Pope said.

"I just don't want to hear from you again. Ever."

"I said all right. The psychiatrist's name is Perry G. Gantt. That's with two *t*'s. He lives in Silver Spring. His phone number's 659-8096. I want you to call him up and tell him that you've referred me to him. Tell him that you think I need help."

"What kind of help?"

"Christ, I don't know what kind of help. You're a doctor. Tell him you think I might be a little paranoid. That's always good. But also tell him that although you're no expert, you think that group therapy might be more helpful than individual counseling."

There was another silence. This one lasted nearly half a minute. Then Dr. Forslund said, "You want to get to someone in his group, don't you? You're trying to get to someone who's a patient of his."

"You are quick, Will."

"I don't like this."

"I don't like it either," Pope said. "But just make the call and then call me back."

"It's blackmail."

"No it isn't, Will. It's not blackmail because I can't prove anything."

"There's nothing to prove."

"Of course there isn't. You won't mind then if I go ahead and call the guy at AP."

"I didn't say that."

"Okay," Pope said. "You make the call to Dr. Gantt, Will, and I'll tell you what I'll do."

"What?"

"I won't call the AP guy and tell him that I can't prove that you're a paid killer for the CIA. How's that?"

The phone went dead in Pope's ear. Dr. Will Forslund had hung up.

21

As Jake Pope hung up the phone in Washington the meeting got underway in the fourth floor suite of the Muehlebach Hotel in Kansas City. The suite had been reserved and paid for in cash by a Mr. Robert Thompson of Salt Lake City. Mr. Thompson had specified that enough furniture be moved out of the suite's living room to accommodate a ten-foot-long table. Seven chairs were now drawn up to the table and it was covered with a green cloth, pitchers of ice water, ten glasses, and eight ashtrays. There were no note pads or pencils.

Against the wall was a large electric coffee urn. It held fifty cups. Cream, sugar, spoons, cups and saucers were carefully arranged next to the urn. There was no liquor. The man who told the Muehlebach Hotel that he was Mr. Robert Thompson of Salt Lake City already had carefully inspected the room, but he was now accompanied by another man who carried a large metal case. Mr. Thompson didn't tell the hotel who the other man was and the hotel didn't ask. The other man's name was Art Balliet. He was from Chicago and part of the time he made his living by doing just what he was doing now: making sure that no one had planted an electronic eavesdropping device in the room. Art Balliet was extremely thorough because, one, he was being paid two thousand dollars in cash plus expenses to sweep the room and, two, because he was a conscientious craftsman who had his reputation to consider, and, three, because he knew that Robert Thompson of Salt Lake City wasn't Robert Thompson at all and that he was really Ralph Hayes of Chicago who worked for Fulvio Varvesi. Art Balliet didn't want to make any mistakes that might come to the attention of Fulvio Varvesi.

It took Balliet an hour to sweep the suite and when he was done he put his gear back into his metal case and told Ralph Hayes, "It's clean as a whistle."

Hayes nodded, took an envelope from his breast pocket and handed it to Balliet. "You can take the next plane back."

Balliet wanted to count the money in the envelope, but he decided not to. He would count it later when he was on the plane or maybe in the cab on the way out to the airport. "Well, thanks a lot, Mr. Hayes," he said.

"One thing," Hayes said.

"What?"

"Don't do any sightseeing in Kansas City."

"No, sir," Balliet said. "I never figured that there was much to see here anyway."

"You're right," Hayes said, "there's not."

After Balliet had gone, Hayes sat down to wait. He poured himself a cup of coffee first and sipped it while he waited. When he was halfway through the cup there was a knock at the door. He got up, crossed the room, and opened the door. Standing there was Fulvio Varvesi accompanied by Jack Sperry, the ex-karate teacher. Both Varvesi and Sperry wore large dark glasses.

Nobody spoke. Varvesi and Sperry entered the room

and Varvesi pointed around it with his right hand. Ralph Hayes nodded. "He just left," he said. "He spent an hour on it. It's clean."

"Okay," Varvesi said and took off his dark glasses.

"How was your ride?" Hayes said.

"You ever been to Topeka?"

"No."

"Well, there's nothing there and there's nothing between here and there, is there, Jack?"

"Not a hell of a lot," Jack Sperry said.

"What time is it?" Varvesi said. He wore a $1600-watch on his left wrist that kept perfect time, but he was one of those people who preferred to have someone else tell them the time.

"Two twenty-five," Sperry said.

"We got five minutes. I'll take a cup of coffee."

Ralph Hayes didn't quite run to the coffee urn, but he moved quickly. When Varvesi asked for something, he didn't like to be kept waiting. After he was served his coffee Varvesi moved over to the window and looked out.

"Kansas City," he said. "This is where everything's supposed to be up to date, isn't it?"

"That's what the song says," Hayes said.

"Well, this hotel isn't much. How old d'you think it is?"

"I don't know," Sperry said. "Pretty old."

"Truman used to hang out here," Varvesi said. "That's what the cab driver was saying. We dumped the car at Avis and took a cab over."

"Who?" Hayes said.

"The cab driver."

"I mean who'd he say used to hang out here?"

"Harry Truman."

"Oh, him."

"Yeah, he said he used to hang out here after he wasn't President anymore."

"That was a long time ago," Hayes said.

"I just barely remember when Truman was President," Varvesi said. "I remember Eisenhower though."

"I can remember Truman," Hayes said. "I was eleven when Eisenhower came in."

"I was ten," Sperry said.

"You guys are old farts, aren't you?" Varvesi said. "I was only three. I can remember him though. Truman, I mean."

The knock at the door interrupted the reminiscing. Jack Sperry glanced at his watch and then opened the door. Four men stood in the hallway. Two of them were in their late twenties. Each carried a suitcase. One of them stared hard at Sperry. The other one kept his eyes moving up and down the hall. The two other men in the hall were older. One was in his mid-forties and had clever brown eyes. The fourth man was somewhere in his fifties, although he looked older. Much older. He also looked tired.

The young man who stared at Jack Sperry said, "We're looking for Robert Thompson."

"Where's he from?" Sperry said.

"Salt Lake."

"This is it," Sperry said and moved back. The oldest man came in first, looked incuriously around the room and said, "I gotta go pee."

Fulvio Varvesi quickly moved over to him. "It's this way, Solly."

"How're ya?" he said.

"I'm fine, Solly."

"I gotta pee first. Jimmy will introduce the boys."

"No hurry," Varvesi said.

"I've had to pee for two hours."

"You should've stopped."

"Wanted to be on time. What time is it now?"

"Two-thirty."

"Okay. Then we're right on time."

The man who had to urinate went through a door and into the other room of the suite. His name was Salvatore Balboni and early that morning, accompanied by the three other men, he had boarded a plane at LaGuardia Airport in New York and had flown nonstop to St. Louis, Mo. There one of the younger men accompanying him had rented a new Chrysler sedan from Avis, using a stolen American Express card and an equally illegal driver's license. The four men had chosen U.S. 40 to drive across the State of Missouri to Kansas City.

Salvatore Balboni was fifty-six. He used one hand to lean against the wall while he urinated. It's those fuckin kidney stones again, he thought. They're coming back. I can tell from the way I pee. He tried to remember an old song that they had sung when he was in the Army during World War Two. How'd it go? I got the gonorrhea, it hurts me when I pea. They had pronounced it "peaaaah" and made it sound like some Mexican was singing it. Salvatore Balboni liked to remember World War Two because he felt it was the last time he had ever been happy.

After the war he had gone into his father's business in Manhattan. It was a highly competitive business, so competitive that his father, Ulderico Balboni, who had a weak heart, had died from the strain in 1949 when Salvatore was thirty.

Some thought that the piano wire that they had

found wrapped around Ulderico's neck might have contributed to the strain on his heart. There were others who thought that the rats might have helped. There were a lot of rats in the cellar on East 22nd Street where Ulderico had been found and during the night they had chewed away most of his face.

For almost a year after his father's death Salvatore Balboni hadn't slept well. He hadn't slept well because he knew that there were those who would like to see him dead. Sometimes he moved three or four times in one night—from Brooklyn to the Bronx to lower Manhattan and then back to Brooklyn again. On those nights he didn't get any sleep at all. By the time he was thirty-one his thick, glossy black hair had turned white. Not grey, but white, almost the color of flour and like flour it had neither gloss nor sheen.

But by persistence, determination, and several rather cunning double crosses, Salvatore Balboni had prevailed over those who would have liked it better if he were dead. Some of his opponents simply vanished. Others were found dead in vacant lots or boarded-up tenements or in lonesome parts of New Jersey where hardly anyone ever went. None of his opponents who were found dead had experienced what might be called an easy death. All had died from pain that must have been excruciating but which was also excellent advertising for Salvatore Balboni. Suddenly almost everyone wanted to be his friend.

A quarter of a century had passed since those days and times had changed and Salvatore Balboni had changed right along with them. Never use muscle when you can use brains, he often counseled his associates and in the twenty-five years that had passed Salvatore Balboni had used his brains to venture into new and heretofore uncharted financial waters. He had gone into the construction business in New Jersey, nicely fleecing the Federal Home Administration out of nearly three million dollars that it had long since given up trying to get back. He had found that there was a ready market for stolen negotiable bonds and for a while he had dealt in them until Wall Street woke up and took remedial measures. His latest venture had found him lending enormous amounts of money to strapped businessmen at enormous rates of interest. It had been and still was an extremely profitable venture, but he now found himself with a large cash surplus that needed to be put to work and this was why he was in the fourth floor suite of the Muehlebach Hotel in Kansas City.

When Balboni came back into the suite's living room he found his three associates seated around one end of the table while Fulvio Varvesi and his two colleagues had taken chairs at the other end. Balboni decided to sit in the middle. He pulled out a chair and lowered himself into it carefully. His hemorrhoids were acting up again and the long drive from St. Louis hadn't done them any good at all. There's another fuckin operation you're gonna have to have, he thought. Fifty-six years old and you're falling apart.

Balboni, because of his white hair, looked more than fifty-six. He could easily have passed for sixty-five or even seventy. He moved like a seventy-year-old, too, slowly and cautiously as if he were afraid that something might crack or break that could never be repaired. After he was seated he looked about the table with tiny black eyes that seemed to miss nothing and suspect everything.

"Okay," he said, "I'm here. Let's get started." He turned his head toward Varvesi. It was a round head with almost miniature features. His eyes were too small and his mouth and his nose were too tiny. Fulvio Varvesi thought he looked like a child who somehow had got to be a hundred and two years old.

"Who're they?" Balboni said, jerking his head toward Ralph Hayes and Jack Sperry.

"My associates," Varvesi said. "This is Hayes and this is Sperry."

"Muscle," Balboni said. "They look like muscle although the blond one there looks like he might have some brains." Ralph Hayes inclined his head toward the compliment, but decided not to say anything.

"I brought my lawyer," Balboni said. "You bring a lawyer?"

"No, Solly, I didn't bring a lawyer," Varvesi said.

"Good. All lawyers do is fuck everything up anyhow, isn't that right, Jimmy?" He looked at the man in his mid-forties who sat at the end of the table. He was James Drei and Salvatore Balboni was the only client he had ever had. He was a chunky man with thinning black hair and skin like dried white paste. Underneath the hair was a good brain which for twenty-five years he had used to keep Salvatore Balboni out of jail. And in doing so he had become rich—rich enough not to mind anymore how Balboni talked to him.

"That's right, Solly," Drei said. "All we ever do is fuck things up."

Balboni nodded. "Those other two punks down there are muscle. I don't call em my associates. I call em what they are. Muscle. One of em is Morry and the other is Joey, but I sometimes get em mixed up. You want their last names?"

"We've already met, Solly," Varvesi said. "While you were in the john."

"Okay," Balboni said. "Up until now you've been talking to Jimmy here about this deal you've got going, right?"

"That's right," Varvesi said.

"And Jimmy here tells me it's real sweet. He don't tell me the details because I don't wanta know the details. All I want to know is the return on my investment. I'm a businessman like everybody else and what I wanta know is if I put a hundred bucks into a deal, how much can I expect to get out of it—and how long's it gonna take me. I wanta know that, too."

"You're not going to believe what I'm going to tell you, Solly," Varvesi said.

"Okay. I'm not going to believe you."

"I'm going to keep it simple."

"That's so I can understand it."

"No, I'm going to keep it simple because I think that's the only way you'll believe me. You want to know how much return you can expect. Okay. You put five hundred into this and you can expect to take maybe two thousand out."

"I knew I wasn't going to believe you," Balboni said. He turned to his lawyer. "You believe him, Jimmy?"

"I've already gone into the figures with Mr. Varvesi rather thoroughly," James Drei said. "He's not exaggerating."

"But it ain't legal, is it, Jimmy?" Balboni said.

"That's the beauty of it, Solly," the lawyer said. "It's perfectly legal. As far as we're concerned, that is."

"But it ain't legal as far as he's concerned," Balboni said, jerking his head at Varvesi.

"Mr. Varvesi will simply supply us with information," Drei said. "We will act on that information to make a speculative investment. The investment will turn out to be most profitable. We will not inquire as to how Mr. Varvesi happened to come by his information."

Balboni turned back to Varvesi. "Okay, let's go back over what's happened. I sent out some feelers that I've got a few bucks lying around that ain't working. The next thing I know you're on to Jimmy here telling him about a deal you've got going. Jimmy tells me a little bit about it and I say, okay, go ahead, find out some more and if it looks good, get back to me. So Jimmy here talks to you some more and comes back and says that if I put in two million bucks, I can come out with maybe four to six million clear and he's being conservative. So I get all excited and say, Jesus Christ, let's go and how do we do it? And you know what Jimmy tells me? He tells me we're going into the commodity market and you wanta know what I do? I spit in his eye."

"I heard all about that, Solly," Varvesi said.

"You know what speculating in commodities is?" Balboni went on. "It's the biggest fuckin, crooked crap game in the world, that's what it is."

"I know, Solly," Varvesi said.

"That's what I told Jimmy here after I got through spitting in his eye. Who the fuck in his right mind's gonna bet on whether the price of wheat and soybeans and pork bellies—*pork bellies,* for God's sake—are gonna go up or down? That's what I asked Jimmy here and you know what he told me? He told me you was gonna rig it."

"That's right, Solly," Varvesi said. "We're going to rig it."

"So I got a little interested."

"I imagine."

"You might say I got more than a little interested."

"I understand."

"And I started doing some research and you know what I found out?"

"What?"

"They rig the thing all the fuckin time."

"I know."

"So where the hell have we been all this time?"

"On the outside looking in, Solly," Varvesi said. "That's where."

"So I got really interested. I mean here's the world's biggest crap game going on and we don't know about it. So I figure well, shit, they probably got all sorts of cops crawling all over the place. But you wanta know what I found out?"

"No cops at all," Varvesi said.

"That's right. They got something down there in Washington in the Department of Agriculture called the Commodity Exchange Authority, ain't that what it's called, Jimmy?"

"That's right," Drei said. "The CEA."

"And you know how big the commodity market is nowadays?" Balboni said.

"It's way over three hundred billion now," Varvesi said.

"Yeah, way over, and they got this CEA down there to gumshoe it and you know how many people they got? They only got a hundred and sixty-nine people. Now how the fuck can one hundred and sixty-nine people keep track of three hundred *billion* dollars, you tell me that?"

"They can't, Solly," Varvesi said.

"And I think it's a goddamn shame."

"What's a goddamn shame, Solly?" Varvesi said.

"That nobody ever told me about this before. Shit,

I knew the commodity market was nothing more than one big crap game, but nobody ever told me they'd let me load the dice."

"That's about how it is," Varvesi said.

"Yeah, well, I'm going in. You work out the details with Jimmy here. But there's one thing I want you to understand, kid. I'm not gonna be greedy. I mean, you were talking about putting in five hundred bucks and taking out four or five thousand. Well, that's so much bullshit."

"That's what you could've done in '72," Varvesi said.

"Maybe. But like I said, I ain't gonna be greedy. I put in two million, take out four million, and I'm happy, you know what I mean?"

"I understand, Solly."

"Okay. Now something else. How long?"

"Maybe two weeks," Varvesi said.

"Jesus. That all? You sure?"

"Three at the most," Varvesi said.

Balboni turned toward his lawyer again. "Okay," he said. "Put it up on the table and let em count it."

The lawyer nodded at the two young men who sat next to him and they lifted their two suitcases up onto the table. They looked at Balboni. "Open em up," he said.

The two suitcases were opened. Both were carefully packed with one-hundred-dollar bills bound in brown wrappers. "We run it all through Panama," Balboni said. "It's pure as snow."

"Count it," Varvesi said. Ralph Hayes and Jack Sperry rose and started counting the money. It took nearly three-quarters of an hour to count the money and while it was counted nobody spoke.

Hayes turned to Varvesi and said, "It's all there. Two million."

"Now I ain't gonna ask for a receipt," Balboni said. "Those two punks down there, their memories are gonna be my receipt, if you know what I mean."

"I understand," Varvesi said.

"But I gotta couple of questions—general information type of questions."

"All right."

"First, when does it start?"

"July eleventh," Varvesi said.

"What's today?"

"July second," Varvesi said.

"So it's just about a week away?"

"That's right."

"Okay. Now I'm gonna ask another question, I'm not gonna ask how, I'm just gonna ask what."

"Wheat," Varvesi said. "We're going to rig the wheat market, Solly."

"Huh," Balboni said, "I thought you were maybe gonna fix up soybeans."

"No," Varvesi said, "we're going to fix up wheat."

22

THAT NIGHT IN WASHINGTON DR. DALLAS HUCKS WAS pretending that he was a member of the Cosmos Club. He wasn't due to meet Noah deGraffenreid there until 7:15, but he had arrived nearly twenty minutes early so that he would have enough time to do his pretending. After signing in as a guest, Hucks ordered a drink, a gin and tonic (specifying Tanqueray gin) and found a comfortable chair near the club's front entrance at 2121 Massachusetts Avenue.

The Cosmos Club had moved only twice since it was founded on November 18 (some say the 16th), 1878, in Major John Wesley Powell's front parlor at 910 M Street, N.W., which was a better address then than it is now. It was founded by a clutch of scientists, many of them astronomers, who for a while were going to call it the Saturn Club, but upon reflection decided that Saturn's reputation wasn't quite what it should be. So they settled on Cosmos, which was kind of grand and all-encompassing and allowed them to admit to membership those who were interested in literature, and later Art with a capital A, which eventually meant that just about anybody, even Noah deGraffenreid, could become a member.

Major Powell, who lost his right arm at Shiloh, is probably the club's most famous founding member. Although nearly everyone recalls his exploration of the Grand Canyon, all too few remember that he was also considered the best one-armed snooker player west of the Mississippi. Henry Adams, great-grandson of one United States President and grandson of yet another, was probably the club's other most prominent founding member although when he died in Washington at eighty nobody paid much attention.

The Cosmos Club first housed itself in some rented rooms in the old Corcoran Building on 15th Street where the Washington Hotel now stands. In 1882 it moved into Dolley Madison's house on Lafayette Square near the White House where it remained until 1952 when it moved into the big four-story Indiana limestone house on Massachusetts Avenue that was previously owned by Mrs. Richard Townsend. Her second husband was Sumner Welles who got to be Under Secretary of State in Roosevelt's Cabinet. There are 44 rooms in the place and when Mrs. Townsend was a girl they hired 34 servants to look after her and her mother and father.

As Dr. Hucks sat, drink in hand, watching some members and their guests arrive, he pretended that he himself was a member awaiting his own guests. He decided that he quite possibly might have invited the first secretary from the British Embassy along with the cultural counselor from the French Embassy, who was known for his wit. And their wives, of course, who were both quite striking but almost shabby when compared to Hucks's own companion for the evening. He hadn't yet got around to giving her a name, but he knew that she would be tall and blond and so stunning that it would make you gasp.

Naturally, there would be a drink or two to start and a bit of deliciously wicked gossip. Then some faultlessly orderly wine, by Hucks, of course, to go with what would prove to be a most memorable meal. But the talk would be the true main course. Ah, the talk! Hucks's guests would be dazzled by their young host's biting wit. They would marvel at the effortless ease with which he served up, along with the soup, one faultless epigram after another. When it came to reducing complicated world problems to a single sentence of astounding logic, Hucks had no peer and he shrugged off the fact that his words would be stolen and shamelessly offered up to His Excellency as the thief's own. It happened all the time.

"You aren't passed out, are you, Hucks?" Noah deGraffenreid said.

Hucks started and looked up quickly over his left shoulder. "No, no, of course not. I was just sitting here thinking."

"I think we'd better go wash our hands, don't you?" deGraffenreid said and led the way, not waiting for an answer.

In the men's room deGraffenreid knelt and looked underneath the closed doors of the five toilet stalls. Then he went over to one of the sinks and began washing his hands, giving particular attention to his nails.

When he was through washing his hands he bent toward the mirror and examined a real or imagined blemish on his chin. Hucks watched him.

"In my car, I have a package for you," deGraffenreid said.

"A package," Hucks said.

"Yes. A package. In this package are three items. One item is a key. The second item is a drug. The third item is a device. A device for opening letters, shall we say."

"There should be something else in the package," Hucks said.

"Oh, really," deGraffenreid said, trying in vain to twist his head around so that he could see what the back of it looked like. "What?"

"Money. There should be some money in the package."

"Oh, I almost forgot. There is some money in it."

"How much?"

"A thousand dollars."

"That's not what we agreed on."

"Didn't we?"

"It's not anywhere near what we agreed on. We agreed on ten thousand. You know that's what we agreed on."

DeGraffenreid sighed and turned. "Hucks, Hucks, Hucks," he said in a sorrowful tone. "You, of all people, surely must recognize the speculative nature of our little venture."

"It was to be ten thousand down and ninety thousand more on delivery," Hucks said.

"I know, but do you realize how tight money is now? It's almost nonexistent, for God's sake. The people whom I represent are putting every dime they can raise into the second—and more profitable phase of the operation. But that doesn't mean they've forgotten our original agreement. You know it doesn't mean that, don't you?"

"I don't know what it means," Hucks said. "All I

know is that I'm supposed to get ten thousand dollars now, not one thousand."

"And you will. When you deliver the material, you'll hand it over to me and I'll hand ninety-nine thousand lovely dollars over to you. Now what could be fairer?"

"I don't like it."

"Of course you don't. But that doesn't mean that you don't understand the necessity for it. You're a very intelligent man. Why, only today I was talking to a fellow member of the club about you. I didn't mention names, of course, but I said I had met this most brilliant chap at the Department of Agriculture and that I was thinking of putting him up for membership. Well, I just went on and on about you. And this chap I was talking to—a really most intelligent fellow, you'd like him immensely—well, he said that if I needed a co-sponsor, well—" DeGraffenreid let his sentence die. He knew from the expression on Hucks's face that the web didn't have to be spun out any further. Hucks was caught, but he still wriggled just a little more anyhow.

"Well, I don't even know if I could afford to be a member. Quite frankly, I was counting on the ten thousand dollars you promised. I wouldn't be going into this thing at all unless I needed money. You know that."

"My dear boy, of course I know that. But you're forgetting one thing. I wouldn't have approached you unless I was sure that you had the kind of quick mind that could appreciate the true nature of our little venture. It is such a delicious little scheme, isn't it?"

"I guess so."

"Of course it is. And in years to come we'll sit right here in the club, when you're a member, of course, and we'll have a laugh about this very night."

"I'm not laughing now," Hucks said. "I really need that ten thousand."

"Nine days," deGraffenreid said.

"Nine days what?"

"Nine days at eleven thousand dollars a day. That's ninety-nine thousand dollars. I do think you could hold out until then."

"Until July eleventh," Hucks said.

"That's right. Until July eleventh."

23

THE FAT WOMAN WAS CRYING. SHE SAT ON THE COUCH across the room from Pope and cried into the Kleenex that she kept taking from her purse. She was about thirty and wore a shapeless brown and white dress and Pope thought she might have been pretty if she hadn't weighed nearly 250 pounds.

She blew her nose in the Kleenex and looked at Pope. "I don't know you," she said.

"I'm the new boy," Pope said. "Jake Pope."

"I'm Dorothy Eaves. You going to be in the group?"

"So it would seem."

"You're early."

"I know."

"You know why I'm early?"

"Why?"

"Because I can't get anything to eat here. That's why."

"You hungry?"

"Oh Jesus God," the fat woman said and started sobbing into her damp wad of Kleenex.

Pope stirred uncomfortably and looked around the room. It was the size of a modest living room, about fifteen by twenty feet, and the walls were lined with

couches and easy chairs that formed a hollow square.
Pope sat in one of the easy chairs. The fat woman sat at
the far end of one of the couches. There were some
lamps on some end tables and a carpet on the floor.
There were no ashtrays. Pope estimated that there were
enough chairs and couches to seat nearly a dozen persons. At one end of the room, behind Pope, were three
casement windows partially covered by tan drapes.
Pope was almost sure that the windows had a view of
the parking lot seven stories below where he had left
his Porsche.

The room was the one that Dr. Perry G. Gantt used
for his group psychotherapy sessions. Pope had met Dr.
Gantt the previous day at seven o'clock in the morning,
the only hour that the psychiatrist had open. When he
had arrived at Gantt's office in the building on Georgia
Avenue, just over the district line in Silver Spring, Maryland, the doctor had looked sleepy and kept rubbing
his eyes.

Gantt had red hair and freckles and Pope thought
he was probably about forty-two. His eyes were green
and partially shielded by Ben Franklin type glasses that
he kept peering over. He was a dumpy man, about five-
eight, who didn't look as if he got much exercise. He
wore white duck trousers, a blue shortsleeved shirt, no
jacket, and wingtipped brown shoes without socks. He
had forgotten to zip up his fly and Pope guessed that
he might have got dressed in the dark.

"Well," Dr. Gantt had said. "It's early, isn't it?"

"That's right."

"You're Jake Pope."

"Uh-huh."

"And—let's see—you were referred to me by Dr.—
uh—Forslund, right?"

"Right."

"Is he your family doctor?"

"I've known him for quite a while. He's not my family doctor, but we know each other pretty well."

"You mean you feel comfortable with him, is that right?"

"That's right."

"Well, let's get a few statistics first," Gantt had said and asked Pope his age, his general health, his address, telephone number, his occupation, marital status, and finally, why he thought he needed psychiatric help.

"Put it in your own words," Gantt had said.

"They're the only ones I've got. Well, ever since my wife died I've been feeling sort of depressed. I just don't seem able to shake it off. I don't want to see anybody; I don't want to go anywhere. I just feel—well—depressed."

"When did she die?"

"Last year," Pope had lied.

"How?"

"She was in a car accident. Alone."

"Do you feel responsible for her death?"

"No."

"Have you felt attracted to anyone since then?"

"You mean any other woman?"

"Anyone," Gantt had said.

"No. Not really. But then I really haven't been out with anyone."

"What do you do most of the time?"

"I stay home. I read some. I watch television a lot. Sometimes I just drive around. You know."

"You see your friends?"

"No."

"Why not?"

"I don't know. I just don't want to see them."

"How about your work?"

"Well, I don't really work. I mean I don't have a job."

"Who pays the rent?"

"I do. My wife left me some money. A lot of money."

"What did you used to do?"

"I was with the Government. With the Senate really."

"What kind of a job was it?"

"I was sort of a researcher."

"I mean, did you have to work with other people?"

"Not very much. Sometimes, I did, but most of the time I worked by myself. Alone."

"Do you come from a big family, Jake?"

"No. I'm an only child."

"Did you get along all right with your father?"

"I never knew him. He got killed at Pearl Harbor."

"Your mother never remarried?"

"No."

"She still alive?"

"No, she died when I was sixteen. In a car wreck—just like my wife."

"Ah," Dr. Gantt had said.

"Ah, what?"

"How did you feel when your mother died?"

"Well, I wasn't happy about it, if that's what you mean."

"Were you sad? Did you miss her?"

"Sure."

"Were you depressed?"

"Yes."

"Would you say that your feelings after your mother's death were quite similar to the feelings that you had—or have—after your wife's death?"

"Yeah," Pope had said slowly, dragging the word out, and hoping that he sounded sincere. "I never quite thought of it like that before."

"You think there's something there that we might illuminate?"

"Illuminate?"

"Look into."

"Yeah, we might illuminate that," Pope had said, latching on to the phrase because he had felt that it might be one of Gantt's favorites.

"What did you do after your mother died?"

"I just—well—went away."

"By yourself?"

"Yes."

"Didn't you stay with relatives or friends?"

"No. I stayed by myself. I didn't talk to hardly anyone for a long time."

"Ah," Dr. Gantt had said again. Then he had looked at his watch. "Did Dr. Forslund mention group therapy to you?"

"He mentioned it."

"He seemed to feel that it might be more suitable for you than individual therapy. I think I tend to agree. Do you know much about group therapy?"

"No."

"Well, it's sort of like family, Jake. We meet and talk about what's bothering us and why. I'm going to recommend that for you. I have three groups. What day suits you best?"

"Thursday," Pope had said quickly, remembering that Thursday was the day that Amelia Hucks attended her group therapy.

Gantt had opened a ledger-like book and studied it briefly. Then he had written something in it. "All right," he had said, "Thursday it is. That's tomorrow, isn't it?"

"That's right," Pope had said.

Dr. Gantt had risen. "I'll see you tomorrow at two then."

"Fine," Jake Pope had said.

By two o'clock the following day the room in which Dr. Gantt held his group therapy sessions had almost filled up. In addition to Pope and the fat lady who cried into her Kleenex there were eight other persons, almost half men and half women. Their ages ranged from the mid-twenties to the late forties. Some of them looked at Pope curiously, but none of them introduced themselves or asked who he was. The fat lady continued to sniffle into her wad of Kleenex. Nobody seemed to pay her any attention.

At three minutes past two Dr. Gantt came into the room, closed the door, and sat down next to the fat lady. He nodded and cleared his throat.

"We have a new member of the group today, Jake Pope. The way we work this, Jake, is that I introduce you to the other members and then you tell us a little something about yourself. I want to emphasize one thing. Anything—and everything—that's said in this room is totally confidential. I just wanted to make that clear at the beginning. Okay?"

"Okay," Pope said.

Dr. Gantt went around the room and introduced each of the nine persons. The only name that Jake remembered was Amelia Hucks. She sat in an armchair behind a pair of dark glasses. She wore tan slacks and a blue and white checked shirt. There was a dark bruise

on her left cheek. The rest of the people Pope gave nick-
names to because it was a convenient way to remember
them. Besides Fat Lady, there was String Bean, Gentleman Jim, Clerk, Housewife, Salesman Sam, Wicked
Beast, and Daddy's Girl.

"Well," Pope said. "I don't know quite where to
begin. I'm—uh—a widower, I guess, and I was born in
West Virginia and went to school there and then went
out to the West Coast for a while and worked there.
After that, I came to Washington where I had a job
with the Senate and met my wife. She was killed in a
car wreck last year and I suppose my problem is that
I've been feeling awfully depressed about it."

"Is that why you're here?" Fat Lady said, "because
you're depressed?"

"Yes. I suppose it is."

"What kind of work do you do?" Clerk asked. Clerk
was a middle-aged man with nervous eyes who kept
putting his glasses on and taking them off. When the
glasses were off he let them dangle around his neck
from a black ribbon.

"I was in research," Pope said, "but I haven't
worked in quite a while."

"How do you eat?" Daddy's Girl asked. She was a
vulnerable-looking little blonde, all curves and dimples,
who sat in one of the easy chairs with her feet tucked
up under her. She giggled after everything she said.

"My wife left me a little money," Pope said.

"Doesn't it make you even more depressed to be
dependent on your wife's money?" Housewife asked.
Housewife spoke with a British accent and kept her
black purse carefully in her lap. She held a pair of white
gloves in her right hand. She was about thirty-five,
Pope guessed, and probably wore a girdle.

"I hadn't thought about it," he said. "Maybe it does."

"You say you're not working at all now?" Gentleman Jim asked. He wore a white double-breasted suit and white shoes and was handsome in a flashy sort of way, Pope thought. He had thick brown hair that curled down over his ears and a mustache that he kept stroking as if he liked the feel of it. Pope guessed that he was about twenty-eight, no more.

"No," Pope said, "I'm not working."

"If you got a job and kept yourself busy, you probably wouldn't be so depressed," String Bean said. Pope named him String Bean because he had pipe-thin arms and legs and a drawn, sensitive face that looked as if it could use more sleep. He was probably thirty.

"What the fuck do you know about it?" Wicked Beast said. Wicked Beast sat as far away from the others as he could. He was a big man, about forty, with a red beard that came down to his chest. He spoke in a deep roar that sounded angry. He wore a continual frown and his blue eyes seemed to snap because he blinked so much. He kept his mouth twisted into a perpetual snarl. Pope decided that Wicked Beast didn't like too many people, especially himself.

"What do you mean what do I know about it?" String Bean said. "I know what depression is. I know plenty about depression."

"All you know how to do is jack off," Wicked Beast said. "Why don't you tell him to keep himself busy jacking off?"

"You're full of shit," String Bean said in a mechanical tone that sounded as if he had said the same thing before many times, but without much effect.

"What I want to know is how Amelia got that

bruise on her chin," the man whom Pope had dubbed Salesman Sam said. He had a hearty let's all have another round voice and a pink face and he grinned a lot. It wasn't much of a surprise when Pope learned later in the session that Salesman Sam was an obstetrician who drank too much.

"You want to talk about it, Amelia?" Dr. Gantt said.

Amelia Hucks shifted in her chair. She reached up and took off her dark glasses. She had two black eyes. "I'm going to leave him," she said, not looking at anyone. "He came home and beat me up again last night. I'm going to leave him."

"When you gonna leave him?" Daddy's Girl said. "You've been talking about leaving him for months, but you never do anything about it."

"Did your husband beat you up?" Pope said.

Amelia Hucks looked at him. "Yes."

"This isn't the first time?"

"No. He's done it before. Plenty of times."

"Why does he beat you up?" Pope said.

She shrugged, but said nothing.

"He likes to beat her up," Housewife said. "That's how he gets his kicks. He's all bent out of shape."

"Let Amelia answer," Dr. Gantt said.

"We get into fights," Amelia said. "Into arguments. He wins them by beating me up. I'm going to leave him."

"When did he beat you up, yesterday?" Pope said.

"Last night after he came home."

"Was he drunk?" Pope said.

"No, he'd had something to drink. Gin. I could smell it, but he wasn't drunk."

"Where'd he been, out with some other woman?" Pope said.

Wicked Beast laughed. "That creep! Christ, he doesn't even fuck Amelia, let alone some other broad. He didn't fuck you last night, did he, Amelia?"

"No," she said, looking at the floor. "He didn't fuck me. He beat me up."

"Where'd he been?" Pope said. "Did he say?"

"He'd been out to dinner. He bragged about it, about being out to dinner at the Cosmos Club. He likes to go there."

"Is he a member?" Pope said.

"No, he's not a member. He's not a member of anything. He's not even a member of the human race."

"I'd leave the cocksucker," Fat Lady said. "I wouldn't let him beat up on me."

"Who'd wanta beat up on you, lard ass?" Wicked Beast said. "Beating up on you would be like beating up on some big, gooey, oversized cream puff."

"Fuck off, sonny," Fat Lady said. "Nobody's talking to you."

"Climb this," Wicked Beast said and held out his right middle finger. Fat Lady ignored him.

"Who does he go to this club with, if he's not a a member?" Pope said.

"Some guy," Amelia Hucks said. "Some guy takes him there. He says he's going to make him a member. That's a laugh. That's really a hardy-har-har laugh. We can't even pay our bills and that shit talks about joining some fancy club."

"What's this guy like who takes him to the club?" Pope said.

"What's the matter, Jake, you think he's queer?" Gentleman Jim asked.

"Who?" Pope said.

"The guy who takes Amelia's husband to the Cosmos Club?"

"I don't know whether he's queer or not."

"Would it bother you if he was?" Gentleman Jim said and smirked.

"Why should it bother me?"

"He's a fag," Daddy's Girl said to Pope, jerking her thumb at Gentleman Jim. "He thinks everybody else is."

"Not everybody, darling," Gentleman Jim said and smirked again.

"Well, I was just wondering who this guy is that takes her husband to the Cosmos Club," Pope said. "I thought it might be his boss."

"It's not his boss," Amelia said. "His boss doesn't even know he's alive. It's some guy over in Georgetown. He's got an antique store over there. DeGraffenreid's. I don't know. Maybe he is queer. Maybe they're both queer. I don't give a goddamn anymore. I'm going to leave him."

"You're all talk and no action, sweetie," Housewife said. "You're always saying you're going to leave him, but you don't. Maybe you like it when he beats you up. You ever think about that? Maybe you like it."

Tears started to trickle down Amelia Hucks's face. She brushed them away with a hand. "I don't like it. I don't like him to beat me up. And I'm gonna leave him, you just watch. I'm gonna leave him. I've got to now."

"Why do you have to leave him now?" Pope said.

"Because—because he said he's gonna kick me out. He's gonna give me some money and then kick me out."

"Is he going to give you a lot of money?" Pope said.

"He said he's gonna give me fifty thousand dollars, that's what he said. He said he's gonna give me fifty thousand dollars and beat me up real good and then kick me out."

"I thought he couldn't pay the bills," Pope said.

"He said he's gonna get the money from this man he's going to that club with. He said they've got some kind of business deal."

"That's a lot of money, Amelia," Clerk said. "Fifty thousand dollars is quite a lot of money. Maybe you should wait around until he gives it to you."

"When did he say he was going to give it to you?" Pope said.

"Next week," she said and started to cry in short, jerky sobs.

"He mention any particular day?" Pope said, trying to keep his question as casual as he could.

"He said—he said he was gonna get one hundred thousand dollars and he was going to beat me up and then give me half of it and then kick me out on my butt. That's what he said."

"But he didn't say when?"

"July eleventh," she said. "He said he was gonna beat me up and kick me out and give me fifty thousand dollars on July eleventh."

"Do you believe him?" Housewife said. "I wouldn't believe the sonofabitch. Oh, I'd believe he'd beat me up and kick me out, but I wouldn't believe anything about fifty thousand dollars."

"You wouldn't believe anybody who shaves, ducky," Wicked Beast said. "You hate all men. Haven't you realized that yet? You hate all men because your sweet old daddy wouldn't let you climb up on his lap, isn't that right, Doc? Isn't that what she told us?"

Pope didn't listen to what Dr. Gantt replied. Instead he watched Amelia Hucks as she dried her tears and plucked at some loose strands of hair. He wondered why Noah deGraffenreid was going to pay Dallas Hucks $100,000 on July 11th. He also wondered whether Dr. Hucks would really give his wife half of it and then kick her out after he got through beating her up. And after he got through wondering about that Pope found himself wondering about how Amelia Hucks was going to spend the money.

24

Parking was no problem for Jake Pope that night down at the bottom of Kalorama Circle where Ancel Easter's three-story house looked out over Rock Creek Park. All the houses in the neighborhood had either two- or three-car garages and virtually the only cars parked on the street were those of the butlers and the maids and the yard men. It was that kind of neighborhood.

The distinguishing feature of Easter's house was its round, three-story turret that was topped with a slate roof in the shape of a dunce cap. Inside the turret, stairs wound up to the second and third stories. The turret even had narrow little slit-like windows that the archers could shoot through in case of attack. The rest of the house, built out of grey stone, sort of clung to the turret.

Thomas J. Fiquette, the ex-vice squad cop, answered the door to Pope's ring. "How's it going, Jake?" he said.

"Not bad, Tom. Yourself?"

"Same old shit. You like fried chicken, I hope."

"Crazy about it."

"Pan gravy?"

"With rice?"

"You got it. Biscuits, too."

"Sounds great."

"You know where he is," Fiquette said.

"I think I can find him."

Pope found Ancel Easter in the living room murmuring to a sick-looking green plant with wide waxy leaves that had grown to a height of about four feet. Easter was not only murmuring to the plant, he was also brushing each broad leaf with a clean white cloth that he kept moistening from a bottle. The plant that was undergoing Easter's ministrations had plenty of company. Plants were all over the living room. They dripped from the mantel, lined the windowsills, and spilled out on to the floor. There were big plants and little plants and medium-sized ones and Pope didn't know what any of them were.

"You really talk to them, like in the cartoons?" he said.

"Why not?" Easter said and went on wiping the leaves.

"What's it got?"

"Spiders."

Pope looked. "I don't see any spiders."

"Scrunch up your eyes and look real close. You can see the little webs where the leaves join the stems."

Pope scrunched up his eyes and looked. "I don't see any webs."

"They're there."

"When did you turn queer for plants?"

"Last year about this time. I'm very trendy."

"Sure you are. You going to offer me a drink or can't you leave your patient?"

Easter nodded toward a tray that held bottles and

glasses and ice. "Help yourself. You can fix me a Scotch and soda."

Pope went over to the tray and mixed two drinks. While he was mixing them, Easter said, "Well, what happened? Did you get in?"

"I got in."

"What was it like?"

"All right, I guess."

"You think it does any good?"

"It gives them somebody to talk to. That seems to be what most of them need—or think they need. It probably amounts to the same thing."

"How was the doctor?"

"He keeps forgetting to zip up his pants, but he seemed okay."

Easter turned to accept his drink. "And Mrs. Hucks, isn't it? How was she?"

"She had two black eyes," Pope said. "Real beauties. There was a bruise on her chin, too."

"Her husband?"

"So she said."

"What else?"

Pope looked around the living room and picked out a comfortable wingbacked chair that was stationed in front of the fireplace. Except for the plants, the rest of Ancel Easter's living room looked as if it might have been ordered by the yard from a catalogue.

"You ought to get married," Pope said.

"So I could beat up my wife?"

"This place needs a touch of something."

"I thought the plants helped."

"It looks like a hothouse."

Easter looked around the room. "Does it really? I never noticed."

"Tarzan would like it," Pope said. "He'd feel right at home. So would Jane."

"Maybe you could give me the name of your decorator," Easter said. "That place of yours has a real nice homey touch to it. Sort of dormitory modern."

"Maybe we both ought to get married."

"Ah."

"You sound like that fucking psychiatrist. What does ah mean?"

"I was thinking of the fair Mrs. Hix. With an *x*. She seems to be lingering on in Washington."

"I thought you were keeping her here."

Easter shook his head and sat down in a chair opposite Pope. "Our business has long since been concluded. Any further business we might have could be just as well handled by phone. Or there's the mail. The mails are still going through. But she lingers on. That's why I said ah. You mentioned marriage. Mrs. Hix is still in town. My keen brain started working and I said ah."

"She's all right."

"Ah-hah."

"Little late in life for you to be turning matchmaker, isn't it?"

"I don't know. She seems to be a most suitable young lady. Nice manners. Good-looking. And she's tall enough for you."

"We already discussed that," Pope said and grinned.

"That she's suitable?"

"That she's tall enough."

"Well?"

"Well, what?"

"Are your intentions honorable?"

"No."

"But you're interested."

"She says she can cook," Pope said.

"Now there's a sound basis for matrimony. Probably the soundest of all."

"I'll give it some thought," Pope said, "but after what I saw this afternoon, matrimony has lost a lot of its attraction."

"The members of the group were having a little marital trouble, I take it."

"A little. Especially Mrs. Hucks. She says she's going to leave her husband."

"The good Dr. Hucks?"

"That's right. He keeps beating her up. She also says that he's going to kick her out so she wants to leave him before he does that. In fact, he says he's going to lay fifty thousand dollars on her, beat her up, and then kick her out."

"Jesus," Easter said. "Where's he going to get fifty thousand?"

"That's what I asked. It seems that he and our old friend Noah deGraffenreid have got a deal working. A hundred-thousand-dollar deal, according to Mrs. Hucks. And it's all going to come true on July eleventh."

Easter looked at Pope for a moment. "You've got something, haven't you?"

"I think so."

"Well, you'd better put it all together for me."

"You'd better put it together for him at dinner, Jake, cause it's on the table." It was Fiquette speaking from the doorway that led to the dining room. "You can bring your drinks, if you want to."

Easter finished his drink in a gulp and put it on a table. "Let's eat," he said. "If we don't, Tom'll pout."

"I ain't gonna pout if you ain't got sense enough to eat when it's hot," Fiquette said.

"Christ, you're sounding more like Stepinfetchit every day," Pope said.

"You oughta see me scratch my head and roll my eyes," Fiquette said. "I got so I can do that real good now."

"I don't think you have to wear that goddamn thing to the dinner table, do you?" Easter said.

Fiquette looked down. "You mean this?" he said, touching the .38 caliber revolver in the hip holster.

"That."

"Well, shit, you never objected to it before."

"Oh, Christ," Easter said. "Let's eat."

The three men sat down at the long table in the dining room that was furnished in the same formal style as that of the living room. There was a chandelier that glittered nicely and a sideboard and tall white candles on the table that would seat a dozen guests comfortably. Fiquette sat at the end of the table near the door that led to the kitchen. Easter sat at the table's other end and Pope sat between them.

"What do you guys do, shout at each other to pass the salt every night?" Pope said.

"It's his idea," Easter said, helping himself from a plate of fried chicken. He had to stand so that he could shove the plate down to Pope.

"If we didn't have a real sit-down dinner, he'd be eatin sardines out in the kitchen, right out of the can," Fiquette said. "Man don't eat enough to keep a bird alive the way it is. You better have some of this gravy while it's hot, Jake." Fiquette watched while Pope helped himself to the gravy. "Shit, you ain't taking no gravy. Come on, man, dump some on that rice."

"See what I mean?" Easter said. "When he's not doing Stepinfetchit, he's doing Jewish mamma."

"Man's gotta eat," Fiquette said. "You know what's really wrong with him, Jake?"

"No, what?"

"He ain't been laid recently, that's what's wrong with him. He stays home and sits around babytalking those fool plants in there. I offer to run him in a couple of real sweet mammas that I got a line on over in Baltimore, but he says he don't feel up to it."

"I remember the last sweet mammas you ran in," Easter said.

"Now what was wrong with them? You tell me that. What was wrong with them sweet little things."

"How old were they?"

"I don't know. Eighteen, maybe twenty."

"You really want to know what was wrong with them?"

"I do. For a fact, I do."

"They couldn't remember World War Two."

"Well, shit, what'd you want, a history lesson?"

Ancel Easter leaned back in his chair and sighed. "I think, Tom, that what I wanted was somebody who could remember World War Two."

"Someone who knew all the words to 'A Nightingale Sang in Berkeley Square,'" Pope said. "Somebody like that."

"I'm getting old," Easter said.

"You ain't getting old," Fiquette said, "you just wanta get married."

"That's what I think, too," Pope said.

"Yeah, well, let's talk about somebody else's marriage," Easter said. "Let's talk about the Huckses'."

"What else do you want to know?" Pope said.

"Whatever you've got."

"Well, from what I got out of that group therapy session, the marriage is on the rocks. He's apparently not screwing her anymore. He's beating her up pretty regularly. He's in debt up to his ears, or rather they are. He tells her that on July eleventh he's going to somehow get hold of a hundred thousand dollars, half of which he's going to give her, after he beats her up. Then he's going to kick her out."

"Must have been quite a session," Easter said.

"She cried a lot. Well, it seems that Hucks has this deal I mentioned going with Noah deGraffenreid. What it is, I don't know; I can only guess. But first of all let's look at what Hucks has to offer, okay?"

"All right. What has he got?"

"Nothing. No money anyhow. He can't raise a dime. So he's going to have to sell something. So what does he have to sell?"

"He works for the Department of Agriculture, right?"

"Right. Now on July eleventh—and that's the date that Crawdad mentioned—there's only one thing going on in the Department of Agriculture. That's when they turn part of the place into kind of a miniature Fort Knox before they release the July crop report. They have all sorts of security measures set up. Guards, sealed off sections, the phones are cut, and they even have a cute little ceremony when at five o'clock in the morning they go down to unlock the box where the crop production information is kept. They even have two keys. Now guess who has one of them?"

"Our friend Dr. Hucks," Easter said.

"That's right."

"Huh."

"That's what I thought. Huh."

Ancel Easter nodded. "So if somebody got that information, they could use it to play around in the commodity markets."

"Maybe. If the information was startling, they could. I mean if the wheat crop, for example, was going to be thirty percent less than what everybody else thought it was going to be, well, it would be pretty valuable inside dope."

"Thirty percent less or thirty percent more," Easter said.

"Either way."

"So you think deGraffenreid might be playing the market?"

"I don't know."

"Could you find out?"

"I don't know that either. Maybe. But I've got to know what I'm looking for. You know much about the commodity market?"

"Just enough to stay away from it," Easter said.

"Where could I get a real quick crash course?"

Easter thought for a moment and then looked at Fiquette. "Is old man Scurlong still alive?"

"Old Commodity Jack? Sure he is. I saw him on the street just the other day. He was scufflin along pretty spry."

"Who's Commodity Jack?" Pope said.

"Commodity Jack Scurlong," Easter said. "He's before your time. Mine too, as a matter of fact. But he was with the Department of Agriculture back in the twenties and went short on wheat one year and retired a millionaire at twenty-six."

"Went to jail, too," Fiquette said. "Did nine months in Atlanta."

"Yeah, it seems that our Jack was using inside information to dabble in the market. Well, when he got out of jail he was broke again, but he somehow scraped up a thousand dollars and went back into the commodity market and six months later he was a millionaire again."

"Then he lost that, too," Fiquette said. "Went flat-ass busted again. That's when he turned preacher."

"Preacher?" Pope said.

"He started lecturing on the evils, ills and pitfalls of the commodity markets," Easter said. "He managed to make a living, but that's about all. Then he got the bright idea that he'd publish a weekly newsletter. Christ, he probably knows as much about the commodity markets as anybody alive so he puts out what's called Commodity Jack's Green Sheet."

"Is it any good?"

"Some people swear by it. They do it from their villas along the Riviera. Jack helped put them there."

"That's all he does, put out this green sheet?"

"It costs two hundred dollars a month to subscribe to it and you've got to go on a waiting list. If somebody dies, then maybe you can get a subscription. There're only one hundred subscribers."

"That's twenty thousand bucks a month."

"So it is."

"Does he still play the market?"

"Jack? Christ, no. He's like a reformed drunk. Half of the Green Sheet is all about the wickedness of specu-.ating in commodities. The other half is how to make a fast buck doing it."

"Can you get me an appointment with him?" Pope said.

"I think so," Easter said. "I'll fix it for tomorrow morning."

"Tomorrow's the Fourth of July."

"Jack won't mind."

25

IT WAS CALLED THE HOPE BUILDING AND POPE WONDERED if it offered any to those who rented its offices. It was a narrow, shabby, nine-story building just south of K Street on Fifteenth, which is bordered on the west by McPherson Square. At ten o'clock on the morning of the Fourth of July there were only five people in the square. Four of them were men who were asleep or passed out on the grass. The fifth was an elderly woman who sat on a park bench and talked to herself while she fed the pigeons out of a brown paper sack.

The lobby of the Hope Building smelled of vomit and Lysol and cheap cigars. There were two elevators, but one of them was decorated with an "Out of Order" sign. The sign seemed permanent. There was some green paint on the walls of the lobby that was just beginning to peel. Somebody had thrown up on the floor and a bucket and a mop stood next to the vomit, but nothing had yet been done about it.

Pope skirted the vomit and punched the elevator's up button. When it came, he got in, and punched the number seven button. The elevator's doors closed and it started moving up, but slowly and with what seemed to be muttered protestations.

At the seventh floor the elevator door clanked open and Pope moved down the hall, guided by the flaked gold paint of an arrow that claimed rooms 701 to 721 were down that way. He stopped in front of the door that had 713 painted on it in black numerals. Beneath the numerals was another painted sign that read, Commodity Jack's Green Sheet, Inc. Beneath that in smaller letters was, John H. Scurlong, President. Pope knocked and while waiting for somebody to open the door or say who's there or come in, he checked Commodity Jack's neighbors. To the left was William Rice, Jobber and Manufacturer's Representative. To the right was something called Metropolitan Industries, Inc. Across the hall was Sally Simmons Real Estate and Insurance. Pope wondered if they had all managed to scrape up their July rent.

It wasn't until Pope knocked the second time that something happened behind the door. A bolt was drawn. A key was turned. Another bolt was drawn and still another key was turned. The door opened perhaps an inch and something blue looked out at Pope. He decided that it was an eye. The door opened wider and Commodity Jack Scurlong said, "Now you'd be Jake Pope, wouldn't you?"

He wasn't very tall, about five-four, and he wasn't very heavy, about a hundred pounds if he kept his shoes on, but he was all dressed up and he moved quickly with a funny little prance, and he was very old, although he had a curiously young voice, high and light, almost a tenor. Once started, he was hard to shut up.

"Mr. Scurlong?" Pope said.

"Come in, lad. Come in. Ancel Easter said you'd

come calling this morning, not that I get many visitors, especially on a holiday like this, but I told Ancel that I'm still on the job seven days a week, just like I've always been, because in my business you've got to keep your eyes open all the time or the bastards'll sneak up on your blind side. Now let's have a cup of coffee, how does that sound?"

"Fine," Pope said. "It sounds fine."

Commodity Jack moved, strutted really, over to a small table that contained an electric kettle, a jar of instant Yuban, a box of sugar cubes, a can of Carnation milk, and three mugs. "How do you like it, lad, black or with just a touch of sugar to take the bite off?"

"Just a touch of sugar."

"You a drinking man?"

"Sometimes."

"I take mine this time of morning with two cubes of sugar and a good big slug of straight bourbon, how does that sound?"

"Great," Pope said.

Commodity Jack reached inside his coat and produced a silver flask. "Holdover from prohibition, lad, now those were the days, I'll tell you; some real shenanigans going on then. Ever hear of Jesse Livermore?"

"Never did."

"The cotton king."

"Doesn't ring a bell."

"Old Jesse cornered cotton his first time out, but of course that was in ought-eight, not the twenties. Pity about old Jesse."

"Why a pity?"

"Walked into the Sherry-Netherland's men's bar, Thanksgiving Eve it was, all dressed up, grey flannel suit, brand-new shoes, nice blue foulard, blue tab-collar shirt, gold pin, ordered a dry martini, drank her down, walked into the men's room, and blew his brains out. November 28, 1940. Sorry to hear about it. Distressed. Here's your coffee."

"Thanks very much," Pope said.

The telephone rang. Commodity Jack put down his own cup, picked up the phone, said hello, and then started listening. He picked up a yellow pencil and made notes as he listened. Pope looked around the room while he sipped at his bourbon and coffee. It wasn't a big room, but neither was it small. It was about the size of what you can get at a Holiday Inn for $32 on a slow night.

One wall was covered with maps. There were maps of the United States, of Russia, of India, of China, of the world, of Argentina, of Africa, and of Australia. There were big maps and little maps and maps that seemed to have been torn from the *National Geographic* and Scotch-taped on top of other maps. Below the maps was a Reuter's newsprinter that stuttered and spoke every few minutes. Next to the newsprinter was a radio, a Sony, with lots of dials and knobs and bands, that looked as if it could pick up either Moscow or the local police calls, depending upon one's mood. Across the room was a bookcase that covered the entire wall and was crammed with books and pamphlets and old copies of the *Congressional Record* and newspapers and magazines. On the floor was a four-foot-high stack of back copies of the *New York Journal of Commerce*. The wall nearest the corridor was lined with metal, four-drawer filing cabinets, some green, some grey. Just enough space was left for the office door, although it could be opened only partway before it banged into a cabinet. The door itself had four Yale locks and three bolts.

In the middle of all this, near the room's single window, was the desk. It was an old desk, scratched and scarred, made out of some dark wood and its surface was covered with graphs and charts and clippings and an electric calculator and three telephones, one of which Commodity Jack Scurlong still had to his ear. Next to the desk was the small table that held the electric kettle and the coffee stuff. There was a swivel chair behind the desk. The only other chair in the room was the wooden one with the straight back that Pope sat in.

The only neat thing in the room was Scurlong himself. He wore a white suit that looked as if it were made out of linen with narrow shoulders, a pinched-in waist, and a belt in the back. Pinned to its lapel was the bud of a red rose. He wore a blue striped shirt with white cuffs and collar. The cuffs were kept closed by gold links and he shot the cuffs every few moments out of what seemed to be nervous habit. His tie was narrow and bright blue and his shoes were black-and-white wing-tips. Commodity Jack Scurlong, Pope decided, was something of a dandy.

He must be at least seventy-five, Pope thought, maybe even eighty. But he doesn't look it. Maybe it's the way he moves.

Even while he was just listening on the phone Commodity Jack was in action. He shot his cuffs, and winked and smiled, made notes, sipped at his coffee and bourbon, found a comb and ran it through his long, white hair, made some more notes, nodded, grinned, and even smirked, made another note, fiddled with some papers on his desk, pulled at his nose, patted his pockets, found a cigarette, lit it, blew three smoke rings, made a note, winked at Pope, shrugged, took off his rimless glasses, breathed on them, polished them with his tie, put them back on, made another note, and fidgeted constantly as though afraid to sit still.

Scurlong had a thin, busybody face with a little black mustache that contrasted nicely with his white hair. His eyes were blue, sky blue perhaps, and shiny hard. They darted quickly about, noticing this and registering that. The face itself was deeply lined with cracks and tiny crevasses, like a piece of fine old rag paper that had been wadded up and then carelessly smoothed out. He had a pink nose that turned rosy at its tip and beneath the little black mustache was a small mouth that couldn't be called prim because its ends kept twitching up too much. His teeth were white and shiny and they may not have been his own, but if they were false, they didn't seem to trouble him. There wasn't much to his chin and this may have bothered him some because every once in a while he would lift it up and thrust it out and hold it there for a while until he got tired, or forgot about it.

It was a smart face, Pope decided, maybe not wise, but certainly clever. It was also the face of someone who had made a few mistakes over the years, but refused to brood about them. Pope didn't think that Commodity Jack Scurlong looked like someone who had much more than a nodding acquaintance with regret.

Finally, the old man said "Thanks very much," and hung up the phone. He looked at Pope. "London," he said.

"On the phone."

Commodity Jack looked at his watch. "Calls every day about this time. Later over there, you know. Time change. Market just closed. Expensive though, these calls. Terrible phone bill. Ghastly. Well, now, Ancel said you want a crash course. Never heard the phrase before. Figured it out. Means intensive instruction, right?"

"Right."

"You interested in going into the market?"

"No. I'm interested in finding out about it though."

"Ever played the stock market?"

"Yes. A little a few years back."

"Never fiddled with commodities though."

"No."

"Thought not. I can tell. Don't know how, but I can. Look at a chap and tell whether he's been in commodities or had gonorrhea. Don't know why, but I can. Never had the clap, did you?"

"No," Pope said, "I never did."

"See. Some kind of second sight. Useful sometimes. Well, where shall we start? Better have a dab more of this first." He reached into his breast pocket, hopped around the desk, and poured another generous jolt of bourbon into Pope's half-empty cup. "Second wing. Fly now. Well, commodities. What are commodities, Mr. Pope?"

"They're various agricultural products, wheat, corn, oats, barley, soybeans, cotton, things like that. In recent years they've included other items. Frozen orange juice. Silver. Lumber. Plywood, and so forth."

"And what are done with these commodities?"

"Well, they're bought and sold."

"Where?"

"In various exchanges. Let's see. There's the Chicago Board of Trade, it deals in wheat and soybeans and stuff like that. And the Chicago Mercantile Exchange which goes in for eggs, live cattle, pork bellies, and sorghums, I think. Then there's New York and

Kansas City and other exchanges around the country."

"And who does the buying and selling?"

"Brokers acting for their clients. Professional traders with the big companies. Speculators."

"Speculators, you say?"

"Yes."

"Nasty word, isn't it? Spec-u-la-tors. Makes you think of shifty-eyed chaps, dollar signs on their vests, big jowls, big cigars, fists full of money. Diamonds on their pinkies. Chaps like that. Terrible."

"Nobody seems to mind," Pope said.

"Mind what?"

"Speculators in the commodity markets. You invest in the stock market, but you speculate in the commodity market. Why?"

"Excellent point. First-class point. Good mind, sir. Well, now, you can buy a share of stock and it's yours to hold and to keep forever. It can go down, up, or stay the same. But it's yours. Right?"

"Right."

"It's an in-vest-ment. But let's take five thousand bushels of wheat. That's what's called a futures contract. You go to your commodity broker. You say, "My Uncle Orville out in Montana's got a wheat farm and he tells me wheat's going through the ceiling. How can I cash in on this wonderful piece of inside dope?' Well, sir, you make a down payment on 5,000 bushels of wheat. That's called a margin. Your down payment is about 75 cents a bushel. Wheat's selling for say, $5 a bushel. Terrible price. Your margin is about fifteen percent. Used to be less, but wheat got volatile, brokers got burned, margin went up. Clear so far?"

"Perfectly," Pope said.

"Okay. But your uncle out in Montana told you

that wheat wasn't going up right away, it was going up in maybe two or three weeks. Big jump then. But you want to buy cheap now and sell high in the fu-ture—mark that word—fu-ture. So you make your down payment, or margin, of fifteen percent on 5,000 bushels of wheat at $5 a bushel. That's what everybody but your uncle out in Montana thinks wheat's going to be selling for in September. That's called a wheat fu-ture. So for a down payment of $750 you control 5,000 bushels of wheat that's worth $25,000. Now when you signed up for your wheat, you signed a contract. You promised to accept delivery of 5,000 bushels of wheat at $5 a bushel from somebody in September. You don't know who. You don't really care. But it's somebody out there who doesn't give a damn what your uncle out in Montana says. This somebody, whoever he is, is selling you 5,000 bushels of September wheat at $5 a bushel. You want to know why? Because he thinks that the price of wheat's going to drop. Of course, he's selling something he doesn't own. Never will own probably. But he's got a contract, too. He's got to deliver that 5,000 bushels of wheat to you in September. Clear so far?"

"Sure," Pope said.

"Well, you've gone *long* in the wheat market and the chap you bought your wheat from has gone *short*. That's what it's called. You think the price is going to rise. He thinks it's going to fall. If it goes up enough, you sell. If it goes down enough, say to $4.50 a bushel, he steps into the market and buys 5,000 bushels of wheat at $4.50 a bushel. Now he's already sold you 5,000 bushels of wheat at $5 a bushel. But when delivery time comes, he can pay you off with wheat that cost him only $4.50 a bushel. So he's made 50 cents a bushel on 5,000 bushels which is $2,500. That's off an investment of $750, which was his margin or down payment. Not bad, huh?"

"Not bad," Pope said.

"Ah, but suppose the price of wheat went up, like your uncle out in Montana said. When you bought your September wheat it was $5.00 a bushel. But it goes to $5.50. So what do you do? You sell. Now who buys it? Well, this chap who promised to deliver you 5,000 bushels of wheat has still got to do it. It's in his contract. He sold you something that he didn't own. He went short. Now he has to go out and buy it. But what does he find? Five dollars and fifty cents a bushel for wheat. That's what. So he has to come up with the extra 50 cents a bushel and instead of making $2,500 on his contract, he loses that much."

"You should write a book," Pope said.

Commodity Jack shook his head. "Spec-u-la-tion is gambling pure and simple. You're betting that the price of something that you never see and never own will rise or fall. Back in sixty-four the value of all futures contracts was a little over $60 billion. Now, it's around $340 billion. It's getting too big. Too fat."

"What's going to happen?" Pope said.

"Collapse. Disaster. A wipeout. Maybe next year or the year after. Total ruin. Awful to think of. They excuse speculation, of course. Say it provides a liquid market. Pure poppycock. Crap game, that's what it is. Look what Russians did. Smart. Clever. Mean, too. Hoodwinked everybody. Especially chaps at Department of Agriculture. Poor sods. Russians come in. Take out checkbooks. Buy 333 million bushels of wheat. More than 246 million bushels of corn. Barley. Sorghums. Soybeans. God knows what. Bought wheat at $1.67 a bushel. Cash on the barrelhead. Poor old Nixon out in San Clemente. He announces big deal. Wonderful news. Russkies going to buy $750 million worth of U.S. grains over next five years. They'd already bought $500 million worth and he didn't even know it."

"Somebody must have known it," Pope said.

"That was back in seventy-two," Commodity Jack said, shaking his head. "Everybody in the commodity market. Cab drivers. Little old ladies. Doctors. Bartenders. People like that. All going short. Wheat selling for $1.67. Everybody swore it'd go down to $1.47. Maybe even $1.40. Everybody got fooled. By year's end it had hit $2.70 and still climbing."

"Nobody went long, huh?"

Commodity Jack tapped his thin chest. "My people. I told em to go long. Curious thing. Kept getting these calls from London. Chap told me his name was Mr. Smith. Nice-sounding chap. Told me every move the Russkies made. Checked it out. Found it true. Put it in the Green Sheet. My people cleaned up. Wretched business."

"This guy Smith. Did he tell anybody else?" Pope said.

"Told a chap out in Kansas City. Mort Sosland. Editor of something called *The Southwestern Miller*. Kept calling him, too. Mr. Smith, I mean. Must have run up tremendous phone bill. Long way from London to Kansas City. Never did find out who Smith really was. Most knowledgeable chap though. Probably Chinese."

"So what happened?"

"The Russkies slickered us. That's what. All legitimate. Cost taxpayers, of course. About $300 million in shipping subsidies. That's Department of Agriculture's fault, of course. Terrible incompetence. Unbelievable.

Senate got mad about it. Called policy inadequate, shortsighted, dictated by outmoded prin-ci-ples. Strong language."

"Whose fault was it?"

"Old man Butz. Secretary of Agriculture then. Chap named Palmby, too. He took nice job with big grain firm. Created lot of suspicion. Nothing proved though. Exonerated. Hah."

"What about the Commodity Exchange Authority, the CEA?"

"Bumblers. Bumbled then, bumble now. Got tip that somebody was rigging Kansas City market. Looked into it. Spent nineteen hundred man hours on it. Lot of hours. But they spent it looking up wrong facts. Incredible."

"Suppose somebody wanted to rig the market, the wheat market say. How would they go about it?"

"Rumor, that's how. Market dotes on rumor. Two types of speculators, actually. Chartists and Fundamentalists. Chartists stick to analysis of price movements. Draw up nice little charts. Charts tell 'em when to sell, when to buy, when to go to bathroom. Fundamentalists misnamed, of course. They take big picture. Weather, famine, governments, things like that. One chap I know, fundamentalist. Went grocery shopping with wife. Bacon $1.80 a pound. Wife refused to buy. Chap went to phone, called broker, told him to sell hog bellies short. Reasoned that if his wife wouldn't buy, other wives wouldn't until price dropped. It did. Chap cleaned up. Made a packet. Another example. Spoke of old Jesse Livermore earlier."

"The cotton king," Pope said.

"Exactly. First time out, Jesse bought cotton. Quiet moves. Gradual. Found himself long 120,000 bales. Rising market. He made it rise, of course. But who would buy? Found a newspaperman on old New York *World*. Fine paper. Headline next morning, 'July Cotton Cornered by Jesse Livermore.' The shorts covered; the suckers rushed in to buy, Jesse unloaded. Slick. Very slick."

"What do you think of the Department of Agriculture's crop reporting service and its predictions?"

"Not bad. Pretty good. Some people swear by them. Chap called Conrad Leslie, private forecaster. He's good too. But something mystic about Department of Agriculture forecast."

"Suppose somebody got hold of that forecast before it was supposed to be released?"

"Impossible. Guards. Locked doors. Sealed blinds. Nobody in or out. Tight security."

"Let's suppose," Pope said.

Commodity Jack looked up at the ceiling. He pursed his lips. "Sell it. Big money. Retire to Majorca. All that."

"How about the guy who got it. What would he do?"

"Make a fortune."

"How?"

"Depended on what the report said. Condition of the market. Rumors around. Things like that. Give you an example."

"All right," Pope said.

"Suppose chap gets report in advance. Report estimates that wheat crop going to be thirty percent short of previous predictions. Instead of 2 billion bushels, going to be 1.4 billion. Chap knows market will react. Shortage of wheat looms. Dollar bread predicted. All that. Price of wheat bound to rise. Chap has to move fast. Goes long 2 million bushels for himself. Goes long

2 million bushels in his cousin Fred's name. Also his Aunt Gertrude's name. Winds up going long, say, 6 million bushels of winter wheat. Okay?"

"Why didn't he put it all in his own name?"

"Against the law. Maximum you can buy or sell in one day is 2 million bushels. Anytime your position reaches 200,000 bushels, you're supposed to report it to CEA. Hah. Some do, some don't. CEA'd probably lose it anyway. No matter. Now you're 6 million bushels long. Say you bought at around $5. Easy figure to play with. You've got your inside information though. You want to maximize it. Start a rumor."

"What kind?"

"The Russians are coming. Use that one again. Market opens with news that crop's going to be short and Russkies are back in the picture. Wheat shoots up in two days to $5.40. You sit tight. The next day it goes to $5.60. By week's end, $6. You dump it. Now then, you went long 6 million bushels at $5 a bushel, right?"

"Right."

"That's $30 million. But you didn't put up $30 million. You just put up $450,000—your fifteen percent margin. Still a lot of money though, right?"

"Right."

"But look at what you made off $450,000 investment. You made $6 million. A dollar a bushel. That's about seven hundred and fifty percent profit. Not bad. Not for a few days' work."

"Now's about the time that the CEA would get a little curious, wouldn't it?"

"Why? You didn't break any law. Everything perfectly legitimate. Up and up. No law saying your Aunt Gertrude and Cousin Fred can't speculate in the commodity market. It's what makes America great.

Risk-taking. Did you have any inside information? No-sirree-bob, you didn't. You just used your common sense. Hah. Chap I used to know. Put out a news sheet like mine. Gave me the idea, in fact. Odd chap. Absolutely mad. Based his predictions of what the market would do on comic strip. Not kidding. Based it on 'Bringing Up Father.' You know, Maggie and Jiggs. If Jiggs blew one smoke ring, meant market would go up. Two smoke rings, down. If he rode steel beam, like he always did, it meant something else, can't remember now. Funny thing is though, chap was absolutely uncanny in his predictions. Right about ninety-five percent of the time. Marvelous record."

"Jesus," Pope said. "But I thought the CEA was something like the Securities and Exchange Commission. I thought the CEA had everything all screwed down."

"Not at all. In the futures market you do pretty much what you please. CEA staff far too small. CEA depends on exchanges to police themselves. Hah. Fox looking after the chickens. Exchanges controlled by big companies. The companies don't like strangers poking noses in. The brokers want volume. That's all. They make a buck on every trade. The more trades, the more bucks. All very cozy. In stock market you have to have about a seventy percent margin or more. Can't go short in stock market unless stock is on an up tick. Not true in commodities. Down, down, down. Chap in CEA told me they can't stop somebody who wants to corner market. They can only move in after he's cornered it and fleeced millions. Then they slap him on the wrist. Fine him maybe $2,500. Maybe not even that. Issue reprimand. CEA is great at issuing reprimands. Congress very unhappy. They want to make CEA more like

SEC. Might this year. Or next. Who knows? Any questions?"

"Maybe a couple," Pope said. "You'd say then that anyone who got the Department of Agriculture's crop report in advance could probably make a killing, is that right?"

Commodity Jack nodded. "If he coupled it with a good sound rumor, he probably could."

"And there wouldn't be much chance of him getting caught?"

"If he stole the report and got caught redhanded? Be in deep trouble. But if nobody caught him actually stealing it, who's going to prove anything? Unusual question by the way. Very."

"I know," Pope said.

Commodity Jack's blue eyes brightened. His tongue flicked over his lips. He picked up a pencil. "Somebody going to steal the report before it comes out next July eleventh?"

"I don't really know," Pope said.

"Possibility?"

"I don't know that either."

"Rumor? I print rumors. Deal in rumors, in fact."

"Not even that. But thanks very much for all your time. You've been very helpful."

Commodity Jack cocked his head to one side. "You sure you're not thinking about going into commodities yourself?"

"What would you suggest?"

"A cold shower," Commodity Jack said. "Then take a long nap. Maybe it'll go away."

26

DON AND MARCIA GANOR WERE TOO YOUNG TO BE CALLED Mom and Pop, but that was the kind of store they ran over on Sixth Street Southeast on Capitol Hill. Don was twenty-nine and Marcia was twenty-seven and they had a son, Arty, just one and a half, who played quietly and even thoughtfully on the floor with such things as cans of Campbell soup and boxes of Arm & Hammer baking soda.

For a while Don and Marcia had worried about Arty. They thought that he might be a little retarded because he was so quiet. They even took him to a doctor, a specialist, and the doctor had smiled and reassured them that Arty was indeed unusual, he was a "good" baby, and if he didn't cry, it was simply because he didn't want to, not because he was slow.

Don and Marcia called their store Ganor's Market and they kept it open seven days a week. They also extended limited amounts of credit and the people who lived in the neighborhood liked the Ganors and were grateful for the credit, especially just before payday, and although the prices at Ganor's were higher than they were at Safeway, everybody agreed that they sure weren't a ripoff like those at the Seven-Eleven stores.

Holidays such as Thanksgiving and Christmas and the Fourth of July were big volume days for the Ganors and they always stayed open. It wasn't so bad working on holidays because they were together and the profits they cleared those days were put into a special fund which was used for the two-week vacation they took each summer in August. They liked to go to Maine in late August.

It was early on July Fourth, about nine o'clock, when the two blacks came in. Don was behind the front counter at the cash register. Marcia was doing something behind the meat case. Arty was on the floor as usual, fooling around with some small boxes of Fab.

"Gimme a Butterfinger," the taller black said to Don.

"You want a big one or a little one?"

"Big one."

Don turned to where he kept the candy behind the counter. "Big ones are a quarter," he said. When he turned back with the Butterfinger he saw the knife that the taller of the two blacks held. It was a kitchen knife. The smaller black held an automatic pistol. It was aimed at Don.

"Stickup, huh?" Don said.

"Just give us the money," the taller black said.

"Take it easy, man," Don said. "Money's in the cash register. I'll hand it to you or you can get it yourself. No trouble. Just take it easy."

"What's going on?" Marcia called.

"Nothing," Don said.

Marcia didn't like the answer. She started around the meat case, still carrying the long knife that she had been using to trim some of the fat off six T-bone steaks.

The smaller black turned. He saw the knife. "She gotta knife," he said and jerked the trigger of his Spanish-made automatic. There was a small bang, certainly nothing unusual on the Fourth of July, and the .22 long bullet struck Marcia in the throat. She tried to say something but couldn't, because suddenly her throat was full of blood. She stumbled forward and fell to the floor.

"You little son of a bitch," Don said and started around the counter. The taller black struck out at Don with the kitchen knife. It caught him in the arm, but Don didn't seem to notice. "I'm going to kill you, you little son of a bitch," he said to the smaller black who promptly shot him twice with the .22 automatic that had been made in Spain.

The taller of the two blacks jumped behind the cash register. He tried to open it, but couldn't figure out how it worked. He looked wildly around and then grabbed the box of Butterfingers. The smaller of the pair grabbed a quart bottle of Canada Dry ginger ale. They ran out of the store and the door banged closed behind them.

Don Ganor tried to raise himself from the floor and crawl toward his dead wife. He tried once, but failed. The second time he tried, he managed to move a foot before he died. Toward the rear of the store, Arty kept on playing with the small boxes of Fab. He laughed once. He was a good baby.

27

BECAUSE BOTH THE RICH AND THE MERELY WELL-TO-DO sometimes kill each other, it was not the first time that Detective Hugo Worthy had been in one of the big, expensive houses that are located in what is sometimes called the Kalorama Triangle. The base of the triangle is Rock Creek Park and its tip points south toward Dupont Circle. Its east leg is Connecticut Avenue and the west leg is Massachusetts Avenue and about the only people who can afford to buy houses in it are the very rich and the embassies of those countries that pump a lot of oil out of the ground. Worthy wondered how much Ancel Easter had spent for his house and when he had bought it, but he decided not to ask.

Instead, he told Easter most of what he knew about the deaths of the young couple who ran the small grocery market over in southeast Washington and by the time he was through it was past nine o'clock on the evening of the day after the Fourth of July.

"The child wasn't hurt, you say?" Easter said.

Worthy shook his head. "No, he wasn't hurt. The girl's mother has him."

"Well, do you still think winos?"

"I'll be honest with you, Mr. Easter. I don't know

what to think. They didn't get any money as far as we can tell. It was all still in the cash register."

Easter nodded. "You look a little beat. Why don't we have a drink?"

"All right. Thanks."

"Scotch or bourbon?"

"Scotch on the rocks would be fine."

Easter mixed the drinks and then handed Worthy his. "Thanks for coming over this evening," he said. "It was very decent of you."

"It was on my way. You've got a nice place here."

"Too big really for just one person."

"I was in this neighborhood three or four years back on a case. It was a couple of streets over on Tracy Place. Maybe you remember it. Murder and suicide. Nice open and shut case, sort of."

"Their name was Sinder, wasn't it?" Easter said. "He was with the State Department and she had money."

"That's it. She killed him and then killed herself."

"With a handgun."

"Right," Worthy said. "With a .38 special. His gun."

"What was the reason they gave out, ill health? I mean he was in ill health."

"Well, I guess you could call cirrhosis ill health all right. But that wasn't the reason she killed him. He had a few little quirks. That's really why he'd stayed with the State Department so long. He didn't need the money. She had plenty. But he liked to be posted places where he could have young maids. He liked to screw them in front of her. You know, make her watch. She put up with it all those years because she didn't want to harm his career, which is what she thought she'd do if she left him."

"Jesus," Easter said. "Where'd you dig all that up?"

"Her psychiatrist. She went to him for about six months secretly. I mean it was a secret from her husband. The psychiatrist advised her to start thinking about what she could do for herself instead of her husband. So she went home and shot him and then shot herself. The psychiatrist took it pretty hard."

Easter shook his head. "The longer I live the less I think I know about what really goes on inside people."

"They do some real weird things, don't they?"

"Do you ever get used to it?"

Worthy stood up. "I won't say you get used to it. But when the initial shock wears off, you can get a little detached. Well, thanks for the drink."

"And thanks for coming by."

"Like I said, it was on my way."

28

THE ATTACHÉ CASE WAS LOCKED TO THE YOUNG CHINESE'S slender wrist. The young Chinese was Raymond Yu and he was twenty-seven years old and not quite five-foot-nine. The man who walked just behind him and to his left was thirty-four and six-foot-one and his name was John H. Batts and he was a licensed, bonded private detective whose instructions were not to let anything happen to the attaché case—or to Raymond Yu, for that matter.

The commodity brokerage firm of Anderson, Maytubby & Jones was located on the ground floor of the Connecticut Avenue office building that had replaced the National Presbyterian Church where Dwight Eisenhower had liked to pray when he was President. Raymond Yu, closely followed by John H. Batts, walked through the firm's entrance and over to the receptionist who smiled nicely and said, "Yes?"

"I'd like to see Mr. Maytubby," Yu said.

"Do you have an appointment?"

"No," Yu said.

The receptionist looked doubtful. She did that by pursing her darkly painted red lips and making her plucked eyebrows frown. "Mr. Maytubby almost never sees anyone without an appointment," she said. "Perhaps somebody else could help you?" She gestured over her shoulder toward the bull pen where a number of sincere-looking young men sat at small desks and talked earnestly into telephones. Behind them on the wall the projected tape of commodity prices flashed past for the benefit of those customers who sat in the half-dozen or so chairs and gazed at the moving prices with expressions that bordered on religious fervor.

"I'm afraid I must see Mr. Maytubby," Yu said. "My name is Mr. Yu. Y-U. This is my card." He laid the attaché case on the receptionist's desk and nodded at John H. Batts, the private detective. Batts produced a key and unlocked the case and raised its top. The receptionist stared for a moment at the neat, banded stacks of one-hundred-dollar bills. Batts let her stare for a moment longer and then closed the case and relocked it.

"I'll—I'll tell Mr. Maytubby that you're here, Mr. —uh—"

"Yu. Y-U."

The receptionist picked up her telephone, punched two buttons on her console set, and started whispering into the phone. Then she hung up and smiled brightly at Raymond Yu. "Somebody will be here shortly to show you to Mr. Maytubby's office," she said.

"Thank you," Raymond Yu said.

The somebody was Mrs. Ethel Quill who had been Lloyd Maytubby's secretary for fifteen years. Ethel Quill had grey hair, a bleak expression, and hands that shook a little in the morning. "Mr. Yu?" she said.

"Yes."

"This way."

Raymond Yu, with John H. Batts close behind, followed Mrs. Ethel Quinn around the bull pen and through a door that led to her office. John H. Batts looked around the office, grunted, and then moved a chair over next to the door which had a sign on it that said "Mr. Maytubby." Batts sat down in the chair. "I'll be right here," he told Raymond Yu.

"Unlock the case first," Yu said.

"Right." Batts unlocked the case and Raymond Yu followed Mrs. Ethel Quill into the office of Lloyd Maytubby.

It wasn't a big office, but it was nicely furnished with pieces that looked as though they might be real antiques. Lloyd Maytubby looked as though he might be a real antique, too. He had a long wisp of white hair that started growing down near the top of his left ear. He combed it over his head so that it almost reached the top of his right ear. He still looked bald, though. And old. His jowls sagged and there were puffy bags under his brown eyes which were covered by thick, trifocal glasses. A shiny slick of saliva had formed itself at the left end of his small mouth. He licked at it sometimes with a grey tongue, but it didn't seem to do much good.

"You wished to see me," Maytubby said after Mrs. Ethel Quill had made the introductions and left.

"Yes," Raymond Yu said. "I want to open an account with your firm. These are my credentials."

He opened the attaché case and let Maytubby look at the packets of one-hundred-dollar bills. Maytubby poked at them with the eraser end of a yellow pencil as if to see how deeply they were stacked. He looked up at Yu.

"How much?"

"One million dollars."

"And what do you wish to do with this—uh—one million dollars of yours?" Maytubby said and licked at his patch of saliva.

"I want to go long on wheat."

"On wheat?"

"That's right. Wheat."

"That would mean that you'd be going long on approximately—"

"On approximately 1.6 million bushels," Yu said. "That's well within the CEA limit of 2 million bushels."

"Yes," Maytubby said. "You're familiar with the commodity market?"

"I'm familiar with the Commodity Exchange Act's rule that the maximum net long that any party may hold or control in wheat on any one contract is 2 million bushels," Yu said in a curiously mechanical tone as if he had learned it by rote.

"You're an American citizen, Mr. Yu?"

"I don't think that's pertinent, but yes, I'm an American citizen."

"And you're quite certain you wish to do this?"

"Mr. Maytubby, today is July sixth. I want to go long 1.6 million bushels today. On the morning of July eleventh I plan to review my position. Acting on certain information I may then possess, I might wish to go long an additional 400,000 bushels."

"On the morning of July eleventh?" Maytubby said.

"Yes."

"Not the afternoon or the next day?"

"No."

"May I ask what this information will be?"

"I'm not prepared to say at this time," Yu said and smiled. "On the morning of July eleventh I may share it with you. Now then, do you think we can do business?"

Maytubby licked at his patch of saliva again. "Yes, yes, indeed," he said. "I see no reason why we can't. No reason at all. There're some forms to fill out, of course, but yes, indeed, Mr. Yu, I think we can do business."

When Yu had gone, Lloyd Maytubby summoned his two partners to his office. The million dollars was neatly stacked on his desk and Maytubby watched his partners' reactions. The younger partner gasped a little, something like the way a goldfish will gasp when it's taken out of water. The older partner clutched at his heart and made little mewling noises before he said, "What in God's name is that?"

"That," Maytubby said, "is exactly one million dollars. The Chinese are going long on wheat."

"Which Chinese?" the younger partner said. "The Reds or the others?"

"Who gives a damn?" Maytubby said. "But if we don't want to get caught on the sidelines this time, we'd better start getting the word out."

"What do the Chinese know that we don't know?" the younger partner asked.

"How the hell should I know?" Maytubby said. "Maybe they know what the wheat crop in China's going to be. Anyway, he waltzed in here and went long 1.6 million bushels today and then told me that he might go long another 400,000 on July eleventh. On the *morning* of July eleventh."

"Christ," the younger partner said. "You mean he might go long before the report's out?"

"Exactly."

The older partner turned pink and rosy with excitement. "They're going to steal it, aren't they?" he said. "The Chinese are going to steal the crop report."

Maytubby gave his patch of saliva a lick. "I don't know what they're going to do," he said. "But we know what we're going to do, don't we?"

The younger partner nodded. "We're going to make a lot of money."

When Raymond Yu left the firm of Anderson, Maytubby & Jones, the attaché case was still locked to his wrist and John H. Batts was still at his heels. The two men walked south on Connecticut Avenue until they came to the Whelan drugstore. They went inside the store and Raymond Yu entered a telephone booth. He closed the door, dropped a dime, and dialed 0.

When the operator came on Raymond Yu said, "I want to place a collect call, person to person, to Mr. Fulvio Varvesi in Chicago."

The Chinese had been hard to find and Fulvio Varvesi had recruited most of them from the University of California's graduate school at Berkeley. Raymond Yu's call was the last of six similar calls and by the afternoon of July 6th, Fulvio Varvesi had contracted to buy nearly 10 million bushels of September wheat.

Each contract that his Chinese agents had bought for him was for 5,000 bushels. He spent $6 million for margin and with wheat bobbing around the $4-per-bushel price it meant that Varvesi would be playing around with nearly 10 million bushels of wheat worth approximately $40 million.

What Varvesi had done was to enter into legal

and binding contracts that he—through his Chinese agents—would receive and take delivery of 40 million bushels of wheat during the month of September. Varvesi, of course, had no intention of taking delivery of a single bushel. He was going to dump it all, all 10 million bushels, as soon as the price hit $5 a bushel, which would mean that from his investment of $6 million he would realize a net profit of approximately $10 million, which he didn't think was at all bad.

"You see," he said to Ralph Hayes and Jack Sperry after completing his call with Raymond Yu, "it's going to work out just beautifully. The brokerage firms are going to spread the rumor that the Chinese are going long on wheat. God knows what it's going to hit by July eleventh when the crop report comes out. It may already be to four and a half dollars by then what with the same rumor coming out of Washington, New York, Chicago, St. Louis and Kansas City."

"That's where you had the Chinamen buying, right?" Hayes said.

"Right," Varvesi said. "Now on the morning of July eleventh, the Chinamen will walk into the brokerage offices and let them all have an exclusive peek at the crop report. We know that the report's going to predict that there's going to be a short wheat crop this year. What we don't know is how short. But once they get their peek at that report they're going to advise every customer they've got to go long and the price of wheat should go through the ceiling."

"Beautiful," Jack Sperry said. "But you're still sure that none of the brokers will go squealing to the CEA?"

Varvesi shook his head. "I picked ones who're

known for their greed. If they see a chance to make a killing, they're not going to tell anybody how they made it."

"And the Chinamen?"

"They're not going to talk either. Each one of them's getting ten thousand bucks for a few hours' work. They won't talk."

"How about the Congressman?" Sperry said.

"That's a different story," Varvesi said. "He's getting antsy. I think you'd better go on down to Omaha and take care of him."

"Okay," Sperry said.

"Then you'd better go from there down to Washington and get in touch with this guy deGraffenreid. Explain to him how things are. That the Congressman's no longer in the picture. Make sure deGraffenreid's got everything else set up, too."

"We'll be in Washington until when, do you think?" Ralph Hayes asked.

"Until when?" Varvesi said. "Until wheat hits five dollars a bushel, that's when."

Ex-Congressman Kyle Tarr met Ralph Hayes and Jack Sperry at the airport in Omaha when they got off the United flight from Chicago. Sperry and Tarr stood around making small talk while Hayes used a stolen driver's license from Utah and a fake Carte Blanche credit card to rent a four-door Plymouth sedan from Avis.

"We could've used my car," Tarr said. "It's parked right outside."

"This makes it simpler." Sperry said.

"How's it make it simpler? We go downtown and

get a steak and a couple of drinks and then I have to come all the way back out here to pick up my car."

"We gotta couple of things to do downtown," Sperry said.

"Why don't I follow you down then?" Tarr said. "Then I wouldn't have to come all the way back out here."

"Then we couldn't talk on the way down," Sperry said. "You don't wanta talk in a restaurant, do you?"

"Nobody has to overhear us, not if we don't yell at each other."

"We're not going to yell at each other. We haven't got anything to yell about."

"Well, I still don't see why I couldn't just follow you downtown so I wouldn't have to drive all the way back out here."

"Do it our way, Tarr, will you, please? Just do it our way."

Tarr was still grumbling when he got into the Plymouth's front seat. Ralph Hayes drove. Jack Sperry, the former karate teacher, sat in the back seat.

Hayes found the exit road from the airport and got on the highway. Tarr was still grumbling about having to drive all the way back to the airport. Sperry looked behind them to make sure that no cars were coming. Then he used the edge of his right hand and broke ex-Congressman Tarr's neck with it.

Hayes didn't look at Tarr. "Is he dead?"

"He's dead," Sperry said.

"Okay," Hayes said and pulled the car over to the side of the highway. He got out and went around to the rear and opened the trunk. Then he went around the right side and helped Sperry carry Tarr's body back and put it into the trunk. Hayes closed the lid of the trunk, made sure that it was locked, and then got back behind the wheel. Sperry got in beside him.

Hayes drove until he came to a spot in the highway where he could turn around and then headed back for the airport. He parked the car in the lot and then he and Sperry went up to the TWA counter and bought two tickets to Baltimore. They paid cash. They had an hour to wait. While they were waiting, Sperry said, "How long do you think before somebody'll find him?"

Hayes shrugged. "A week maybe."

Sperry nodded. "Yeah, that's how long it took last time, a week."

29

JAKE POPE SAT SLUMPED DEEP IN A CHAIR, A DRINK BALanced on his chest. His feet were up on Ancel Easter's desk. It was the evening of July 7th and almost everyone but the most senior partner of Gilmore, Easter, Timothy, and Stern had gone home. The most senior partner was seated behind his desk telling Jake Pope what was known about the deaths of a young couple who had operated a Mom and Pop grocery in southeast Washington.

"And that's all?" Pope said. "I mean that's all that Worthy knew?"

"That's all," Easter said. "Although there is the other thing."

"What?"

"He called me today. He wanted to know how much I'd charge to handle his divorce."

"What'd you tell him?"

"I told him that I didn't take on much divorce work anymore, but that we had somebody here in the firm who'd be glad to talk to him, and for him not to worry about how much it would cost."

"You're a saint, aren't you?"

"Just a candidate."

Pope swallowed the last of his drink, swung his feet to the floor, and stood up. He put his glass down on a copy of the *Wall Street Journal*. "Well," he said, "I'll go see Hucks."

"He's not going to like it."

"No. Neither will his wife."

"Who're you going to be?"

"I guess I'll be Jake Pope, private eye. I've still got my old credentials from the Whetstone firm out in L.A. I can flash those at him."

"Well," Easter said, "I guess it's all right if you take her along."

"Faye?"

"Yes. Who's she going to be?"

"Faye Hix, my loyal and trusted associate. Sidekick. Deputy private eye. Hell, I don't know. She's going to be the corroborating witness if Hucks says anything worth corroborating. You said I was going to need one."

"I said you'd need some corroborating evidence. Why don't you strap a tape recorder on your leg or something?"

"I never could work those things," Pope said.

"What did Mrs. Hix say when you asked her?"

"She said she thought it sounded like it might be fun."

When Pope and Faye Hix drew up in front of the home of Dr. and Mrs. Dallas Hucks in Fairfax, Pope cut the engine and switched off his lights. It was 8:35 P.M.

"They're home, aren't they?" Faye Hix said.

"It looks that way. Were you hoping they wouldn't be?"

"A little, I guess."

"You can wait out here."

"No, I'll go through with it. What am I supposed to look like?"

"Like yourself."

"I mean what am I?"

"You remember all those prison matrons you see in the jailbreak films?"

"Uh-huh."

"Look like them."

"Stern visaged," she said. "Sort of dykish."

"Right."

They got out of the car and made their way up to the front door. Pope pushed the door bell. Chimes sounded somewhere in the house. They were one-tone chimes. When nothing happened, Pope pushed the door bell again. This time the door opened, but not much. Amelia Hucks had come to the door. She didn't looks as if she were expecting company.

"Yes?" she said.

"Hello, Mrs. Hucks," Pope said. "Remember me? Jake Pope. I was in your group therapy the other day. Thursday. I'd like to see your husband."

"I—I don't understand," Amelia Hucks said. "You were in group and now you want to see my husband. I don't understand why you want to see him."

"I think he's in trouble, Mrs. Hucks," Pope said and smiled.

"Trouble? What kind of trouble?"

"I think I'd better talk to him first."

The confusion that had spread itself over Amelia Hucks's face was replaced by alarm. Her eyes widened and she bit her lip. She bit it hard. "You're not going to tell him about what I said in group Thursday, are you? You're not going to tell him about that?"

"I think you'd better tell him I'm here."

"Who is it, Amelia?" It was Dallas Hucks's voice, calling from somewhere in the house.

"It's somebody here to see you. A man. And his wife."

"I'm not his wife," Faye Hix said.

"That's right. You said your wife was dead, didn't you?" Amelia Hucks said.

"This is Mrs. Hix. My associate."

Dr. Dallas Hucks appeared at his wife's side. He didn't look as if he were expecting company either. He wore old khaki pants and a blue shirt. On his feet were white sneakers without socks.

"Yes?" he said. "What is it?"

"I'm Jake Pope, Dr. Hucks. I'd like to talk to you."

"What about?"

"About Noah deGraffenreid for one thing."

"He was in group," Amelia Hucks said. "He said he was depressed because his wife was dead."

"What'd you tell him?" Hucks said to his wife. His tone was harsh, almost mean.

"I didn't tell him anything," she said, but Amelia Hucks didn't lie too well.

"I don't think your neighbors need to hear all this," Pope said. "May we come in?"

"I don't have to talk to you," Hucks said.

"No, you don't. But I think you'd better."

"Well, all right," Hucks said after a moment. "We might as well get it over with."

He led the way. Faye Hix was next, followed by Pope. Amelia Hucks brought up the rear. She was chewing on her lower lip now.

"Sit down anywhere," Hucks said and lowered himself into a tan easy chair. Pope sat on the living room's couch. Faye Hix sat beside him. Amelia Hucks started to sit down on a straightbacked chair, but her husband said, "I don't think you need to hear any of this, Amelia."

"I think she does," Pope said. "Sit down, Mrs. Hucks."

Amelia Hucks looked at her husband who shrugged. She sat down on the straightbacked chair. She was wearing blue jeans and a white shirt, but she sat on the chair primly, her knees close together, not much hope on her face, like a girl who knows that nobody's ever going to ask her to dance.

"Who are you anyway?" Hucks said.

Pope reached inside his jacket and produced the black folding case that Judge John Whetstone had given him years before. There was a picture of Pope and a reproduction of his license to be a private investigator, but it had expired long ago. He held it out anyway. "I'm a private investigator. The name's Pope, Jake Pope. This is Mrs. Hix, my associate."

Hucks didn't reach for the folding case so Pope put it back in his pocket. "All right," Hucks said, "what do you want?"

"How well do you know Noah deGraffenreid?" Pope said.

"Not well," Hucks said. "I've met him."

"You know what he does?"

"He's in the antique business."

"You ever borrow any money from him?"

"No."

"You sure?"

"Of course, I'm sure. I know who I borrow money from."

"You know anybody else who's borrowed money from him?"

"No. Nobody."

"Did you know that deGraffenreid makes a business of lending money to people?"

"No."

"Do you know he's a loan shark? You know what a loan shark is, don't you?"

"Yes, but I don't know that he's one."

"Do you know that deGraffenreid's also a fence? You also know what a fence is, don't you? A fence is a receiver of stolen property. In deGraffenreid's case, stolen antiques. He sells them through his shop."

"I don't know that he's a fence."

"Take my word for it," Pope said.

"Why should I take your word for it?"

"So you can stay out of trouble, that's why. How much money do you owe?"

"That's none of your business either."

"You owe around twenty-two thousand, don't you? That's not including the two mortgages you've got on your house. Twenty-two thousand dollars is a lot of money."

"But it's still none of your business. Are you from a finance company?"

"No. I'm not from a finance company. How are you going to pay off this twenty-two thousand—with the hundred thousand you're going to get from deGraffenreid?"

There was nothing but venom in the look that Hucks shot at his wife, but she didn't see it. She was looking at her toes. "I don't know what you're talking about," Hucks said.

"I understand that you and deGraffenreid have a hundred-thousand-dollar deal going. What is it, stolen antique furniture?"

"There is no deal."

"That's not what your wife says. Your wife says after the deal between you and deGraffenreid goes through, and you get the hundred thousand, you're going to give her half and then throw her out, isn't that right, Mrs. Hucks?"

Amelia Hucks kept staring at her toes. She shook her head.

"My wife lies a great deal," Hucks said. "She lies to get attention. She's even going to a psychiatrist because of this and some other problems she's having. You do lie, don't you, Amelia?"

Amelia Hucks still didn't look up. "Yes," she whispered. "I lie."

"Those bruises she has on her face," Pope said. "Did you do that to her?"

"Do you mean have I stopped beating my wife?"

"Something like that."

"She fell. You fell, didn't you, Amelia?"

"Yes," Amelia whispered, still fascinated by her toes. "I fell."

"What happens on July eleventh?" Pope said.

"I don't know," Hucks said. "I don't know of anything that's going to happen on—when did you say, July eleventh?"

"That's right. July eleventh."

"It doesn't mean anything to me."

"It doesn't?"

"No."

"I thought that's when deGraffenreid was going to pay you the hundred thousand."

"There is no hundred thousand."

"I keep forgetting," Pope said. "You work at the Department of Agriculture, don't you."

"You seem to know everything else, why ask that?"

"You like your job?"

"Yes, I like my job."

"You're a GS-14, aren't you?"

"Yes."

"What happens at the Department of Agriculture on July eleventh?"

"A lot of things are going on there all the time."

"But I thought something special happened on the eleventh?"

"No. Nothing special."

"Isn't that when they put out the estimate on wheat and corn?"

"Yes, they put that out on the eleventh."

Pope was watching Hucks carefully. But there was nothing yet. Hucks's eyes weren't blinking too fast. He wasn't sweating. He wasn't massaging his hands together or fidgeting or squirming about. He was meeting Pope's gaze easily as he lay slumped back in the tan easy chair. He almost seems to be enjoying it, Pope thought. Maybe he thinks it's a contest, a battle of wits. Well, maybe it is.

"I thought that was a pretty important report."

"What do you mean important?"

"Well, they go into a lockup condition down there, don't they? They seal off part of the department. Cut off the phones. And then at five o'clock in the morning they come down and open the box where the reports have been collected. Isn't that what they do?"

"That's right."

"There're two keys to that box, aren't there?"

"Yes. There're two keys to it."

"And you've got one of them."

"That's right."

"What would happen if somebody got to the box early? What if somebody got all that information on what the wheat crop or the corn crop is going to be, could they sell it?"

"That's impossible."

"You mean to sell it?"

"To get the information. It's held under very tight security."

"About the tightest in Washington, isn't it?"

"Yes."

"It would almost have to be an inside job, wouldn't it? I mean to get that information."

"It's all in code anyway," Hucks said. "Even if somebody got it, it wouldn't do them any good unless they could decipher the code."

"Where do they keep the code—I mean the key to the code?"

"In the Secretary's office."

"You mean in his office in a safe there?"

"No, it's under his control though. His jurisdiction."

"You work in the Secretary's office. I mean in the executive section."

"Yes."

"You're an Assistant to the Assistant Deputy Director for Programming, aren't you? That's a pretty impressive title. Does that mean you have access to the code?"

"That's classified information."

"That means you do have access," Pope said. "Well, now, let's see. You have one of the keys to the mailbox where the reports are kept. You have access to the code. So if it were going to be an inside job, you'd be a pretty likely candidate, wouldn't you?"

"Nobody's going to steal those reports. It's impossible."

"Okay, it's impossible. But let's just pretend that somebody stole them. How much do you think they would bring? Just a guess."

"I don't know."

"A hundred thousand dollars?"

"I don't know."

"That's what Noah deGraffenreid's going to pay you for them, isn't it?"

Hucks stood up. "I think that's about enough. You can leave now. Anytime."

Pope didn't move. He yawned instead, or pretended to. Then he stretched. "On June twenty-eighth. You remember June twenty-eighth, don't you?"

"I said you can leave now," Hucks said. "I'm not going to answer any more of your questions, so you might as well go."

"On June twenty-eighth you had dinner at the Cosmos Club with Noah deGraffenreid, didn't you?"

"No more answers."

"You don't have to answer it. The club records say you did. Some time during the evening you and de Graffenreid went into the men's room. You or de-Graffenreid looked under the toilet doors to see whether you were alone. You then proceeded to enter into a conspiracy in which you agreed to sell information to deGraffenreid. The price was one hundred thousand dollars. The information was to be the gist of the Department of Agriculture's July eleventh prediction of what this year's wheat and corn crop will be. Now this is all fact, Hucks. This I know and can prove. So I've only got one more question."

"Get out!"

"What are you and deGraffenreid going to rig, corn or wheat?"

"Get the fuck out of my house!" Hucks yelled.

Pope still didn't move. "Wheat?" he said.

Hucks strode over to his fireplace, seized a poker, and turned toward Pope. "If you're not out of here in five seconds, I'm going go wrap this thing around your neck."

"I think he wants us to go," Pope said and got up. Faye Hix also rose. "Well, thanks for all your cooperation," Pope said. "You ought to call deGraffenreid, you know. Tell him I dropped by."

"You've got two seconds," Huck said.

"We're going," Pope said. "Good night, Mrs. Hucks."

Amelia Hucks didn't look up. She continued to sit quite still on the straightbacked chair, her knees together, her hands clasped in her lap, her head down. She seemed to be very interested in her toes.

Outside in the car Jake Pope put the key in the ignition, but he didn't start the engine. "He's going to steal it," he said.

"How do you know?" Faye Hix said.

Pope shrugged. "I just know."

"Back in there, is that what you used to do for a living?" she said.

"Something like that."

"I don't think I would have liked you then. I didn't like you in there."

"Did you like him?"

"No. I didn't like him, but I felt sorry for her."

"How'd you feel when he picked up the poker?"

"I was scared. Weren't you?"

"Yeah, I was scared."

"What are you going to do about it?"

"About him? I'm going to tell Easter and let Easter fix it. It's up in Easter's league now."

"Can he fix it?"

"I don't know."

"What if he can't?"

Pope shrugged. "Then I might go long on September wheat."

30

THE SECRETARY OF AGRICULTURE KEPT AN OLD DOG IN his office, a huge mutt that was the result of the improbable mating of an Irish wolfhound with an English sheepdog. The dog, whose name was Brewstie, sometimes farted at staff meetings and the Secretary would draw on his large and carefully assembled stock of barnyard humor to make some awful joke, which everyone dutifully laughed at.

The Cabinet member who presided over one of the largest of the Federal bureaucracies was Fred C. Clapperton and he always used his middle initial as though afraid that he might be mixed up with some other Fred Clapperton. He was the product of the Midwest, Iowa to be precise, and he had been born and reared in Des Moines, which is not exactly a hamlet, although he always liked to refer to himself as a country boy.

He was also the product of Cornell University and the checkerboard square company, which is to agribusiness what General Motors is to the auto industry. Clapperton had studied his agricultural economics at Cornell and he had put what he had learned into practice for the checkerboard square people who had appreciated his no-nonsense approach to the business of agriculture. For Secretary Clapperton was convinced that farming is no longer a way of life, if it ever was, but a business that should be run exactly like any other business, and those small farmers who couldn't hack it without hanging on to the Government tit should get out of it and go get jobs up in Detroit or someplace. The Secretary preached his philosophy up and down the land and as a result he was the darling of the American Farm Bureau Federation, the Chamber of Commerce, the National Association of Manufacturers, the commodity traders, and others who have a deep and tender concern for those who produce the nation's food and fiber.

About the only thing that Ancel Easter knew about agriculture is that food didn't taste the way it had when he was a boy. Easter was cooling his heels, an expression he had never quite fully understood, in the Secretary of Agriculture's outer office on the afternoon of July 8th. So he had time to reflect about what he knew of the business of farming and concluded that it was virtually nil, except that in some instances a farm could serve as a valuable tax shelter.

Easter had met with Jake Pope at eight o'clock that same morning. Pope had described his session the night before with Dr. Dallas Hucks.

"He didn't crack?" Easter had asked.

"If I'd had just one more little piece of the puzzle, he might have."

"But you didn't and he didn't."

"No."

"It's all pretty circumstantial evidence."

"So is a trout in the milk."

"Thoreau, right?"

"Right."

Easter sighed. "Well, since we're a little short on facts, maybe he'll be impressed by my brilliant presentation."

"And your obvious sincerity," Pope had said, "Don't forget that."

"I won't," Easter had said as he reached for the telephone.

His first call hadn't been to the Secretary of Agriculture. Although Easter had met Fred C. Clapperton upon several occasions, they had not exactly warmed to each other. So Easter called the chairman of the Senate Agriculture Committee and the Senator had called the Secretary and informed him that he would deem it a great courtesy if he would take time from his busy schedule to grant Easter an appointment.

The appointment had been set for 3 P.M. and at 3:20 Easter was still waiting. At 3:25 Secretary Clapperton had asked his executive assistant what was next on the schedule.

"Ancel Easter. He's waiting."

"Now there's a city slicker, if I ever met one. You know what he wants?"

"No idea."

"Philadelphia lawyer, too," the Secretary said.

"I think he went to Harvard."

"That's just as bad. Well, get him in here."

After Easter was ushered in and after the two men had shaken hands and exchanged meaningless pleasantries, the Secretary said, "What can I do for you, Mr. Easter?"

"I have reason to be convinced, Mr. Secretary, that certain parties both within and without your department are trying to arrange a money harvest."

"What the hell's a money harvest?"

"I think you would agree that that's what happens whenever somebody succeeds in rigging the commodity market."

"You're saying somebody's out to rig the market?"

"That's right."

The Secretary leaned back in his highbacked chair and put one foot up on his desk. "That's pretty hard to do nowadays. I don't say it's impossible. I just say it's a pretty hard thing to do. We keep those jaspers on pretty short rein. Let me ask you this. How they going to do it?"

"As the result of a rather careful private investigation, I am convinced that they will have advance access to your July eleventh crop report."

Clapperton snorted. "That's like saying somebody's going to steal the gold out of Fort Knox. I don't want to brag, but we run a pretty tight ship around here when that crop report comes out. Why, I even had the FBI come over and go over it for us. They gave us an A-number-one rating."

"I appreciate the security measures that you've taken," Easter said. "However, I'm convinced that an employee within your department has devised a method of circumventing them."

"You got his name?"

"I do."

"Well, you gonna give it to me?"

"His name is Dallas Hucks."

Clapperton took his leg off his desk long enough to

write the name down on a yellow legal pad. His big dog farted and Clapperton laughed. "By God, Brewstie, we'll need to light a match after that one." He leaned back in his chair and put his foot up on his big desk again.

"Well, that's a pretty serious charge to level against somebody, Mr. Easter."

"I realize that."

"This fellow—what's his name—"

"Hucks," Easter said.

"Yeah, Hucks. I never heard of him. What's he do?"

"He's an economist, I believe."

"Not Schedule C, is he?" Schedule C was the designation given to political appointees.

"No, he's Civil Service. A GS-14, I understand."

"And he's gonna steal the crop report and do what, take a flyer in the market?"

"I have reason to believe that he intends to sell it."

"For how much?"

"For one hundred thousand dollars."

"Shit, he oughta be able to get more'n that for it."

"The person to whom he plans to sell it is Noah deGraffenreid."

The Secretary took his foot down from his desk. "Never heard of him either." He picked up his pencil again. "That Noah like Noah in the Bible?"

"Yes."

"How do you spell that last name?" Easter spelled it for him.

"What's this fellow deGraffenreid do, he a trader?"

"He's an antique dealer," Easter said. "He's also a loan shark and quite probably a fence."

"Doesn't sound like he'd know much about how to rig a commodity," the Secretary said. "That's a pretty ticklish business."

"It may be that deGraffenreid is merely the Washington contact for others."

"Now we're getting down to business," the Secretary said. "Who's this deGraffenreid fronting for?"

"I don't know."

The Secretary sighed, took out his corncob pipe and filled it from a can of Prince Albert. He doesn't have a pipesmoker's face, Easter thought. He'd like to look folksy, but his eyes are too sly. He's got a banker's eyes, and a sheriff's mouth, and a preacher's nose.

"You don't know?" the Secretary said.

"No. I don't."

"You just *think* he might be working for somebody else?"

"That's right."

"You got any hard evidence that this fellow—uh—Hucks is planning to make off with the crop report?"

"Purely hearsay. I might add, Mr. Secretary, that I wouldn't have asked for this meeting if I'd had sufficient evidence. I would have turned it over to the Justice Department. What I'm doing is presenting to you the results of a rather careful investigation. This investigation has convinced me that Dallas Hucks plans to obtain and to sell information contained in the July eleventh crop report."

"Let me ask you something else. Let me ask you how come you got mixed up in investigating one of this department's employees?"

"It was brought to my attention by my former partner, Mr. William Gilmore."

"Crawdad Gilmore?"

"That's right."

"He died just a while back."

"Yes, he did."

"Pretty old man, wasn't he?"

"Ninety-three."

"So where'd he get the notion that somebody was going to rig the commodity market?"

"Mr. Secretary, Mr. Gilmore didn't get the notion, as you put it, that somebody was going to rig the commodity market. Certain information came to his attention, he relayed it to me, and I had an investigation carried out."

"Took a lot on yourself, I'd say."

"Yes, I suppose I did."

"Well, I'll tell you what I'll do, I'll take this matter under advisement. But I'm pretty sure that nobody's going to be able to bust our security. We had the FBI check it out, you know."

"So you told me. I might add only one other thing, Mr. Secretary. Should it come to light later that someone has actually succeeded in rigging the commodity market through access to the crop report, I would feel it incumbent upon me to advise the proper authorities that you had been given the facts of my investigation."

"In other words, you're gonna tell em that you told me so."

"I would feel obligated to."

"Well, now, I'm gonna tell you something, Mr. Easter. I do appreciate your taking time off from what must be a mighty busy schedule to come down here and tell me how to run the Department of Agriculture, but we're sort of country down here, we like to run our own shop, so if I don't exactly panic over what you've just told me, I hope you'll understand."

Easter rose. The dog farted again. "Thank you for your time, Mr. Secretary."

"Don't mention it," Fred C. Clapperton said.

When Easter had gone, the Secretary summoned his executive assistant. "What's next?"

"You have to give that award to that 4-H kid."

"Aw shit," the Secretary said. "Ever hear of somebody called—wait a second—Dallas Hucks?"

"No, should I?"

"He's a GS-14, works around here someplace. You might check him out. Wouldn't do any harm, I guess."

"What do I check him out for?"

"That fancy lawyer thinks he's gonna steal the crop report."

"Sweet Christ," the executive assistant said.

"That's what I thought."

"Where'd Easter get that idea?"

"Said he got it off his ninety-three-year-old partner who got himself killed a couple of weeks ago."

"Ninety-three?"

"Ninety-three."

"Well," the executive assistant said, "I'll check it out."

"Don't bust your ass."

"Don't worry," the executive assistant said, "I won't."

31

THEY DECIDED TO STEAL THE CROP REPORT A DAY EARLY. It was Noah deGraffenreid's idea really. He came up with it after Dallas Hucks had called him in panic about the visit that he had received from Jake Pope.

"He knows," Hucks had said. "We can't go through with it now. He sat there and told me that I was going to steal it and that he knew I was going to steal it and how much you were going to pay me for it. It's all off. I'm just not going to take the risk."

In low, precise tones that were almost soothing, deGraffenreid explained to Hucks just what bones would be broken in what particular order unless he went through with the theft of the report. "You might walk again with a cane, but it would be a very long time before you did."

"But he knows!" Hucks said.

"He knows you're going to try to steal it on the eleventh."

"He knows everything."

DeGraffenreid ignored him. He was thinking. "Actually, all that information is there now, isn't it? I mean they mail it in from the states on the first so the eleventh is really just an arbitrary date, isn't that right?"

"It's usually all there by the third or the fourth," Hucks said.

"Then you can steal it tonight, can't you, before the lockup conditions go into effect?"

"But I tell you he knows—"

"He won't know anything," deGraffenreid said. "He'll never be able to prove anything. I assure you, Dr. Hucks, if I thought there was any danger of your getting caught, I would certainly call it off. Because if you were to be caught, I'd be implicated two seconds later. Somehow I have the feeling that you talk too much. Far too much."

"I told you how somebody overheard us in the men's room—"

"We've been all over that. Let's concentrate on what we're going to do, not what we've done. Is there any reason why we can't obtain the information tonight?"

Hucks thought for a moment. "No," he said finally. "None."

"All right, then just move everything up a day."

"I'll still meet you at the same place?"

"Exactly," deGraffenreid said.

"If I'm late, you'll know I've been caught."

"You're not going to be caught," deGraffenreid said.

DeGraffenreid recognized the voice when it came over the phone in his antique shop on Wisconsin Avenue. It was the voice that had called him the previous day to inform him that ex-Congressman Tarr was no longer "in the picture." DeGraffenreid hadn't asked what had happened to Congressman Tarr. He decided that it would neither be polite nor smart.

The voice belonged to Ralph Sperry. It was Sperry who had informed deGraffenreid that everything would proceed according to schedule with the exception, of course, of ex-Congressman Tarr's participation. Sperry hadn't thought it necessary to inform deGraffenreid that Tarr lay folded up with a broken neck in the trunk of a rented car at the Omaha airport.

"You'll be dealing directly through us from now on," Sperry had said.

"How will I get in touch with you if something should happen?"

"You think anything's going to happen?"

"Well, no, but—"

"We'll be in touch with you. When you get the stuff, you'll bring it to the airport at six A.M. We're going to fly it to wherever it has to be flown."

"How'll I recognize you?"

"You think you need to recognize us?"

"Well, I was just thinking—"

"We'll do the thinking from now on. When you get to the airport, go to the first pay phone on the right like you were going to take a shuttle to New York, okay?"

"Yes."

"We're gonna tape a locker key underneath the phone. Put the report in the locker, take your money out, and then put the key back where you got it. Clear?"

"Clear."

"Okay. Now we'll be calling you every two hours from now on, just to make sure everything's going okay. If you got any problems, we'll talk 'em over."

So when Ralph Sperry had called just after de-Graffenreid had finished talking with Dallas Hucks, deGraffenreid said, "We have a problem, but I think I've already resolved it."

"What kind of a problem?" Sperry said.

"There's some sort of investigator on Hucks's tail."

"Shit," Sperry said.

"No need to worry. We'll simply obtain the information one day early. The investigator thinks that everything's going to happen on July eleventh. We'll make it happen on July tenth instead."

Sperry thought it over for a moment. "Yeah," he said. "I like it. I like it very much. July tenth's tomorrow, isn't it?"

"It's tonight, really," deGraffenreid said.

The executive assistant to the Secretary of Agriculture called his secretary into his office and started going through some notes that he had made to himself. There was one note that puzzled him. It read, "Dallas Hucks—look into—July 11th."

"Oh, yeah," he told his secretary. "Get in touch with personnel. Get me their file on Dr. Dallas Hucks. I think he's a GS-14."

"When do you want it?" the secretary said.

"What's today?"

"The ninth."

"Tomorrow will be okay."

After Jake Pope got through hearing about Ancel Easter's meeting with the Secretary of Agriculture, he said, "You don't sound as if you're exactly delighted."

"I'm not," Easter said. "I have the feeling that I blew it, although I can't think of what else I could have said. I even made him a mild threat."

"Do you think he'll move on it?"

"Perhaps. But it's nothing we can count on."

"I think," Pope said, "that it's time for me to shift my attention from the thief to the fence."

"To deGraffenreid."

"Right. I think I'll nose around today and see whether there's anything new that I can find out. Then I'll start sticking pretty close to him."

"Let me know," Easter said.

"If I get anything startling, I'll call you," Pope said and hung up the phone after saying good-bye.

The Department of Agriculture is composed of two buildings that sit astride the lower end of Independence Avenue between 14th and 12th Streets, just south of the Mall. They are dull-looking buildings without much architectural style, although they do give off an air of lasting solidity, which is probably all that can be expected from Government buildings.

It had been a long day for Dr. Dallas Hucks. He had arrived at the department at his usual time in the morning, at 8:30. Somehow, he had got through the day, mostly by shuffling papers from one side of his desk to the other. At 5 P.M., his secretary had come in to say that she was leaving. He told her good night and said that he would be staying on for a while. A while had lasted for nearly five hours.

At 9:45 Dallas Hucks left his office on the second floor of the South Building and made his way to the locker room in the basement. The locker room was used by the Government Service Administration guards. They kept their coats there along with their dinners, which most of them brought to work. Hucks went quickly down the row of lockers until he came to the one that was number A-13. He opened it, took out the Thermos flask, twisted off its top, and dropped in the red and blue capsule that had been given to him by Noah de-Graffenreid. Hucks didn't know what was in the red and blue capsule. He really hadn't wanted to know.

When he screwed the cap back on the Thermos, he noticed the name that was taped on it. The name was that of its owner, Collin Strong.

Collin Strong was forty-three and he had been a GSA guard at the Department of Agriculture for three years. This was the third time that he had drawn the assignment of guarding the mailbox in which the crop estimates were kept. Collin Strong was a heavy man, almost fat, and he liked the assignment because it let him sit down for his entire eight-hour shift. Strong liked the four to midnight shift because it meant that his wife was always asleep by the time he got home. Collin Strong didn't much like his wife.

At ten o'clock on the dot, Collin Strong would leave the mailbox unguarded for just long enough to go back to his locker in another area of the basement and get his dinner. He would bring his dinner back and eat it while seated next to the mailbox. For three years, his dinner had consisted of exactly the same thing: a Thermos of coffee; two Spam sandwiches, and a piece of homemade pie.

That night Collin Strong followed his usual routine exactly. At ten he fetched his dinner from his locker. By 10:20 he had screwed the top back on his now empty Thermos flask and put it inside the brown paper sack. By ten forty-three he was fast asleep having ingested approximately 320 milligrams of phenobarbital.

At 10:45 Dallas Hucks left his office and made his way to the mailbox. The first key he used was the one whose custody he had been charged with. The second key was the one that had been made by the locksmith six weeks ago. The locksmith, an acquaintance of Noah deGraffenreid, had met Hucks at the Independence Avenue entrance to the department. He had been wear-

ing a uniform with Acme Locksmith Company written
on its back in red letters. He had also been carrying a
tool kit.

The locksmith had followed Hucks down to the
basement. Hucks had pointed at the mailbox. Then he
had left. The locksmith had gone to work on the lock
while Government workers flowed past him. They had
seen the man working on the mailbox and although
some of them knew that it was the same box that was
kept tightly guarded when lockup rules were in effect,
each assumed that the locksmith was now there because
he had every right to be there.

The locksmith, after finishing his work, had turned
the key over to Noah deGraffenreid who had turned it
over to Dallas Hucks who was now opening the mailbox. Collin Strong stirred, muttered something in his
sleep, and Hucks paused. When he was sure that Strong
was not going to wake up, he opened the mailbox and·
removed the 44 red-X envelopes. He quickly put them
into a briefcase, locked the mailbox and left.

Hucks made his way back up to his office. He
opened the briefcase on his desk. He removed the envelopes. Then from the bottom of his desk he took the
third item that Noah deGraffenreid had given him. It
looked like an aerosol spray can, except that it had an
almost razor-thin bill attached to the spray part. Hucks
held up his left hand and aimed the bill-like thing at it.
He pushed down on the button on the top of the can
and jerked back his left hand. A jet of hot steam had
hit the hand, almost scalding it.

Hucks took the first envelope from his briefcase.
They were Manila envelopes, eight by ten inches, and
they had a large red X printed across their fronts. Hucks
inserted the thin bill of the aerosol-like can underneath

the lip of the flap on the back of the envelope. He pushed the button. The hot steam shot underneath the flap. Slowly, Hucks peeled it back. He removed the contents of the envelope and hurried across the hall. The Xerox machine was already on. Hucks Xeroxed the contents of the envelope, returned to his office, and replaced the original material in the red-X envelope. He then resealed the still sticky flap and looked at his watch. The entire operation had taken 37 seconds.

Hucks did exactly the same thing to the other 43 envelopes. He then replaced them in his briefcase and headed back for the basement. Collin Strong, he saw, was still asleep in his chair. Hucks unlocked the mailbox, replaced the envelopes, re-locked the two locks, stood up, and looked at his watch. The theft had taken 31 minutes.

Hucks reached out and started shaking Strong by the shoulder. The man came awake slowly, fighting his way out of the drugged sleep.

"You were asleep," Hucks said.

"Huh—huh—who you?"

"I have one of the keys to this box," Hucks said. "I was working late so I just thought I'd check on it. You were asleep."

"Asleep—I wasn't asleep."

"You were sound asleep," Hucks said. "What's your name?"

"Strong. It's Collin Strong."

"I'm going to have to report this, Mr. Strong."

"This is the first time it's ever happened. I've been working here three years and I swear it's the first time it's ever happened."

"Well, I don't know," Hucks said. "Maybe we can forget it this time. But I certainly wouldn't mention the fact to anyone that someone found you asleep down here."

The guard shook his head. "I don't know what happened. I sure won't tell nobody." He shook his head again. "I sure don't know what happened."

"You fell asleep," Hucks said. "That's what happened."

Dallas Hucks signed out of the Department of Agriculture at exactly 12:05 A.M. on the morning of July 10th. He got his car out of the lot and drove north on 14th Street. On K Street he turned left, and then right again on 15th Street. At R Street, he turned left again and followed it to Connecticut Avenue. He turned north on Connecticut Avenue and drove until he came to the Taft Bridge. Just before he got to it, however, he turned right on Belmont, found a place to park, got out of his car, and made his way back up the steeply sloping street to Connecticut Avenue.

He saw the figure of the man standing halfway across Taft Bridge on its east side. He started toward the figure, carrying his briefcase. When he was about forty feet away, he saw that it was Noah deGraffenreid. Hucks increased his pace.

DeGraffenreid was leaning casually on the bridge railing. He smiled at Hucks. "Everything went all right, I see."

"Perfectly," Hucks said and patted the briefcase.

"The key to the code's in there, too?"

"Everything. It went as smooth as silk."

"Well, I have something for you," deGraffenreid said. "Some money."

"It's about time."

DeGraffenreid started the swing as soon as his hand

left his jacket pocket. The short iron pipe struck Hucks on the left temple. He staggered, stunned, and almost fell. DeGraffenreid caught him by the crotch and rolled him up and over the side of Taft Bridge, a favorite site for Washington suicides. Hucks screamed all the way down and it was a long way down, almost ten stories.

Noah deGraffenreid looked around, picked up the briefcase, and started walking slowly north on Taft Bridge.

32

THE TWO BLACK KILLERS OF CRAWDAD GILMORE WERE
out early on the morning of July 10th. It was just after
dawn as they walked down the west side of Wisconsin
Avenue on the edge of Georgetown. On the east side of
Wisconsin was a Safeway store and the Schrader Sound
Company. On the west side was a row of narrow houses
that had been transformed into shops and offices.

"Look at that blue house, man," the shorter of the
two killers said.

"Shit, man, that house ain't blue."

"What is it, if it ain't blue?"

"It's purple, man, any fool knows that."

"You callin me a fool?"

"No, you ain't no fool, man, you just dumb. You so
dumb you smell. Look at you, hair all nappy, eyes all
pink, you ain't nothing but one big stink."

"That's just my fine smell that your mother digs
so well that—"

"Hey, man, look," the taller one said.

"Yeah," the shorter one said, "I'm looking."

That early in the morning there were only a few
cars parked in the metered zones on Wisconsin Avenue.

The two blacks had already passed a brown, dusty Porsche. Ahead of them, in front of the huge house that one of them had insisted was purple, was parked a grey Mercedes 280 SE. A man in a brightly checked cream and tan sports jacket was coming out of the blue house. He carried a briefcase.

"Look at that," the shorter of the two killers said.

"Let's go," the other one said.

The man carefully locked the door of the blue house and headed for the Mercedes. He was bent over unlocking the car's curbside door when the taller of the two blacks said, "Hey, man."

Noah deGraffenreid straightened and turned. He looked coolly at the two blacks. The taller one held a knife. The other held the Spanish-made automatic pistol.

"Beat it," deGraffenreid said.

"Give us some money, man," the black with the pistol said.

"I said beat it."

"What you got in that case, man?"

Noah deGraffenreid opened the door of the Mercedes. "I told you to buzz off. If you don't, you're going to get big trouble."

The taller of the two blacks grabbed for the briefcase. DeGraffenreid snatched it back and swung it at the black's head. The shorter black shot deGraffenreid in the stomach. DeGraffenreid looked down in surprise. He dropped the briefcase. "Why you little shit," he said and took a step toward the black with the pistol. The black backed up and shot deGraffenreid again. DeGraffenreid went down on his knees, mouthing something to himself, and the black with the pistol shot him for the third time in the head. DeGraffenreid died as he fell to the sidewalk.

The shorter of the two blacks snatched up the briefcase. The taller one found deGraffenreid's wallet and stuffed it in his pocket. They looked around wildly and then began to run north on Wisconsin toward the brown, dusty Porsche.

Inside the Porsche, Jake Pope tried to time it just right. He kicked the curbside door open just as the two killers drew even with it. They had no chance to dodge. They raced into the door and bounded back, sprawling on the sidewalk. Pope was out of the car, a lug wrench in his hand. The shorter of the two killers tried to claw the Spanish gun out of his pocket. Pope brought the lug wrench down on the killer's right wrist. It snapped and the killer began to cry. Pope put his foot on the neck of the taller black, bent down, and jerked the Spanish pistol out of the shorter black's pocket.

"Don't move," Pope said, "or I'll put one of these in your kneecap."

A car stopped and a man got out. He was a short, stocky man with grey hair and green eyes. "What the hell's going on here?"

"They shot a guy just up the street," Pope said. "Can you call the cops?"

"Jesus Christ," the stocky man said. "That one you got your foot on. How old's he?"

"At least twelve," Pope said.

"And the other one?"

"Thirteen," Pope said. "The other one must be all of thirteen."

33

THE WITNESS ROOM HAD NO WINDOWS. IT HAD AN OAK table and six chairs and two tin ashtrays that nobody was likely to steal and it was located next to Juvenile Court in the Superior Court Building at 4th and E Streets, Northwest.

Detective Hugo Worthy was a little nervous about Jake Pope being in the witness room. "It's all right for him," Worthy said, nodding at Ancel Easter who sat in one of the chairs at the oak table. "He's their lawyer, God knows why. But, hell, you're not their lawyer."

"Just consider me an amicus curiae," Pope said.

"It'll be my ass if anybody finds out," Worthy said.

"It'll be all right," Easter said. "This is only the preliminary hearing."

The door to the witness room opened and the two killers came in. They were handcuffed to each other and to Arthur Calloway who was big and black and a U. S. Federal Marshal. Calloway nodded at Worthy. "You got about ten minutes," he said.

"Thanks," Worthy said.

Calloway carefully unlocked the handcuff that was fastened to his wrist. "Sit over there," he told the two killers. They sat down in two chairs, still handcuffed to each other. The shorter one wore a white cast on his right wrist. Calloway nodded again at Worthy. "I'll be right outside," he said.

"Which is which?" Pope asked after Calloway had left.

"The taller one is Bobby Goad," Worthy said. "He's thirteen. The shorter one is Willie Hurd. He's twelve. They're cousins."

"You the mothuh fuckuh who broke my arm," Willie Hurd said to Pope.

"Uh-huh," Pope said.

"I'm Ancel Easter," the lawyer said. "I talked to your aunt and she's agreed that I should serve as your lawyer. Is that all right with you two?"

"We ain't got no money," Bobby Goad said.

"We'll worry about that later," Easter said. "I want to ask you a few questions and then we'll have to go in and talk to the judge. I want you to tell me the truth, because if you do, I can probably make it easier for you. All right?"

The two killers looked at each other. "They gonna put us in Lorton?" Bobby Goad said.

"No," Easter said. "They're not going to put you in Lorton."

"We don't wanna go to Lorton."

"You won't have to go there. I promise you that. Now, do you want to answer some questions?"

They looked at each other again. "Awright," Bobby Goad said.

"Where did you get the gun?"

"Found it," Willie Hurd said.

"Where did you find it?"

"In a car."

"Where in the car?"

"Glove compartment."

"What else was in the glove compartment?"

"Box of bullets."

"Where was the car?"

"In Georgetown."

"You go over to Georgetown much?"

"We go over there some."

"You live over on Thirteenth and T, don't you?"

"Yeah. We live over there."

"With your aunt?"

"Yeah. We live with her."

"Who else lives there?"

They looked at each other again. "I got two brothers," Bobby Goad said. "They little, but they live there. He got three sisters. They live there. Then there's Duke. He live there."

"Who's Duke?" Ancel Easter said.

"Friend of my aunty."

"What's Duke do?"

Bobby Goad shrugged.

"What's your aunt do?"

"She on welfare."

"How many rooms in your aunt's apartment?"

"Two," Willie Hurd said. "She's got two rooms."

"And you live there and Bobby lives there and your aunt and Duke and five other children live there, is that right?"

"Uh-huh."

"So all nine of you live in two rooms?"

"Duke, he don't sleep there all the time," Bobby Goad said. "Sometime he get drunk and don't come home."

Ancel Easter nodded. "How long had you had the

gun before you decided to stick up the old man with the watch?"

"Couple of days," Bobby Goad said. "We just playin with it before that."

"Who showed you how to use it?"

"Duke," Willie Hurd said. "He show us."

"When you got the watch off the old man," Easter said, "why didn't you sell it? Why'd you keep it?"

Bobby Goad shrugged. "Nevah had a watch like that."

"Shit, man," Willie Hurd said, "you nevah had no watch at all."

"You liked the watch," Ancel Easter said. "That's why you kept it?"

Bobby Goad nodded.

"Why did you shoot the old man?"

Willie Hurd shrugged. "He coming at us. Gun went off. We didn't go to shoot him."

"And the old man in the liquor store and the young man in the alley and that man and his wife over in Southeast?"

Willie Hurd looked at Bobby Goad. Then he looked away and said something, mumbled it really.

"I didn't hear you," Ancel Easter said.

"It got easier," Willie Hurd said.

Ancel Easter sighed. "You said you go over to Georgetown a lot. When do you go over there?"

"Mornins," Bobby Goad said.

"Early mornings?"

"Uh-huh."

"Why do you go in the early mornings?"

"Me and Bobby can't sleep," Willie Hurd said. "We gotta sleep in one bed, me and him and the three littlest ones and it get too hot so we gets up and goes over to

Georgetown where it's cool and it's nice and there ain't hardly nobody up and they got trees. They got lotsa and lotsa trees in Georgetown."

"And that's why you were over there when you tried to take that briefcase away from the man on Wisconsin?" Easter said.

"Uh-huh," Willie Hurd said. "We wanted to be where it was cool and they had trees. Me and Bobby like trees."

"And why did you pick him?" Easter said.

Willie Hurd shrugged. "Because he was like the first one—the old man."

Easter's voice tightened. "How was he like the old man?"

Willie Hurd shrugged again. "He was the only one up."

34

THE PRICE OF WHEAT WENT TO HELL WHEN WORD LEAKED out of the Department of Agriculture that its July crop report had been stolen either by the Mafia or a skilled band of Red Chinese agents. Five days later, by the time that Secretary of Agriculture Fred C. Clapperton called a press conference to straighten things out, rumor had hammered the price of wheat down a dollar and it looked as if it might drop even farther.

Clapperton, who was never comfortable with the press, appeared even more nervous than usual. He always sweated easily and under the hot TV lights he looked very much like a small-town banker who had been caught at the airport with a satchel full of money.

No, he said, it was not true that the crop report was stolen by a team of Chinese secret agents. Yes, it was true that the report was stolen by a trusted department employee. No, it was not true, it was a damned lie, in fact, that previous thefts of crop reports had been covered up. Yes, it was true that he himself had been tipped off that the report might be stolen. No, he did not ignore the tip; he took immediate steps, but because of security reasons he was not at liberty to divulge just what those steps had been. No, he had not submitted his resignation to the President and had no plans to do so. No, he had no idea what the dead employee had planned to do with the stolen report.

The reporter from the Chicago *Sun-Times* had been flown into Washington to go after the story. His normal assignment was the Chicago police and he found the United States Department of Agriculture no great shucks.

"When was it that you learned that a big wad of mob money had gone long on September wheat?"

Clapperton used his sodden handkerchief to mop at some of the sweat that was streaming down his face. "I—I haven't heard that rumor."

"You ever hear of a guy called Fulvio Varvesi?"

"No."

"They fished him out of Lake Michigan day before yesterday which was when wheat went down to three dollars and two cents a bushel. Somebody had shot him in the back of the neck. Twice."

"I'm afraid I don't understand the question."

"I haven't asked it yet."

"I see."

"If everything had worked out normally, I mean if you had issued the crop report without any problem, what do you think might have happened to the price of wheat? I just want a guess."

"I'm making a pure guess, but it probably would have risen. The report estimated a twenty percent drop in wheat production."

"But because of all these rumors floating around, the price of wheat almost fell out of sight. If Varvesi had gone in with somebody on a deal to rig the market

and drive the price of wheat up, that somebody might
be a little unhappy, right?"

"I'm not sure that I understand your question."

"Let me ask you another one. Are you gonna look
into the rumor that the Mafia was out to rig the price
of wheat or are you gonna turn it over to the FBI?"

"If such an investigation is begun, we will, of
course, cooperate in any way that we can."

The Chicago *Sun-Times* reporter shook his head.
"Are you sure you haven't sent your resignation over
to the White House?"

While the Secretary of Agriculture was being tor-
mented by the press, Ancel Easter's big grey Cadillac
limousine swung into the access road that led to Dulles
International Airport. At the wheel was Thomas J. Fiquette, the former vice squad cop. In the rear were Jake
Pope and Faye Hix. It was mid-morning and Pope was
reading the *Washington Post*. He folded it and said,
"Huh."

"What does huh mean?" Faye Hix said.

"It means the price of wheat's down to three-oh-
two."

"What's going to happen to her?"

"To whom?"

"To that little woman we saw out in Fairfax. Mrs.
Hucks. I keep feeling sorry for her."

"Well, she'll have some insurance. They figured out
that Hucks didn't commit suicide after all."

"She'll need more than insurance."

"She has her psychiatrist," Pope said. "And her
group."

"That's not much of a comfort."

"It must be better than none."

Faye Hix shook her head. "I also keep thinking about those two kids. They weren't kids, they were children. What's going to happen to them?"

"I don't know," Pope said. "I suppose they were children. One was barely twelve. The other one was twelve going on thirteen. Nothing good's going to happen to them. Nothing good has ever happened to them. They found a gun and some bullets and used them. When the psychiatrists get through with them, I suppose they'll lock them up for a while."

"For how long?"

"I have no idea," Pope said. "When I broke the older one's wrist, he started to cry. Did I tell you that? He cried like a child, not like a killer."

Faye Hix put her hand on Pope's arm. She smiled at him. "Do you really think I'll like it on the boat?"

"Sure," he said. "You'll like it fine."

"What if I don't?"

"Well, you can always go back to your ranch."

She shook her head. "No. Not anymore. I told Ancel Easter to sell it. Just like that. I said, 'Mr. Easter, I want you to sell my ranch.'"

"What'd he say?"

"He said fine, he'd do it. I thought it would take a lot of—well, I don't know what I thought it would take a lot of."

"You keep forgetting that you're rich now," Pope said. "The rich can hire people to buy this and sell that. They can hire people to look after the details. This gives them time to count their money."

"Oh, my God!" she said. "Stop the car."

"What's the matter?"

"Granddad. I forgot Granddad. I left him on the dresser in the hotel."

"You want to go back?"

Faye Hix thought about it. "Could I call from the airport? Maybe I could call from the airport and tell the hotel to send Granddad over to Ancel Easter. Do you think he'd mind?"

"Who, Easter?"

"No," she said. "Granddad."

The maid in the fifth-floor room of the Madison Hotel had finished making the bed and was starting to dust the furniture when she noticed the grey metal canister sitting on the dresser. She picked it up, shook it, and when it didn't rattle, she tried to twist off its top. When the top didn't twist, she gave it a hard pull and it came off suddenly and the fine grey ashes spilled all over the blue carpet.

Damn, she told herself, now you've gone and made a mess. She bent down and picked up the handle of the vacuum cleaner, switched it on and, humming to herself, pushed it back and forth across the carpet. The Electrolux vacuum cleaner neatly sucked up into its innards all that was left of Crawdad Gilmore, the hammertoed friend and adviser of six Presidents.